FORTUNE COOKIE

Books by Joanne Meyer

HEAVENLY DETOUR

FORTUNE COOKIE

Published by Kensington Publishing Corp.

FORTUNE COOKIE

Joanne **Meyer**

KENSINGTON BOOKS
http://www.kensingtonbooks.com

KENSINGTON BOOKS are published by

Kensington Publishing Corp.
850 Third Avenue
New York, NY 10022

ISBN: 0-7582-0262-8

First printing: March 2004
10 9 8 7 6 5 4 3 2 1

Printed in the United States of America

For Gloria

Acknowledgments

I'm indebted to the following for contributing their expertise toward this project: Mr. Willie Freeman, Security Director for Newark Public Schools, who was the former NYPD Supervisor at the 84th Precinct, Brooklyn, New York; Dr. Francisco M. Cervoni, First Physicians Group, Sarasota, Florida; and Dr. Danielle Green.

As always, it fell upon my husband, John, to take on the task of first reader. I am grateful for his support and honesty. Again, I tapped the resources of my children: Ellen, Howard, and Ken, and thank them for sharing their knowledge and professional experience in the fields of law and real estate.

No author could be luckier than to have the support of fellow writers who understand and tolerate the ongoing angst of coping with deadlines and life's ongoing crises (which always manage to cross paths at the same time).

Thanks to my agent Alice Martell for always being there for me and to John Scognamiglio, the most encouraging editor an author could hope for.

A graveyard for over-the-hill cars and trucks—old, battered, paint-peeled cars, wrecked pickups, treadless tires, mounds of metal and jackknifed junk. At first nothing moved, then without warning, a small creature darted out from underneath an abandoned Jeep. Rosie hesitated, but this was no time for distractions, no room for mistakes. This dream had its own agenda. The area was deserted and growing darker by the moment. Only one streetlight was working, not enough to penetrate the gathering dusk. She had to find him before it was too late, but the nearest street sign was facing in the opposite direction, and she was losing her concentration. She searched for a landmark, but the light was fading, the landscape dissolving into mist, and one can't hold on to a dream that's seen its end. Rosie awoke shivering with fear and her message for the day. . .

Chapter 1

SOMETHING IS ABOUT TO OCCUR THAT WILL CHANGE YOUR LIFE COMPLETELY.

The thought grabbed her in the stomach like cramps after a cold pizza, so she knew it must be true. Natalie "Rosie" Rosenstein had a gift, something she was born with thirty-three years before. Some would call it a sixth sense—others, intuition or ESP. Be that as it may, there were many times Rosie wished she hadn't been so blessed, like the advance notice she'd received just before her sixteenth birthday, for instance.

Your sixteenth will not be sweet. And true enough, her boyfriend at the time, whom her mother referred to as "that loser from the East Bronx," stood her up. Of course she broke up with him on the spot, but no amount of anger erased the hurt. The only good thing to come out of the incident was that she learned to pay more attention to that inner voice. And now, the foreboding that had awakened her this morning began to haunt her: *Something terrible is about to happen,* it echoed.

Her first look in the bathroom mirror confirmed that nothing was in sync for her this day. She bent her head forward and berated herself for not finding time for a much-needed touch-up. Rosie carried her family's sturdy, gene-patented, brown hair. Healthy, it was true, with natural heavy waves—but brown? In these days of *It costs more, but I'm worth it,* nothing could be more boring. So once she'd escaped the confines of her mother's heavy reach some years before, she'd concluded that auburn was meant to be her true shade; it was Mother Nature who'd made the mistake. Rosie was much too critical of herself. Others saw her as smart and attractive with dark lucent eyes, the color of ranch mink, a perfectly proportioned five-foot-four-inch figure and a terrific sense of humor. She attempted to focus on some of these positive traits as she showered and dressed. Facing the mirror for a last-minute check, she took in the powder blue two-piece Kasper linen and nodded. Not bad. She could imagine her mother urging her to get a husband before she lost her figure. *Thirty-three, Na-ta-lie,* she'd warn, sending the syllables of her name on patrol, *now is not the time to dillydally.* Ida Rosenstein would never let up until the mission was accomplished.

All during the morning's commute from Oceanside into

Brooklyn, her forebodings increased. What terrible thing was in the works? Whatever it was would occur today. These psychic predictions were seldom wrong.

Upon unlocking the office door around eight-thirty, the earlier bulletin gained momentum and shape: *The catastrophe has to do with Grace.* Indeed, the latter's private office was still dark. Rosie played devil's advocate with herself: Does it really make sense to worry about Grace? She's one of the pluckiest, most independent women you've ever known. Why, she could be a role model for strong-mindedness. Besides, the delay will give you more time to make coffee, check messages and organize today's court appearances.

But when her boss, a successful attorney who specialized in matrimonial law, still hadn't arrived by eight-forty-five, the back of Rosie's neck began to tickle, and she was convinced that her early morning clairvoyant attack was on the money. Grace Osborne was never late. The legal assistant reached for the phone and dialed her boss's home. After three rings, the answering machine picked up, and Rosie caved in to her earlier flash. This was the start of it. Her intuition never failed her. Besides, her hands were cold—another sure sign, especially since the office's old air-conditioning system hadn't fully cranked up from its weekend rest.

By nine, she was fighting to control the panic, but her stomach muscles contracted, and she felt herself getting hyper and fidgety. She swept back a fistful of russet waves—or *cheveux châtaine claire,* as her onetime French lover Jean Marc would have said. Rosie hadn't thought of that lying bastard in more than five years. Oh! how she'd been taken in by his accent. Anything he said had sex smeared all over it. Guess that's why she put up with the louse for as long as she did—two years of sheer waste. Now, after that fleeting reminder, she just as easily pushed him out of her life again.

Her boss was due at court in fifteen minutes. What the hell was Rosie supposed to do? The judge would be pissed. Heck, it didn't take much to get Judge Conroy angry. Well, she'd better get her ass across the street; maybe she'd think of something on the way over. Still hoping for the best, Rosie ripped off a sheet of yellow paper from a nearby legal pad, scrawled a note with a black marker and placed it on the floor just inside the office entrance where (if the gods were smiling) Grace would see it. Whispering a silent prayer, she grabbed her bag, locked the door behind her and headed over to Supreme Court, Matrimonial Division, praying her so-called gift was off the boil.

Rosie was stopped by several acquaintances as she entered the courtroom. She was considered by many to be the Jewish version of *Today* host Katie Couric (before the latter went blond of course). Nearly always upbeat, the legal assistant had a talent for remembering everyone's current dilemma. However, her good nature did not extend to schmucks, and there was one in particular, Arnold Feltman, who was signaling wildly from the far end of the first row. Rosie did a masterful job of ignoring him.

After exchanging a few words with Lou Caruso, the court officer, Rosie slipped into a seat four rows back and watched the action in front of her. For the lawyers and their assistants, it was the usual Monday-morning schmooze, mostly catching up on weekend adventures. They sat around trading stories and jokes until a door behind the bench opened. The court clerk broke away from a conversation he was having with someone in the front row and moved forward to declare the beginning of yet another week in court.

"Part five now in session," he announced, and Rosie thought she'd lose her breakfast. Another week in the crazy world of deadbeat dads, drunk moms, abusive spouses and lost children had commenced, but her boss was nowhere to be seen. An hour and a half later, all other court business having been cleared, the lawyers and other observers remaining were waiting for the trial to begin. It was Grace's case, a dispute that had seen its share of motions and show-cause orders, conferences and other legal delays. Too much effort had gone into this for her not to be here. Rosie glanced up at the ceiling and beyond, searching for inspiration, but God was not online this morning. She might have known. Ever since her day started, Rosie's well-ordered life had gone straight down the toilet. And the earlier message replayed itself like a phonograph needle stuck in a dusty groove: *Something is about to occur. . . .*

In desperation, she made eye contact with Lou. During their earlier conversation, she'd shared her bad news. Now he, too, checked the doors, shrugging his shoulders in sympathy. Finally, Rosie, along with all those present, heard the announcement: ". . . the case of *Schreiber v. Fisher.*"

Rosie's brain kicked into action. This is it. What'll I do?

More shuffling as opposing counsel, Harvey C. White, and his client, Hans Schreiber, moved forward to the counsel table. White was admired for his legal mind, generally well liked by his colleagues, and someone who had been very helpful to Rosie when she first started working for Grace four years before. In court, however, one could count on White to put all friendships aside and go to the wall for his clients no matter what kind of scumbags they were. Hans Schreiber was a case in point.

A most unlikeable man, Schreiber was petitioning the court to grant him full custody of his son so he could move their permanent residence from Brooklyn to Manhattan. From where she sat, Rosie had a good view of the tall, beefy-faced man with the shaved head who resembled, she thought, an ill-tempered Mr. Clean. His divorced wife, who protested that Hans was a violent person, was fighting the motion. If Schreiber won, no one would envy the boy. But a law guardian had been appointed, and Rosie was pretty sure she would recommend custody be granted to the mother. Forensics was another part of the equation. But it would be difficult to imagine any psychologist favoring a wife beater. In the long run, it was the judge who would determine the boy's final fate.

Rosie's boss represented Schreiber's ex-wife, Jane Fisher (who'd been thrilled to get her name back), a tentative soul who had broken away from the abuse-driven bastard and was just learning to stand on her own. Grace Osborne's job was a formidable one since Harvey White was a brilliant lawyer who rarely lost a case. But Grace had her own reputation, and Rosie had been planning to sit in on this one and, hopefully, watch Grace kick ass. Now that pleasure would have to be delayed.

With an uncertain expression, Jane Fisher (sans lawyer) rose halfway out of her seat and paused in mid-squat, obviously at a loss regarding her next move. Rosie had the uncomfortable vision of the pleasant lady about to plunge down onto a toilet seat. She pushed the notion aside and concentrated instead on creating an excuse for Grace's absence—something that wouldn't give the entire courtroom an opportunity to laugh too hard.

Judge Conroy was flipping through some papers in front of him, so it was several seconds before he realized that the parties of the second part were not in place at the table.

"And? I'm waiting"—Conroy checked his watch and drummed his fingers—"but not too patiently." He faced the court directly now, the permanent scowl that sat between his brows deepening, enhancing the shape of his receding hairline. "May I have the honor of seeing Attorney Grace Osborne and her client seated in front?"

His sarcasm was scary, so Rosie hesitated a second or two before leaping into the jaws of uncertainty. "Your Honor . . . um . . . Natalie Rosenstein, Ms. Osborne's assistant."

A few good-natured snickers greeted the paralegal who, for most of her life, had almost never been referred to as anything but Rosie by her friends, which was fine because she'd always hated her given name, Natalie. Of course her family persisted, but she had no control over that.

"That's lovely to know, Ms. Rosenstein, but right now I'm more interested in the whereabouts of Ms. Osborne."

"Yes, Your Honor, but—"

The judge stared at her over the top of his reading glasses, displaying unusual patience, but he was not smiling.

"Ms. Osborne has been unavoidably detained, Your Honor," Rosie finally stated. "I'm certain she's on her way. Uh—a recent problem with a wisdom tooth might have unexpectedly flared up." That sounded okay to her. After all, who among us could not sympathize with such a painful possibility? She would have elaborated even more, but good sense dictated she had better quit while ahead.

Concern, raised eyebrows and dubious expressions reacted to Rosie's attempt to cover for her boss. Most present did not envy her; some were sympathetic; all had experienced their share of this particular judge's wrath. Wise guy Arnold Feltman, who was out of the judge's view, threw Rosie a nasty wink and shook his head slowly from side to side, all of which could best be translated as, *Who are you kidding?* She knew the creep was using this opportunity to get back at her for turning down all his attempts to get into her pants, and easily pushed him out of her mind as she set about the more important task of assuaging Judge Conroy. The latter must have gotten a pretty good night's sleep because he flicked his hand at her and began checking his calendar.

Harvey White, a distinguished-looking man in his early fifties, stood and cleared his throat "Your Honor, my client is anxious to establish residence in Manhattan with his son."

"I'm sure he is, Counselor, but nothing of the kind has been decided yet."

"Yes, Your Honor, but we would appreciate it if the case would not be put over beyond next week."

The judge muttered something unintelligible, finally opting for Wednesday of the following week, calling upon Rosie to confirm if the date was okay for her boss. Adjournment was an everyday occurrence in the courts and, while an inconvenience, most in the profession took it as a matter of course. So she was off the hook for now, but that still didn't solve the problem of what happened to Grace. Rosie slipped out of court at the first opportunity and double-timed it back to the office, quietly celebrating Judge Conroy's unusually pleasant humor.

The automatic coffeemaker had kept the coffee hot, so Rosie poured herself a cup after retrieving her undisturbed note from the floor. *I knew it,* she thought, and was more convinced than ever that something bad had happened. If she could only just push ahead to the next level of cognizance and get to the solution. Rosie dialed Grace's home number again on the outside chance the lawyer had overslept. Who was she kidding? Now was the time for action.

She flipped through the phone book in Grace's top drawer, aware of the futility. Her boss was a loner. Outside of joining some of the courthouse regulars for a drink now and then, Grace didn't socialize. No close friends, no special relationship that Rosie was aware of, no one to contact in an emergency, except some family in Iowa that Grace had referred to once or twice but never in too much detail. So, what next? Rosie sipped her coffee. Time to bring in the marines. She pulled the phone closer and punched in a number. An answering machine picked up.

"Mike Bartel. Please leave a message and I'll get back to you."

"Hi, Mike. Rosie here. Listen, I need to speak to you. It's kind of urgent. I'm in the office, but just to cover all bases, I'll also try your pager now. Either way, get back to me." She paged him immediately after and left the office number.

The private investigator had only been working for Grace for three or four months, but so far, he was batting a thousand. Grace was pleased with him, so Rosie had every reason to believe he'd be of help. At this point, she had no idea how she was going to pay him, but her inner sense told her not to let that stand in her way.

It didn't take five minutes before the phone rang.

"Law Office of Grace Osborne," she responded, silently praying it was either Grace or Mike.

The latter's raspy voice boomed, "What's up?"

"In a nutshell, Grace is gone—zappo, vanished!"

A pause. She could almost hear the wheels turning.

"Okay, since when?"

"Since this morning. She never came in, and there's no answer at her place."

"What the hell time is it? Eleven o'clock? It's Monday morning, for God's sake. She's only a couple of hours late, right? What's the panic?"

"Grace is never late. I've been working for her for almost four years, and she's always in early, mostly before me." What did she have to do to convince him? "Listen, Mike, she had a case scheduled this morning—with Judge Conroy, okay? She never showed."

"Conroy, huh?" The investigator blew a small breeze into the phone. He'd been around the courts long enough to know most of the players. "Give me her home address. I'll run by her place and check it out. You'll either see me or hear from me in an hour."

Rosie gave him the information and hung up, trying to conjure up what might have happened. Could Grace have gotten a call over the weekend from Iowa about some catastrophe with her family? Sure, but she would have called me. Okay . . . maybe one of her hardship heroines (that's what Rosie called the women clients on whose behalf her boss was always going the distance) had contacted Grace for some unscheduled assistance. Rosie had warned her that her good deeds might not be appreciated by some of her clients' enemies. Then she got this awful feeling. *No, it's not something that innocent.*

Sheesh! Why couldn't she just turn off the bad stuff? She put her hands over her ears and shook her head, knowing full well she had no control over the incoming data. These inspirations appeared like the hidden messages found inside Chinese fortune cookies and were often just as cryptic.

She grabbed the phone when it rang ten minutes later and strived for a voice that didn't sound like it was boiling over.

"Law Office of Grace Osborne."

"Well, ah know that, honey," the pseudo-Southern accent crooned. It could be none other than Arnold Feltman.

"What do *you* want?"

"Listen, Rosie," he fell back into his New York mode, "I know we've had some difficulties in the past . . ."

"You got that right!"

"Well, about this morning, you can forget that tooth fairy shit. Everyone knows you were covering for your boss. Word has it that she was a no-show this morning. Whazzup?" Then Feltman switched to his I'm-really-a-good-guy voice: "Why don't you let me help?"

Rosie bit back the obscene phrase that came to mind and forced a deep breath. If ice could freeze to a deeper level, her next comment would keep meats and poultry safe for a year: "Noooo thank you, Arnold."

There was a momentary pause. ". . . Call me, sweet thang, if you change your mind."

After she hung up, Rosie muttered aloud, "Not if I were choking and you were the only airway tube."

It wasn't ten minutes later that the phone rang again. She picked it up, ready to let loose if it was Feltman, but Mike's familiar voice punched out some disturbing news. "Yeah, it's me. She's not at home. That's a definite. Wait there. I'm coming in. Twenty to twenty-five minutes. Take down my cell number if you need me before." He waited just long enough for her to repeat the number before hanging up.

His tone was mysterious, and Rosie began shivering even before the next flash hit her: *Something really awful has happened, and if action's not taken soon, you'll never see Grace again.*

Chapter 2

Mike Bartel arrived at the office fifteen minutes later. Her mother would describe the tall, thin, former NYPD detective as a *langer loksh,* comparing his long legs, narrow hips and slim waist to a noodle. Of course, Rosie's mother was barely an inch over five feet herself, so anyone much taller than a Lilliputian was intimidating.

At six feet, two inches, Mike was impressive in his own right. In his mid-forties, his battle-weary face spoke of frontline experience dealing with the city's seamier population. Gestures like raised eyebrows substituted for whole sentences like, *Are you sure you want to stick with that lie?* and went a long way toward saving hours of interrogation. Oh, yeah, Mike had an intimidating manner. Creases surrounded his iridescent blue eyes, and when he didn't get enough sleep, which was often, the bags underneath tended to become more prominent, and the grouch in him escaped. In spite of that, and in a rough sort of way, he was handsome, with hair the color of wet sand and a crooked smile that invited all sorts of fantasies. Quickly, Rosie reviewed her miserable history with men and reminded herself that it was always the good-looking ones who caused the most destruction.

"To all intents and purposes," Mike began, glancing at his watch, "Grace is missing about three hours. Convince me this a crime."

"Okay, you can label it anything you want, but in the four years since I'm working for her, Grace has never not shown up for a court appearance."

". . . In four years?"

She nodded—eyes hard, lips pressed together as if she were daring him to argue with her about it.

He zeroed in on the pretty face with the large intelligent eyes that were presently focused on him. She was trying her damndest to sell him on, what was to her, some serious stuff. "Okay, talk to me about some possible recent troubles in her life—boyfriends, money, enemies—like that."

Rosie let a couple of seconds pass before shaking her head. "I'm thinking, but nothing comes to mind."

"How about something to do with work. Was she handling any dicey cases lately?"

"Oh, yeah! The one from this morning, as a matter of fact. Hans Schreiber, wife beater *extraordinaire,* is looking for custody of their son, a sweet little boy. Grace's client is the ex-wife, who's fighting him on it, and well she should. That jerk shouldn't be permitted custody of a turtle."

"Let's start there, then. Give me the guy's address and whatever else you have, and I'll check him out."

Rosie hurriedly searched through a pile of papers on her desk and found what she was looking for. She scribbled down the information Mike needed and offered him something extra besides. "For what it's worth, I knew something terrible happened when I woke up this morning. Now I know whatever it is has to do with Grace's disappearance."

He stared back at her, waiting for her to elaborate, but

Rosie had said all she'd wanted to and now sat back in her own misery.

"Care to expand?"

Frowning, she swept back a miscreant wave that had fallen forward, dismissing him. "I'm not sure you'd understand."

"Try me." His eyes crawled all over her.

"Let's just say I have a sixth sense."

He shot her a quizzical look, did the eyebrow thing and waited a beat, but Rosie offered no further explanation. A search through some of Grace's other current clients turned up nothing more than the usual dreck and assortment of misfits.

"Okay, I'll get started with this," Mike said, and shoved the Schreiber info into his pocket, waiting. (They always had something extra to add.)

"You know, Grace is kind of a loner—doesn't go out much."

"Everybody's got something they don't share with the world."

She caught his hard look, then thought again about Jean Marc, the charismatic freeloader who'd deluded her into thinking she could trust him with her heart. She wound up supporting him by getting the only job available to an American lacking the language in the Paris of the nineties: washing dishes at a Kosher restaurant in the Jewish district where the owner (married, of course) considered the act of grabbing her ass as part of his due. She'd lied to her family in her weekly letters, not able to admit even to herself she was being used.

"Yeah, I guess you're right," she finally responded. "I'll try to think of some other possibilities."

"You do that. I'll get going with what I've got here." He paused at the door. "Call me if you hear anything."

Mike was a good PI, Rosie thought, maybe the best. He'd certainly earned Grace's respect. She felt a stab of concern. What a good friend she'd turned out to be! Rosie remembered their first meeting: Grace, with her natural Norwegian blond beauty—a real *shikseh* face, her mother would say. Ah, but she was gracious—helpful, too, not like some of the shitty bosses Rosie had worked for after returning from France. Of course, attending night classes at the same time had added to her burden, but she'd stuck with it and finally gotten her college degree. Then came the search for a job, one that interested her and offered some respect. Becoming Grace's special assistant provided that opportunity. Now she had to do all she could to bring back her friend. *But if we don't find Grace soon, there's not going to be a happy ending to this story.* Rosie jumped when the phone rang and pushed the ominous premonition aside.

"Law Office of Grace Osborne."

"Rosie, hi! It's Carolyn."

It took only a minute to connect the familiar voice of Carolyn Hughs, another lawyer who specialized in family law. Although she was born and raised in New York, Carolyn was an Anglophile. She simply *adored* England and had adapted her speech to sound as British as possible. As a result, "can't" became *cahn't* and "should not" turned into *shan't,* etc. But Rosie's discomfort had nothing to do with accents. She knew that Grace and Carolyn had been close friends at one time, but somewhere along the line they'd had a falling-out. Oh, they didn't let it interfere with business. Rosie knew they still carried each other's names on their malpractice insurance, meaning each still covered for the other if anything went awry. But she also knew the two were no longer close buddies.

"Where are you calling from?" Rosie asked, recalling that Carolyn had not been in court that morning.

"At the office, dear. I was away for the weekend. Just got in and heard about Grace not showing up this morning. What's going on? And is there anything I can do?"

Now you see? That's pretty decent. Rosie never understood what Grace had against the woman. She seemed okay, and had always treated Rosie with respect.

"Well, that's nice of you to offer, but there's nothing I can think of at the moment."

"I understand Judge Conroy was most decent."

"Actually he was."

"Is it true that Grace has disappeared?"

"I . . . I'm not sure where you heard that from, but . . ."

"Look, it's quite all right. You don't have to say any more. Grace and I have had our differences, but we're both professionals, and I do want to help. Please know that I am here for you."

Rosie was touched. "Thanks, Carolyn, for your call. I'll let you know."

Grace's unexplained absence made no sense at all. Then again, much about Grace was a mystery. She was especially careful about not revealing much about herself.

Mike returned to the office about eleven. "Anything?"

She shook her head. "What did you find out?"

He pulled up a chair. "How much do you know about Grace's personal life?"

"You're answering a question with a question? Maybe you're a lawyer, too. Let's start over."

"Nope, I'm not a lawyer. And you're not stupid either."

"Okay. I don't know anything about her personal life. At work, she's tough but fair. She listens, and she goes to bat for her clients. Now it's your turn."

"Okay, Grace's personal life. Seems she has—or should I say had?—a relationship with a guy by the name of Marcos—Nikki Marcos. Name sound familiar?"

There wasn't a soul with an IQ over fifty who hadn't read something about the Greek tycoon in one of the gossip columns, or seen his photo with some actress or royal princess. Rosie's dark eyes flashed back at him. "Where on earth did you get that from?"

"I didn't expect you to react any other way. Look, accept what I'm telling you. I've got my sources."

"That's garbage. . . ." Rosie stared off in the distance. "I would have known. I mean . . . a relationship? With Nikki Marcos? Nah. Grace never . . ."

"Never mentioned it? That's not surprising. The guy is married, but that's not the bad news. The bad news is that this Marcos has an iffy reputation. No one denies he's rich. Besides his international hotel chain and rare gem investments, he probably owns half of Greece and then some. The worst part is there are rumors he uses his money to manipulate top government officials all over the world. Interpol flagged him way back in the eighties—that's more than twenty years ago—but no one ever got any hard evidence. Money buys a lot." Mike watched her reaction carefully.

"Getouttahere! You must be confusing Grace with someone else. Grace is a straight arrow, focused—a professional, for God's sake!"

"All of that is true. She also has a life, another life, that is—one that involves Nikki Marcos."

Mike's news hung in the air like three-day-old fish. Neither spoke. Only the telephone broke the silence.

Rosie grabbed the receiver. "Law Office of—"

"It's lunchtime, sweet thang. Maybe a platter of pasta at Theresa's will cheer you up."

"I'm busy, Feltman. Please stop bothering me." She hung up.

A question hovered on Mike's face. "Care to share?"

"Oh, some jerk that won't take no for an answer."

He grinned, enjoying her discomfort. "Listen, your personal life is none of my business, but we can't count anyone out now."

Rosie gave Mike a two-sentence outline. "Guy's a sleaze. Nothing I can't handle."

"Right. Maybe that's what Grace was telling herself up until today."

"I'm telling you, Feltman's a jerk. Doesn't have the brain power of a pigeon. I'm convinced his parents bribed the powers that be to get him through law school and the bar exam." After venting, though, she wound up giving Mike the pest's full name and particulars.

"I'll look into it—discreetly," he added, and barely covered a smile when he saw her annoyed expression.

Rosie was beginning to have feelings of another sort but dismissed them. She had no room in her life for a man, especially a good-looking guy who was full of himself. Even as she underscored the thought, she could imagine her mother raging on. "You're almost thirty-four years old and still single! When I was a girl, we called that an old maid. And there's no excuse for it. You're a beautiful girl, Na-ta-lie, with those big brown eyes . . . such long lashes . . . gorgeous hair—like expensive mahogany! . . . and a figure? *Gotteniu!*" . . . and on and on and on. . . . *Agrrrrrrh!* Her mother made a terrific P.R. person, but that's not what she needed in her life.

Mike hesitated. "There is one other thing."

Rosie looked up, mentally scrambling for an excuse as to why she wouldn't go out with him—yet.

"Since this actually does appear to be a missing-persons case, we need to report it to the authorities."

Rosie covered her disappointment. She had subconsciously swallowed her mother's campaign. "Uh, I know you're right. It's just that, once we do that, it becomes official. If Grace should materialize tomorrow, say, seems there'll be a lot of explaining to do."

"You appear to be a smart lady. What do you think are the odds of Grace turning up tomorrow?"

Rosie seemed to be mulling this over. "All right," she said after a pause. "How do we go about it?"

"I'll take care of it. Just lock up when you leave. Oh, and you better give me your home telephone number in case I hear anything tonight."

She hesitated only a minute, then wrote it out for him, dismissing for the moment all other possibilities. But she wouldn't deny the slight fibrillation occurring in her chest.

He paused at the door. "Oh, and I made a copy of Grace's photo taken at last month's dinner for the mayor." He held up a glossy five-by-seven picturing Grace seated at a table with several other lawyers and two judges. Yes, she was a knockout, all right, with hair the color of new corn, cool gray eyes and a small, perfect nose that preserved its dignity by not turning up. The only wanton feature was her mouth, appealingly full and sensuous. If Nikki Marcos was putting his fortune at Grace's feet, it was likely that he wanted to own this vision, but what did he have that Grace could not ignore—besides money, that is? And speaking of that good stuff . . .

"I have to tell you that even if this is true about Grace and Marcos, she was not that kind of person." Mike's eyebrows were climbing up his forehead.

"I know what you're thinking—it's the money—but Grace is a plain and very sincere person. She doesn't go in for all that razzmatazz."

"So what do you think lies at the heart of their relationship?" His sarcasm dripped like heavy syrup on a cold morning.

"Did you ever stop to think it might be a four-letter word, like 'love'?"

Mike passed "smile" and went directly to "laugh," and that reached her.

She didn't try to hide her annoyance. "You're a piece of work, you know?"

But Mike let it wash over him. "You plan on coming in tomorrow?"

She nodded coldly.

"Because someone from NYPD will be in touch. We're not wasting any more time. Oh, and you have my cell if you need me." He closed the door softly behind him.

Once in the hallway, Mike grinned. Not bad, he decided. She's got brains and just enough hot sauce to keep it interesting. The only problem is that sixth-sense shit—a little weird. He shook it off, concentrating instead on the immediate problem: Rosie's short list. This Arnold Feltman sounded like a creep, all right, but he could wait. Hans Schreiber had far more possibilities. Pretty coincidental that Grace came up missing on the very day Schreiber's custody case was to be heard.

The home address Rosie had given him was off Fulton Street near the Bedford Stuyvesant area. He didn't expect Schreiber to be home at this hour. The guy's business—a watch repair shop—was in lower Manhattan on Canal Street, and that's probably where he was. Good! Let's see what his neighbors think of the sonofabitch who beats his wife. Fifteen minutes later, Mike pulled up to a typical residential street near Tompkins Park.

The houses looked like they were all stamped from the same vintage, early twentieth century, he would guess, and solidly built. None were huge, but they all sported heavy-duty redbrick exteriors meant to last a lifetime. Narrow two-story jobs, he guessed they all had basements. Gnarled old oak trees stood guard along the sidewalks, their branches so laden with leaves that little sun seeped through to the small emerald carpets that abutted the redbrick fronts, making it seem like Christmas in July. Mike approached an older woman who was wheeling her shopping cart up the walkway next to Schreiber's.

"Excuse me," he said pleasantly. "I sure do love this section—so pretty, so natural. My wife and I are looking to buy in this area. Would you happen to know if anything is available?"

"Why, yes, as a matter of fact I do," she said. "Your timing is good."

He retained an interested expression, waiting for her to elaborate. "There's a nice couple—elderly people—who've got the last house on the corner. I think they're talking about relocating to Florida. Can't take the winters anymore. Know what I mean?"

"Sure do." Whereupon he made up some story about having arranged for his parents to do the very same thing two years before.

"You're a good son."

Mike turned on his choirboy smile. "Oh, well . . ." But he was really thinking he'd invested five whole minutes in talking with this lady, and he still hadn't found out a thing about Schreiber. Better push another button.

"You know what? I've got a five-year-old, and I think my family would be better off in the middle of the block. Less traffic to worry about." The expression on his face took on the manner of someone who'd come close to winning the lottery but lost completely when the last number was pulled.

"Wait a minute." His savior brightened. "There's a strong possibility that my next door neighbor will also be leaving the area." Her face fell. "If the bastard gets custody of his son, that is."

"Oh?" His eyebrows moved up in glorious wonderment. He exercised great control and refrained from clapping his hands or dancing a jig. "Who is he, and do you think I might talk with him?"

She formed a serious expression and lowered her voice. "His name is Schreiber—Hans Schreiber."

"Oh? Is something wrong, Mrs., ah, Miss . . ."

"Mitchell—Mrs. Mitchell. Anne, to you."

He grasped her hand. "Just call me Mike. Uh, Anne, you seem nervous. What's wrong?"

Of course she poured out her heart. Most women did to Mike. He could put on that kind of face. When she was through, Mike gathered that this Hans Schreiber was a demon with a nasty temper. According to Anne Mitchell, she'd heard loud yelling on numerous occasions, followed by the sounds of a woman weeping.

"He keeps to himself mostly, but I wouldn't ask him for the time of day if I could help it."

"I'll take that under advisement. And you say he's looking for custody of his child?"

"Can you believe it? The poor little kid, and the mother's so nice. That man has no right . . ."

Mike made small talk for another few minutes, then scouted the vicinity in search of corroborating opinions. He was able to catch another neighbor down the block, several shop owners and a waiter at a nearby German restaurant, who was only too happy to tell Mike "vat a cheap sonofabitch ist der Schreiber." The private investigator came away secure in the opinion that Hans Schreiber was a selfish, volatile, misogynist—capable of violence. Was he involved in Grace's disappearance? He was certainly at the top of the list—right alongside Nikki Marcos.

Chapter 3

Rosie pulled in front of her parents' house on East Olive Street in Long Beach, thinking wistfully about the scotch she much preferred over the Manichewitz her mother would offer. She hadn't been able to make it for dinner this past Friday and had been granted dispensation until tonight, which explained some of her ambivalence. She wouldn't have her sister to help dilute the visit, either. Julie was involved with hubby and kids this night. What else was new? The spotlight would be entirely on her—not something she relished. Either her mother would interrogate her about her current social life, or she knew an absolutely wonderful single man that would be perfect for her. Her father, no doubt, would be focused on some baseball game on television. It was his happy escape route. And where did that leave her? Watching the clock.

Of course she felt guilty the moment her mother enfolded her in her arms. That's what Jewish mothers were best at: embracing and reproaching. But the familiar surroundings—her dad propped in front of the TV screen watching the Yankees, the wonderful aromas floating from her mother's kitchen—did contribute to the "coming home" atmosphere that made her feel good. So why was she always so ambivalent?

"Wash your hands, Na-ta-lie, I'm putting dinner on the table."

"Honestly, Mom, I'm not a child."

By way of response, her mother gave her "the stare"— *funkelaugen,* her German grandmother used to say. It was enough to end the discussion. Rosie watched her disappear into the kitchen, a short, plump woman whose once-dark waves were now unashamedly silver.

"So what's new, Na-ta-lie?" her mother inquired soon after they were seated at the table. Rosie had just bitten off a hot chunk of potato latke. What a tainted talent for timing the dear woman had!

"Not too much," Rosie managed, scalding her throat as she swallowed the burning clump. Her statement was immediately followed by a shovelful of guilt: *Don't lie. She'll know immediately.*

"Na-ta-lie, what are you not telling me?"

Do I know my mother or what? Rosie was beginning to believe she'd acquired her aptitude for clairvoyance in response to a need for self-preservation. Well, now she had a choice. She could either continue to fabricate, in which case the entire evening would afford Madam Sherlock Holmes an excuse to probe, or she could simply tell the truth. She chose the latter.

"Grace didn't show up for work today."

"Why? What happened?"

Rosie glanced at her father, who had left the TV on in the other room but was, to all intent and purpose, still tuned in. He had no interest in the dinner conversation.

"Don't know, Mom. We're looking into it."

"Don't talk with your mouth full, dolling."

Rosie put forth an outline that some might call creative. In order not to alarm her parents, she eliminated all references to Grace's alleged relationship with Nikki Marcos and presented a scenario that made the whole episode sound like Grace simply took the day off. Rosie forced her voice into a monotone to disguise any excitement she really felt about the disappearance and sighed as though she was bored by the whole thing. Her mother frowned, unsure, so Rosie took it a step further.

"The brisket's wonderful. Nobody makes it as good as this. Right, Pop?"

He barely nodded. Her father said yes and amen to everything. The line of least resistance, he called it.

"So, dolling," her mother continued, "tell me, what else is new?" (Translation: Are you seeing anyone romantically?)

"Nothing much. You know, we've been so busy at the office."

"Busy, shmisy—what does that have to do with your personal life?"

"Mom, please don't start."

Rosie was immediately sorry. Her mother put on her "hurt" face. She was good at faces, her mother was. Probably should have been an actress on the Yiddish stage. Rosie wished she had controlled her big mouth. Guilt rolled over her like an extra blanket on a humid night. Now she had to find a way out of this and fast. Maybe she should play her "Feltman" card. *Yucch!* She'd rather walk barefoot over hot coals. Well, there's nothing like the basics.

"I'm sorry, Mom. Guess I'm just tired."

Her mother nodded an acknowledgment of the apology, but Rosie detected a gleam of triumph.

Don't tell me I've been caught in one of her traps again!

"Uh, dolling, I want to speak with you about something else."

Here it comes, she thought, and I walked right into it. And who is she fooling with the *something else*. There's only one thing on her mind.

"Don't make a 'no' when I tell you about my wonderful news."

Shit! She's done it again. But Rosie forced a smile—anything to keep the peace. "What would that be?"

Turned out this one was a dentist. Her mother went into orgasmic ecstacy describing the perfect son of her dearest new friend, a widow who recently joined their synagogue. "When I saw them at services last Friday, she introduced me. God must be watching over us, dolling. Can you imagine? A dentist!"

Her mother uttered this last in a prayerful whisper, she shouldn't get a *ki'neh-hurah* because she was boasting.

Various excuses vied for position in Rosie's brain. *Too busy* was overused. Think! *Another man?* Asking for trouble, but what else did she have? "Well, Mom, I'm not sure it would be right at this time."

"Not right? Explain, please."

"Um, there's another guy, possibly, a lawyer actually, who's been asking me out." This was not a lie, if one could consider Feltman a member of the human race.

"A lawyer?" A dubious shadow crossed her mother's face. "Is he Jewish?"

"Actually, he is." Again, she was not lying.

"Well, we'll see. . . . This is a good one, this dentist. And his mother is a doll."

Rosie couldn't resist. "Why do you suppose he isn't married yet?"

Her mother shrugged. The gesture could be interpreted as "maybe he's not so good-looking, but what difference does that make?" or "he's very smart and he's got a *doctor* in front of his name, so stop asking questions." Then her eyes brightened with malice. "If you hadn't wasted all that time living in Europe, we wouldn't be playing catch-up now."

Well, that was true enough. Her mother should only know that it was not just Paris but a deceitful Frenchman who had taken the best years of her life—and that wasn't the worst of it, but why go into that now? Rosie knew when she was beaten and changed the subject quickly, asking about her sister Julie and the kids. This last was a real button pusher. Just getting her mother onto the subject of her grandchildren meant Rosie could sit back, relax and continue eating without acquiring an ulcer.

After dinner, her father went back to the living room to watch the rest of the ball game while Rosie and her mother cleared the table. They had a little more discussion about Rosie's possible engagement to either a dentist or a lawyer, and when they finally said good night at ten o'clock, Ida Rosenstein was a happy woman. Rosie, of course, gritted her teeth all the way back to Oceanside. The ongoing saga of her doomed love life was nothing to boast about, and her mother's reminder of her European fiasco was about as welcome as a herpes infection. Yet every once in a while (just like a repetitive nightmare) she replayed her Paris experience.

Rosie had left college one year before graduation because she was bored, and the jobs that followed were equally unfulfilling. Remembering that era was as inviting as grave digging, but once begun, the process was hard to turn off. Was it really ten years ago that the spirit of adventure moved her to redefine her life so drastically?

As the plane touched down at Orly Airport, she began questioning her sanity. Where did she get this crazy idea anyway? Her French was weak; she knew no one; and her funds were limited. Fortunately, she'd been able to make temporary living arrangements with the help of her former French professor. But where did she go from there? *You are about to have the adventure of your life,* her sixth sense insisted. (Yeah, easy for you to say!)

After the plane arrived at the gate and the doors were finally opened, she followed the crowds to *Passeport Contrôle* and allowed the excitement of a new life to overtake her. After all, this was Paris! What could be bad? She was even getting up the nerve to practice her French, but the guy behind the cage just looked at her, stamped her passport and waved her on. And then she saw *him.* The cute guy from the plane who'd sat three rows in front was smiling at her. *Sheesh!* Her stomach felt like it was on a runaway elevator, but she managed to smile back.

"Oh, allo again!" came the sexy voice with the undeniably authentic accent.

"Hi . . . er, *bonjour!*"

"*Bonjour, mademoiselle!* Your first visit to France?"

"Yes." (Oh, God, that accent! It sounds like he's asking to massage my shoulders.) She took in the let's-get-to-bed gray eyes, the tall, but typically slight European build and the handsome face.

"Well, I hope you enjoy your vacation." But his expression seemed to shout, *and you will, if we get it on.*

"Thank you." (And I shall, if I get to see you again.) "Actually, I'm hoping to stay longer than just a vacation." (Just in case you're curious—Oh, please, be curious.)

"Oh? Then perhaps I might have the pleasure of seeing you again." (Translation: Telephone number, please.)

(Yesss!) "I'm sure that would be pleasant." (Mom would tell me to play hard to get. Thank God she's not here, because on top of everything else, I'm sure he's not Jewish.)

They finally got around to the introductions, and the next thing Rosie knew she was sharing a taxi with Jean Marc Brulard who, with his fair skin, sparkling gray eyes, salon-styled blond hair and sweet smile, was the embodiment of the forbidden gentile. How could she resist? And how could she know that their torrid, two-year affair would peak long before the first year was over? But because she was too stubborn to admit her mistake, and because Jean Marc had the inside track on every valley and curve of her body, Rosie allowed it to limp on for yet a second year.

About the only reward worth crowing about after living in Paris for that length of time was that Rosie finally became fluent in French. Oh, yes, one other thing: Jean Marc introduced her to his neighbor, Madame Volante, a spiritual woman of uncanny ability who encouraged Rosie to embrace her powers of clairvoyance.

She was a pleasant lady, this Madame Volante, with her ice white hair and startling blue eyes that were able to penetrate even the most private thoughts. Yet, she never took advantage. Her ability to guide a novice through the maze of self-discovery was the basis of her talent. Rosie's friendship with her more than filled the empty hours when Jean Marc would go off on his occasional assignments to film documentaries, many of which took him out of the city for days at a time.

So Rosie allowed that the strange visions she'd had as a child—the premonitions, the foreknowledge, the sixth sense that alerted her in advance of a happening—all stemmed from a gift not to be denied. "Trust yourself," Madame had insisted, and Rosie complied. It stood to reason, therefore, that Jean Marc's desertion after two years came as no surprise.

Rosie limped back to the States, older, wiser, but definitely not looking for love.

Chapter 4

Rosie lived on the second-floor apartment in a two-family home on a pleasant tree-lined block in Oceanside about five miles from Long Beach. Like most of the other structures in that area, the Spanish-style stucco house sat on a narrow lot, not more than forty feet across and eighty feet deep. A walkway led to the entrance, which was located on the side of the house, and inside the small vestibule, a long flight of wooden stairs led to Rosie's rented apartment. It was a little after ten when she returned home, but Rosie decided it was not too late to call Libby.

Libby Goldfarb was her oldest friend. They had a history together that included early playground rejection, teen angst, and clumsy feel-up tales about their first boyfriends. Even Rosie's escape to Paris hadn't altered their friendship. When she returned, they simply picked up where they'd left off. The only difference between them now was Libby's priority to get married. She was in love with her boss. Fine for her, but Rosie's experience with Jean Marc had made her wary about getting involved in any close relationship, or so she said.

Unfortunately, the years were leaving heavy footprints on her friend. Libby swung back and forth between hog heaven and starvation, although the latter was never long-lasting. Basically, she had three wardrobes: full, fuller, and over-the-top. Oh, but she was smart, loyal and had a great sense of humor, this last being the selling point whenever one of Rosie's dates had a friend who was willing to double.

Unlike Rosie, who had to commute back and forth to Brooklyn, Libby lived less than fifteen minutes from her job as a receptionist for a gynecologist whose office was in Rockville Centre (and with whom she had been having an affair for three years). Dr. Aaron Finkel, a married no-goodnick, was good at promises, though, and an expert at shtupping. So, as Libby said (often), *until something better comes along . . .*

Her friend picked up on the second ring, so Rosie launched right into her news: "Had some really bad happenings today."

"Oh, God, what? Did someone—?"

Quickly, Rosie told her friend about Grace and what the authorities were doing about it. "The police have started an official investigation, plus the ex-detective that Grace hired a few months ago to help her out on some of her cases is also looking for her. Shit! My life's been turned upside down."

"Do you have any—you knows?" Libby was well acquainted with Rosie's special powers.

"Only that something really awful has happened, and it's urgent that they find her soon. But other than that, no inkling as to just *where* she could be."

Libby sympathized with her friend. "If there's anything I can do . . ."

"You'll be the first one I'll call."

They spent another ten minutes hypothesizing, but came to no conclusions. "Stay in touch," Libby said, which was really not necessary because unless there were some shocking changes in Rosie's life, who else would she call?

★ ★ ★

Beware of enemies wearing disguises. Rosie awoke the next morning with a headache and the latest bulletin from ESP Central. She shut off the alarm and stared hard at the ceiling. Sun streaked through the slats of the Venetian blinds, stroking the walls in bright, vertical slashes. She wanted to return to the safe embrace of sleep, but Grace's disappearance pushed itself front and forward. What in the world happened? People just don't simply vanish. Rosie padded toward the bathroom and splashed cool water on her face. As she studied her reflection in the mirror, another thought struck her. Suppose Grace was . . . no longer alive? She didn't want to believe that. Whatever happened could be explained—and fixed. But even as she offered these platitudes to her reflection, Rosie knew she was deceiving herself.

She stumbled through her early morning routine in the small one-bedroom apartment, taking small comfort from Gabby, her cat, who seemed to know instinctively that her mistress was not to be fooled with this morning. The smart feline dived off the bed and into a chair, watching cautiously.

Rosie noticed and came over to pet her. "Sorry, Gabs, things are not going well for us at the moment."

Among other things, economics was a large issue. Her sweet job, secure up until yesterday, was suddenly an unknown quantity. She feared falling back into the hole she'd found herself in after two wasted years in France and the four more it took to find her groove after returning to the States. And what about Grace? A sudden chill made her spine tingle, but a glance outside revealed nothing but an innocent July morning. Shaking off all negative thoughts, Rosie dressed, fed Gabby and headed to the train station.

★ ★ ★

When she unlocked the office door just before nine, everything was just as she had left it the day before. She glanced at
Grace's empty office, checked the answering machine, found
two messages and pushed the play button even before plunk-
ing her bag on the desk.

"Hi, there," Arnold's voice crooned. "Didn't want you to
think I'd deserted you, my little *k'naidel*. It's eight-twenty-
five, and I'm in. Call me."

Rosie pushed the delete button and passed to the second
message. It was Mike, informing her that he'd filed a missing
persons report on Grace with one of his buddies in the police
department, and she could expect to be contacted this morning. She rolled her eyes at the unhappy prospect. But even before that interview, Rosie knew she had to set matters straight
with Judge Conroy and fess up that Grace was indeed missing. Then there was Harvey White. Whatever she thought
about his client, White was entitled to move forward with his
case. And what about Grace's client, the ex-wife? The poor
woman would now have to reestablish a rapport with yet another empathetic listener. Where to begin?

Rosie had learned a lot about the law since working for
Grace. Her disappearance was an inconvenience for the
courts, but it would gum up the system only briefly. There
were always others to step into the breech, and to that end,
she'd better get started. But as she reached for the phone to
begin the unraveling process, the front door opened after a
firm rap, and in walked two faces she'd never seen before. They
turned out to be detectives from the nearby precinct on Gold
Street.

"Natalie Rosenstein?" the first one asked.

"Detectives Parsons and Marino from the Eighty-fourth."
They flipped two badges at her.

"Yes, I got a message from Mike Bartel that you'd be by this morning."

"Need to ask you a few questions," the one who turned out to be Adella Parsons said. A dynamite-looking woman with a smooth, coffee-colored complexion and beautiful almond-shaped eyes, she appeared to be about the same age as Rosie.

"I figured. I'm making coffee. Can I offer you some?"

Rosie got a "sure thing" from Adella and a grateful nod from her partner, Chris Marino, so she added extra scoops of coffee and water to the automatic coffeemaker before plugging it in. She slumped down onto her desk chair and waited for the detectives to settle on the couch before speaking.

"This is a first for me. Tell me what you need to know. I want my boss located as quickly as possible."

"Why don't you take it from the top?" urged Marino. A few years younger than Mike, this detective was a clean-cut representative of New York's finest. Not quite six feet tall and broad-shouldered, he wore his brown hair regulation short and moved like an athlete. One could assume he had a hard time fighting off the ladies.

Rosie took a breath. "Well," she began, and stared off into space for a few seconds. "I'm not exactly sure. Came in yesterday, and Grace was not here." She quickly added that her boss usually beat her to the office. "She is a workaholic." Then she told them about the hearing before Judge Conroy scheduled for yesterday morning. "Grace takes her work seriously—and is always prepared. I'm not saying she wins all her cases, but she never knowingly lets a client down. And she was never a no-show—never."

Rosie went over to the table and filled two mugs for the detectives, indicating the milk and sweetener. The detectives asked a lot of the same questions that Mike had the previous day, and Rosie pointed this out as she repeated the same answers.

"Yeah," Marino acknowledged, "these are the basics. Have to begin somewhere."

He seemed an experienced detective, this Marino. His partner, Adella Parsons, was almost the same height. She looked tough, like you wouldn't want to mess with her if you were on the wrong side of the law. Her questions were sharp. And Rosie noticed that she didn't take any notes—and guessed she didn't have to.

When the detectives paused, Rosie decided to ask some of her own questions, directing the first to Marino. "Mike indicated that he had some connection with your precinct. Why do I have the feeling that you two worked together?"

He grinned back at her and nodded. "Yeah, we were partners. That was before Mike decided to go into business for himself." He said this without any hard feelings. His present partner smiled, and Rosie gathered none of this was news to her.

"That Ms. Osborne's office?" asked Marino, pointing to a closed door.

"Yes it is."

"Let's have a look," he said, rising from the couch. He wasn't asking permission.

Rosie opened the door and switched on the lights. Grace's office was not huge, maybe twelve by fourteen feet, but it was more than adequate for the lawyer's purposes. Her desk, two chairs, some bookcases and a file cabinet filled most of the space. But the focal point was the view that could be seen through the window directly behind her chair. It overlooked Court Street, a prime spot, or as the real estate agents would say: location, location, location! Office rentals were huge, and good spaces were at a premium.

Rosie frowned as the detectives began poking around. But she needn't have worried. Grace kept a neat desk, and there was nothing much to disturb.

Adella Parsons indicated the phones on the desk. "Private line?"

Rosie nodded. The detectives exchanged glances, and Marino asked Rosie if she had an extension for it on her desk. She shook her head no.

Adella Parsons looked to her partner. "Phone company?"

He nodded, and by way of explanation explained they would obtain a list of recent calls made from Grace's private line. Rosie didn't object, but she wondered about lawyer/client privilege. Then she reminded herself that the focus here was finding out what happened to Grace.

"While we're at it," Marino said, "we'll also get a tap on your main line, in case you're contacted by whoever's involved in this."

The three chatted another ten minutes, interrupted by the telephone several times. They were mostly fellow lawyers; the mystery was beginning to spread like a rash.

Rosie apologized for the inconvenience. "Bad news travels fast, I guess."

Just as the detectives were getting ready to leave, Carolyn Hughs arrived. Rosie introduced the attractive lawyer, noticing Marino's eyes lingering an extra few seconds. At five feet six inches, Carolyn was a traffic stopper, all right, with buttery blond hair, wide gray eyes and long, sweeping lashes. She made the most of her height by draping her "runway" figure in expensive clothes, and the exacting care with which she applied her eyeliner and mascara would make a professional cosmetician nod with satisfaction.

When introduced, Carolyn responded with "delighted," her typically British affectation. There was a long pause until

Adella Parsons finally cleared her throat and Marino made a show of looking at his watch. The two headed for the door.

Carolyn pointed toward the coffeemaker after they left. "Can you spare any of that?"

"Sure thing."

The other rattled a bakery bag she was toting. "Nothing like some sweets to cheer us up." She tore open the bag, exposing two freshly baked pastries. "Ta-dum!"

Rosie poured coffee for her guest, who pulled a chair closer to her desk. "This is very nice of you, Carolyn."

The latter waved a dismissive hand. "No matter what slight difficulties Grace and I had, I was always fond of you, Rosie." Her words were clipped, precise.

"I appreciate that." (But why am I suddenly uncomfortable?)

"As a matter of fact, I'm quite concerned about you," the other went on. "I mean it. Tell me what I can do."

Rosie was uneasy. She was torn between her appreciation for Carolyn's support, and loyalty to her boss (who, she knew, disliked the woman). "Well, not really anything right now. The police are involved, and Mike Bartel is also looking into it." But another thought hit her. "Wait a minute; there is something. The Schreiber case was up yesterday. When Grace didn't show, I sort of gave Judge Conroy the impression that she was merely delayed, so he continued the case."

Carolyn brightened. "Oh, I can take care of that!"

"You can?"

"Most certainly."

But Rosie was skeptical. "Even I know that Conroy is anything but a piece of cake."

Carolyn smiled confidently. "Leave it to me. I shall make it all better. I promise . . . you'll see." She laughed confidently.

"I'm thinking that you'll probably have to take over the Schreiber case if . . ."

Carolyn cut her off. "Oh, I'm sure Grace will be found and the matter resolved, but if that's not the case—God forbid!—of course I'll take it over. And, Rosie, if the worst does happen, I should like you to consider working for me."

Rosie's stomach floundered like a fish on a dry dock. She stammered something about how flattered she was, and then protested that surely Grace would be located soon, and life would return to normal for all.

When Carolyn left fifteen minutes later, instead of feeling relieved, Rosie felt guilty. It's my heritage, she reasoned. Jewish people have to feel guilty in order to feel good. Another thought struck her. Now I'm beholden to Carolyn. Wait'll Grace hears about this. Before she could even wonder about the odds of that happening, the private line rang in Grace's office.

It was a soft tone, normally inaudible when Grace's door was closed. But Rosie had neglected to pull the door shut after the detectives left. The muted tones of the private phone beckoned to her now like a chocolate eclair to a dieter. Should she or shouldn't she? Maybe it was a client? Maybe it was . . . Oh, hell! Why didn't she just answer the thing and stop guessing?

Rosie clutched at the receiver. "Hello?"

She heard breathing, then a soft-spoken male voice with an accent asked for Grace, and Rosie commanded herself to reply calmly. "She's not here at the moment. May I take a message?"

There was a polite refusal, and a click on the other end indicated the connection was broken. She stared at the phone, the echo of her pulse beating in her ears. She knew. *That was Nikki Marcos.*

But when Mike arrived a few minutes later, Rosie found herself unwilling to share the event. A believer in gut instinct, she held back and let the private investigator lead off.

"Understand Chris Marino and his partner were over."

Rosie nodded. "Did they learn anything new about Grace's disappearance?"

Mike shook his head. "Not yet. They're checking out her place and canvassing the neighbors as we speak." He studied her a moment. "Anything happening on this end?"

Rosie's cheeks flushed like a microwave on high. She remembered to shake her head no while fussing with some papers on her desk, but when she looked up, Mike's eyebrows had risen a half inch. (It's my mother's fault that I don't lie well.) "How can somebody just vanish?" she squeaked, continuing to stare back at Mike with as much moxie as she dared. Maybe she should just tell him about the mysterious call on Grace's private line and get it over with. "Carolyn Hughs was over," she finally managed. "She wanted to help, but I didn't have any suggestions."

"How about your secret lover?"

Rosie jerked her head up, but Mike was grinning.

"You mean Arnold? Puleeze!"

"Seriously, nobody gets a free pass. Tell me about him."

Rosie wasn't sure if Mike was playing his detective card or trying to get personal, and what was it about the latter that intrigued her? She said nothing, but felt a vaguely familiar turmoil brewing. *My God!* she could almost hear her mother yelling while clutching her chest, *not a doctor, not a lawyer, not even Jewish!* Rosie shook off all temptations. This time, she was on her mother's side. "What do you want to know?"

"Like, how long has this Arnold been chasing you? Did you ever actually go out with him? Did he ever threaten you? And, what kind of relationship did he have with Grace?"

She satisfied his curiosity on all counts, keeping her tone neutral. "As for his relationship with Grace, there was nothing outside of court that I know of."

Rosie couldn't help notice that Mike was ogling her. *He's looking me over like a smorgasbord at a Jewish wedding. I know he's going to ask me out.*

Mike continued to stare her down, saying nothing for several minutes after Rosie had finished, then he blurted, "How would you feel about having a drink with me after work?"

(I knew it!) So why was she having trouble breathing? She heard the word "yes" escape her mouth and thought she would pass out. (My mother will absolutely die.) Rosie didn't need any special power to realize she was on the verge of doing the same. Oh, but she was loath to get involved again . . . and with a private investigator yet! They have all sorts of deductive powers. She stared at the closed door for several seconds after Mike left, willing her heartbeat to return to normal. It took a few minutes more to get back to serious work.

Right before she left for lunch, the phone rang. Rosie snatched at the receiver, hoping for a miracle, but it turned out to be Judge Conroy's clerk, Sam Nicholson.

"Hi, Rosie, the judge would appreciate it if you could stop by chambers around ten to one today." (Translation: Be there at the appointed hour if you value your freedom.)

"Of course. Uh . . . what kind of mood is the good judge in today?" Rosie and Sam had traded quips together on numerous occasions, so she knew she wasn't taking that much of a chance.

The clerk didn't hesitate. "Don't worry. You'll get to sleep in your own bed tonight."

"Okay. See you later."

She glanced at her watch and realized she barely had time

for a fast sandwich, so she locked the office and ran to Nathan's two blocks away. She slid onto an empty seat at the counter, realizing too late that Arnold was near. She could smell his spicy aftershave. Sure enough, he was perched two seats away, and when he spotted her, there was no holding him back.

"Do you mind?" He nudged at the person sitting between him and his intended prize. "My girlfriend and I would like to sit together."

Rosie rolled her eyes in annoyance as the guy moved over and Arnold plopped his chubby frame on the stool next to her. It was apparent that Arnold didn't exercise too much self-control when it came to food. His round cheeks spoke of too many bagels with cream cheese and lox, topped off by too many blintzes and God-knows-what-else. The effect was that of a pubescent bar mitzvah with a too-short haircut. "I'm not staying, Arnold. Save your breath for someone who appreciates it."

His brown cocker spaniel eyes pleaded to hear otherwise. "Now, is that any way to treat a good friend?"

"I'm not in the mood, Arnold."

When Gus, the owner, approached, Rosie recited her order without pausing for a breath. "Lean corned beef on rye with mustard to go, please, and a Diet Coke."

"Put that on my check," Arnold interjected.

"Do that and you'll never see me in here again!"

Poor old Gus looked from one to the other, shrugged his shoulders and swung around to fill the order.

Arnold leaned over. "I don't understand you, Natalie. Why can't I get through? I really like you. Be nice!"

She pressed her lips together in annoyance. "Please do not call me Natalie! That's a typical example. You have no sensitivity. You—" She paused suddenly. Why did she owe him an explanation? In a calmer tone, she concluded, "Honestly, Arnold, this will go nowhere."

"How do you know? You've never given it a chance."

Rosie could feel her mother standing over her, reminding her that time was running out—almost thirty-four and still not married. But a sudden vision of herself lying flat under this schmuck was enough to spur her forward.

"Arnold," she managed through clenched teeth, "a wise person once told me not to waste time on a losing proposition. For old time's sake, I pass this along to you."

He stared at her a full minute, his expression devoid of his usual good humor. "All this time I was under the impression you were playing hard to get."

"I'm sorry if you were misled."

When Rosie left the restaurant minutes later, she felt guilty. She'd never seen Arnold looking so sad.

Rosie's appointment with Judge Conroy was not the stressful visit she'd imagined. In fact, the judge was curious about Grace's disappearance, empathetic as well. Grace had often told her that judges were radically different when in their private chambers and before they donned their robes, but this was her first experience with the phenomenon. Her interview with Judge Conroy certainly bore this out. Ensconced at his desk and surrounded by plants, paintings and well-worn law books, Conroy was actually human. He had a warm, sincere smile and displayed more patience than she'd expected. So Rosie relaxed and poured out her story. While she spoke, he tilted back in his chair and placed his interlocked fingers behind his head. A few seconds of silence passed before he offered his comments.

"Grace Osborne has been trying cases in my court for five years. I've spoken with her in chambers often and know her to be a hardworking advocate."

"That's so true."

"Furthermore," he continued, "she is respected by all her peers. I can't think of a single person who would want to do her harm."

"I know, Your Honor. That's why it's so difficult to fathom."

"So, Natalie—or is it Rosie? Where does this leave you?"

"Unless Grace returns soon, looking for a job, I guess."

The judge smiled. "I can think of a half dozen law offices that would be glad to have you."

Was this the monstrous Judge Conroy talking? She returned his smile. "Thanks for your vote of confidence. I guess I'll have my hands full for a while seeing to it that Grace's cases are covered."

The judge gave her the names of several people who would help her work through that part of it, and they parted on what Rosie could only describe as incredibly, unexpectedly, cordial terms. She headed back to the office, still holding out the hope that all of this was a bad dream.

Chapter 5

Adella Parsons raised her eyebrows and nodded at her partner when the two conservatively attired men entered the squad room. "Think these are our guys."

Marino craned his neck and called out, "Over here." He stood halfway to welcome them, extending his hand. "How you doing? Marino and Parsons. Thanks for coming over."

"Lesnick and Masterson," said the one nearest. "So what's the story?"

Adella studied the two FBI agents and wondered where her career might have stood now if she'd gone through with her original plans to join up. Neither one looked older than thirty-five. They were clean shaven, dressed in generically appropriate suits and ties and their shoes were polished. Nothing unusual—just two undistinguished-looking guys who could meld into any crowd. Adella was certain they had promising futures, decent benefits and, except for the bad press the bureau and the CIA shared after September 11, respect.

Marino gestured to the two chairs he had just pulled over. "Here's the deal. We got a missing person's report filed late yesterday. A lawyer—name of Grace Osborne. Last seen . . ."

He picked up a pile of notes, but Adella interjected, "Friday, late afternoon."

"Family? Friends?" asked Masterson, the taller of the two.

Adella offered some details, including Grace's relationship with Nikki Marcos. Neither flinched. "She was in the middle of a custody case," continued the detective, "a client who was trying to prevent her ex-husband from leaving the area with their son."

"Okay," the one identified as Lesnick said. "Between that situation and the Greek boyfriend, there's every possibility the missing attorney has been kidnaped and taken out of the state. What else can you tell us?"

The four spent the next half hour sharing details that might help locate Grace Osborne. After Lesnick and Masterson left, Marino shrugged his shoulders. "Whatever it takes. The clock's ticking." They both knew that the passage of time was their worst enemy.

Rosie didn't recognize the two men who knocked on the office door about a half hour later. At first, she thought they were going to ask her to take a message for the lawyer who had the office across the hall from Grace's. That was not unusual. But when they addressed her by name, she felt her stomach flutter in dismay. Oh, please don't let it be bad news!

"How can I help you?" she managed, thinking if her mother knew about this, she'd remind her how uncomplicated her life could be if only she'd get married and let her husband worry about such things.

"FBI Agents Lesnick and Masterson," said one, holding up some identification.

Rosie scrutinized his ID carefully while trying to collect herself. She wondered if he could hear her pulse thumping against the side of her neck. "And you are?" she stared at the other.

"Martin Lesnick, ma'am." He, too, held out his ID.

"The FBI . . . well . . . How can I help you?"

They explained what Rosie had already surmised, that the Bureau had now joined Marino and Parsons in searching for Grace. Well, the more the merrier. She gladly answered their questions, particularly since they seemed interested in finding out more about Hans Schreiber. Rosie filled their ears with what she knew about the creep. But then they inquired about Nikki Marcos. To that end, she didn't have much to report. As she made clear, she'd never met the guy, but that was soon to change.

When Grace's private telephone rang later that afternoon, Rosie knew instinctively who it was. *It's him.* She hurried into the other office and snatched up the receiver.

"Hello!"

A beat passed and she could sense disappointment on the other end. "Grace Osborne, please."

Rosie steeled herself against the mysterious male voice with its soft, foreign accent. "Who's calling please?"

"Am I speaking with Ms. Rosenstein?"

"Yes," she whispered, sucking in air.

"You know who this is."

"Yes."

"Don't be frightened. I mean you no harm. I'm concerned about Grace."

"We all are," she responded honestly.

"Maybe we can help each other." His voice was silky, exotic, mesmerizing.

Rosie felt herself responding to his candor. "How?" she asked.

"Meet with me."

"When? . . . Where?"

"Now. Close the office. When you leave the building, walk toward Montague Street. Turn west, toward Clinton."

She glanced at the clock on Grace's desk: four-thirty. "How will I know you?"

"I'll know you." The phone went dead.

Rosie's hands were clammy; her heart was racing; yet she was afraid to lose this contact. Her inner voice commanded her to trust Nikki Marcos. *It's the only way to find out what happened to Grace.*

That did it. Rosie grabbed her purse and turned off the lights, but just as she was about to lock the office door, she remembered that she'd agreed to have a drink with Mike at the end of the day. She turned back and reached for the phone. Purposely bypassing Mike's cell phone number, she left a message on his office answering machine instead. Something unexpected had come up, and she'd get in touch with him tomorrow. She felt guilty about not letting him know about Marcos, but her intuition suggested it was not the time to share this confidence. Locking the door behind her, she carefully checked the hall and departed the building via the back stairs.

Slipping out the service door of the building, Rosie checked left and right on her way to the corner. She headed west on Montague Street as directed. A late-afternoon breeze promised possible showers. Who would mind that? The whole city could use a break from the summer's humidity.

She walked slowly, scanning the faces in front of her. What would this mysterious guy look like? She still couldn't imagine Grace hanging with this character and wondered, for the umpteenth time, how they met. Slowing her steps as she neared Clinton Street, Rosie searched the vicinity for any possible candidate. As she waited at the intersection for the light to change, a mile-long limousine with darkly tinted windows pulled alongside the curb next to her. The rear door opened a crack and she recognized the now-familiar voice.

"Please join me, Ms. Rosenstein."

Sheesh! Rosie was sure she'd have a heart attack before this day was over. She hesitated only a couple of seconds before moving toward the car. As she approached, the rear door opened wider, and the man who stepped out and gestured for her to enter would stop any woman's heart. Well over six feet tall, broad shouldered, with long, crisp silvery hair secured in a ponytail, his black eyes held hers in a grip as strong as steel. To say the effect was powerful was like describing rocky-road ice cream as simply cold and sweet. The description can't do the calories justice. Rosie took in the movie-star good looks, the custom-made black silk suit, smelled testosterone-scented cologne and entered the car thinking, my mother is going to kill me!

As she settled back into the soft, padded luxury, the mysterious Nicholas "Nikki" Marcos introduced himself, inquiring, "And may I call you Rosie? Grace has spoken of you often, and I feel like I know you."

She nodded dumbly, imagining her mother's reaction to all this. *First, she'll shake her head and cluck her tongue. And then she'll wag her well-trained forefinger under my nose until I admit the error of my ways and promise never to do it again, and then, as further punishment, she'll make me go out with the dentist! In the meantime, just in case I don't wind up dead in an alley, I'd better pay attention.* But it was his accent, foreign, hypnotic, sexy, that sent her back in time:

Jean Marc—two four-letter words, reminding her that **F** referred to French accent; **U** stood for utterly gorgeous; **C** equaled conniving cockroach; and **K** signified the kick in the ass he gave her. How he'd conned her! And to think she'd given up more than two years of her life to a devil with the talent to fuck her brains out at night and shove her out the door in the morning to go wash dishes at a kosher restaurant. And all the while the sonofabitch was cheating on her! Oh yeah, she'd found out about that.

Rosie shook off her trance and tried to focus on the mysterious man beside her, admitting once again her weakness for foreign accents. Oh, but this one was also drop-dead gorgeous. And she didn't have to wonder why, even though the guy had a cloudy reputation, Grace would fall hard for him. Oh my gosh—Grace. She'd almost forgotten.

Marcos leaned forward and spoke to the driver in a language Rosie literally took for Greek. She did not understand one word, and could only hope he hadn't ordered her execution. Before leaning back, Marcos pressed a button on the console in front of them and the partition lowered, revealing a minibar and glasses.

"Care for something to drink?" he offered.

She shook her head. "No, thank you."

A shrug of his shoulders suggested she had no taste, and he leaned forward, reached for a cut-glass decanter and poured some liquid into a crystal glass. He extended his hand. "Won't you try some ouzo?"

"No, thank you," she repeated, aware that her voice was tight.

Marcos lifted his eyebrows but didn't try to hide his smile. "You do not have to be afraid, Rosie. I mean you no harm."

"Truthfully, I'm very nervous."

He nodded. "I know. All the more reason for you to have a sip." He brought the glass to his lips and downed the contents in one gulp, then poured some into a second goblet and extended his hand once more.

Rosie assumed he was showing her the stuff wasn't poison. She accepted the glass and studied the colorless liquid for a second. *What the hell.* She took a sip, immediately grateful for its analgesic effect.

Now Nikki Marcos was smiling openly. He had white, even teeth, and his dark eyes sparkled with genuine pleasure. "Good!"

He poured some more ouzo for himself. "Now, can you tell me," he began softly, "what might have happened to Grace?"

She looked directly at him. "Truly, I don't know."

"Have you talked with anyone? I assume the police are aware of her disappearance."

Rosie hesitated for only a moment. "Yes. And Grace's own private investigator is looking for her as well."

Marcos nodded. "Mike Bartel."

"Yes."

"Do you trust him?"

She thought the question strange. "Yes. Why do you ask?"

He shrugged his shoulders. "I suppose Grace does. Otherwise she wouldn't have hired him for her own work."

Rosie nodded, very much aware that Marcos seemed well informed of Grace's life. Plus, he continued to speak of her in the present tense, which was reassuring. Rosie was desperate to know that Grace was indeed still among the living.

"Where shall we begin to look for her?" he prodded.

"Frankly, I hoped you might know."

Marcos shook his head sadly. "She's never done this before."

"Never," Rosie echoed.

"I thought maybe someone connected with one of her cases . . ." His voice trailed away. Then he turned toward her, suddenly alert. "But Grace told me something about your, ah, special talents, so perhaps you can enlighten me?"

Rosie was wondering if he would broach the subject. "Look, Mr. Marcos . . ."

"Please, call me Nikki."

"Look, ah . . . Nikki, Grace gives me more credit than I deserve." But she knew he was waiting for her to say more. "I'm not a fortune-teller. I don't even know where these thoughts come from."

"Nevertheless, you do have . . . special thoughts?"

"Sometimes."

"And do you have any particular insight about Grace in connection with her disappearance?"

Rosie stared back at him, feeling almost as if he were the one who could read her mind. "You don't want to know."

"Try me."

"My feelings are . . . not good."

Marcos inclined his head. "Oh?" His voice took on a challenging tone. "Could you be more explicit?"

"I'm not sure you want to hear this, but I feel almost certain that, uh, something terrible has happened with Grace."

He stared back at her.

"I woke up with a bad feeling yesterday morning. Look—that's how it is with me. I can't explain it. But I knew for certain when I got to the office and Grace had not arrived that my premonition, or whatever you want to call it, had to do with her."

"Do you have any ideas—or *premonitions*—as to what exactly happened?"

She hesitated. "Not yet. Sorry."

Although Marcos was looking at her, she knew his mind was elsewhere.

"Look," she continued, "Grace is more than my employer; she's my friend. I've loved working with her. She always treated me well, and I'm just as anxious to find out what happened as you are."

"Of course."

"I'd like to go home now." She felt stupid—like she was in grade school asking for permission to go to the bathroom.

But Marcos nodded and smiled at her while jotting down a telephone number. "You can reach me at this number anytime, Rosie. May I expect to hear from you if you have any news?"

"I want to say yes, but as long as Mike is handling the situation, I can't promise to contact you right away." She wondered if she'd been a little too honest, but he nodded as though he understood.

"Grace always said you were—how do you say?—a straight shooter. Please remember, I do not mean you any harm."

She believed him.

Then he spoke to the driver, who pulled over to the curb. Marcos opened the door, and Rosie skittered over, preparing to exit the car, but he turned toward her and held up his hand. "I've instructed Theo to drive you home. He has the address. Good night, Rosie." He stepped out and closed the door, and the limo took off, leaving her with a lot of unanswered questions. One thing struck her: Marcos really cared for Grace. She could not know that, besides Grace's own mother, who was now past seventy, Nikki Marcos was the only person who knew the lawyer's true story.

★ ★ ★

Grace was nine when her father died. Her mother had no skills outside of homemaking, so she went to work on the assembly line for a company that manufactured farm equipment. The long hours kept her away from Grace, who did most of the cleaning and cooking for the two of them and tried to keep up her grades, the one thing she cared about. Then her father's brother came to live with them in Council Bluffs. At first, the young girl thought this would be good—to have a man in their house again. She would later discover it was no such thing.

She was almost ten when he came to her room the first time. She did not understand why he was touching her that way, and then it began to hurt. He put his meaty fist over her mouth and whispered, "If you wake up your ma, I promise I'll hurt you twice as much the next time." So she lay there, trying not to think of what he was doing to her, knowing only that it was wrong. When he finally finished, he left the same way he'd come in—ever so quietly. Three days went by before he returned. This time, she was ready for him.

When he opened her door, young Grace saw his silhouette framed against the light in the hall and reached under her pillow for her father's old gun, which she'd loaded with bullets. "If you take one more step, Uncle Ben, I'll pull this trigger. And don't think I don't know how 'cause my daddy taught me."

She saw him hesitate, then plant his feet. "Give me the gun, Grace, honey. I ain't gonna hurt you."

She cocked the pistol. The sound made him step back. "One . . ."

"Aw, that's no way to act, baby. C'mon, give me the gun now."

"Two . . ."

"Okay, okay. There's no need to get nervous. Maybe you jest don't feel good tonight?"

"I don't feel good about you any night—or any day, for that matter. And if you bother me again, I *will* tell."

He backed out of the room, making *tsk tsk* sounds. The next day, Grace waited outside the factory for her mother. It did not take long for the child to unburden herself. An hour later they arrived home in the sheriff's patrol car. Fifteen minutes after that, Uncle Ben was gone.

The event made a deep impression. Maybe there are other girls like me who don't know what to do, Grace thought. She promised herself she would be there for them. Years later, in her first job after passing the New York Bar Exam, Grace was filing some papers late at night for the large firm that had taken her on, when she came across an interesting case. A seven-year-old girl was found wandering alone late at night in Manhattan's Central Park. She related that she'd been abducted by an older man just looking for company. He'd taken her to his apartment on Central Park West and kept her for a week, despite her pleading to be returned to her family. This night, after he'd fallen asleep, she'd managed to climb up on a chair and release the locks on the apartment's front door and escape. Though grateful to find her alive and have her back, the family sought revenge. The man in question was a member of a prominent Middle Eastern family, and he claimed diplomatic immunity.

The firm thought the case was iffy and didn't want to spend too much time on it, but Grace was adamant about seeking justice. The girl's story was too similar to her own nightmare to ignore. Finally the firm's hierarchy issued an ultimatum: Forget the case or forget the job. Grace chose the case. She spent many hours researching the details. When she finally got in touch with the family, the girl's uncle made her an offer: Money was no obstacle; all bills would be paid, plus her time, of course, if she would dedicate herself to seeking justice. She agreed, and was amply compensated. When the abductor's family finally settled, Grace's contingent fee was more than enough to set up her own practice. The lawyer continued to focus on matters involving children. It was the only thing that made sense. And she remained close to the young girl's family, especially Nikki Marcos, the girl's uncle, who'd fallen in love with the dedicated advocate.

Chapter 6

The doorman eyed Mike as he approached the fashionable building on Eighty-first and Park, where Grace lived. "Help you?"

Mike flipped open his wallet and flashed an official-looking card at the man. "Yeah, you can let me into Grace Osborne's apartment. I've got a warrant." He waved a paper in the air. The other had no way of knowing that the paper contained nothing more than an overdue notice on his electric bill.

"Oh, all right. Let me get Henry to open up for you. I can't leave the door." He pick up a wall phone and punched in some numbers. After a brief exchange, he nodded at Mike. "Be here in a sec."

"Meantime," Mike said, "maybe you can help me out with something. By the way, what's your name?"

"Cawley—Frank Cawley."

"Well, Frank, can you tell me when you saw Ms. Osborne last?"

"Ah, let's see. I was off on Friday . . . so, Thursday—I saw her last on Thursday."

"And everything was normal, would you say?"

"Yeah, I guess. The car service picked her up at eight in the morning, as usual. She seemed fine."

"And you haven't seen her since?" Mike pressed.

"No. Like I say, I was off on Friday. Didn't see her over the weekend or since." As he spoke, the service door opened and a heavyset man in his fifties approached. "This here's Henry Warnick," the doorman finished.

"Okay, Frank, thanks for your help." Mike turned toward the other man and gave him the once-over. "How you doing?"

Warnick looked up and blinked.

"I'm Detective (kuch-kuch-kuch)."—Mike began coughing and covered his mouth, so that no real last name was discernable. "I need to get into Grace Osborne's apartment."

Henry Warnick glanced toward Frank Cawley, who nodded. "It's okay. He's got a warrant."

As they headed toward the elevators, Mike asked, "Did you know Ms. Osborne long?"

Warnick didn't face him directly when he answered. "Couple'a years." His voice was tight, as if he resented being pulled out of his sanctuary, wherever that was.

Oh, an attitude—that's all I need, thought Mike. "Think you could help me out here?"

"Got nothin' to say. Don't know nothin'. I mind my own business."

"Yeah?" Mike turned up the thermostat: "WELL MAYBE YOUR BUSINESS IS MY BUSINESS. HEAR WHAT I'M SAYING?"

"I hear you."

"Good. Now maybe you can tell me when you saw Ms. Osborne last."

The elevator stopped at the eleventh floor; the doors opened, and they stepped out.

"Don't remember. They call me when they need somethin' fixed. Maybe a month ago, maybe less. Leakin' faucet."

Mike shook his head in annoyance.

"Notice anything different about Ms. Osborne whenever it was that you *did* see her last?"

"Wouldn't know. We didn't have no personal thing between us." He unlocked the door to apartment Eleven F and stood aside to let the detective in.

But Mike grabbed his elbow and swung him back toward the door. "I'd like you to stay with me for now," he said, his eyes wide. Then he smiled, his bright white teeth reminding the other of a shark. They moved inside.

Everything appeared to have been left as though the owner had just stepped out and would be back shortly. Toothbrush, hairbrush, bottles of lotion and perfume—everything waiting. It all looked as though she stepped away, fully expecting to return before the end of the day. Mike dismissed the maintenance man and searched the rest of the apartment, but came up empty-handed. He checked his watch, locked the door and left.

Mike was surprised to find the office closed up when he stopped by for Rosie around five. What the hell kind of game is this? He checked his pager, cell phone, and finally, his office machine before finding her message. And he was even more pissed after that. What is this? Some kind of cutsie act? He headed for Casey's Tavern down the block and, after downing his first scotch, was comforted enough to concede this did not appear to be Rosie's style. Not that he really knew Rosie, but what had attracted him in the first place was her honesty. One didn't find too many broads like that these days. Hell, there'd only been one other woman in his life he'd ever trusted. Come to think of it, maybe she was the only one that ever existed. Mike held up a finger to Casey and nodded. No words were necessary. A second Chivas Regal on the rocks, no water, no lemon and no nonsense were exchanged for his empty glass. The sweet sound of Ella Fitzgerald's "But Not For Me" slid out from the jukebox, and Mike let the music and the memories gather him in.

He loved the old jazz classics; so did Monica. They liked nothing better than to sit quietly at the end of the day, sipping wine, catching up and listening to Frank, Ella, Louis, and the rest. Often, dinner got postponed until after they made love. That was what was so special about Monica. She didn't go by any timetable—until the end, that is. In the months before she died, they talked about "the train." And when they listened to Ella's version of "Sentimental Journey," they just held hands. Didn't have to talk; Ella did it all: *Gonna take a sentimental journey / sentimental journey home.* . . . Cancer, the robber who steals irreplaceable jewels, stole his love one morning in early December four years before. Nobody would ever take her place. So why should he worry about some broad who stood him up? Fuck her. "Casey, hit me again, pal."

Chapter 7

Her friend Libby was happily dipping chunks of hot, crusty Italian bread into seasoned garlic oil when Rosie met her at Luigi's in Island Park for dinner. "Sorry," Libby said, "but I was just starved."

"Not to worry," said Rosie, "I told you I might be a few minutes late." She plunked her bag down on the seat next to her and scanned the immediate area. "I'm definitely ready for a glass of wine. You?"

Libby thrust her oil-sopped prize into her waiting mouth. "Mmm . . . this is so good!" She shoved the bread toward Rosie. "Have some."

"Maybe afterward. Ah . . ." She'd finally caught the attention of a nearby waiter and ordered a glass of merlot. Her friend shook her head. "No thanks."

Rosie seemed surprised. "You okay?"

"I've been listening to the news," Libby said, ignoring the question. "Is it true there are no leads at all?"

Rosie shook her head. "Unbelievable! Grace has just completely vanished."

"The police? That guy, what's his name?—nothing?"

"His name's Mike. No, nothing."

Rosie took a minute to study her friend whose cheeks now stood out like two ripe apples. (She's added at least another four pounds since we met last week, but she looks so . . . so pretty! New makeup or what?) The waiter brought the wine and took their dinner orders. After he left, Rosie told Libby about Nikki Marcos.

Libby squealed with shock and delight. "Getouttahere! A limo? Ouzo? Sounds like a Greek godfather."

Rosie grinned. "Don't know about that, but I found him rather, um, charming."

The other's thumb and forefinger held yet another crust hostage over the garlic oil and nodded wisely. "It's the charming ones you have to be careful with."

Rosie eyeballed Libby. "And speaking of charming ones, how's your good friend, Dr. Fingers?"

"Dr. *Finkel* is very well, thank you!" But she was blushing.

Rosie eyed her friend, who appeared to be gaining weight by the mouthful, and was tempted to ask some pointed questions but something held her back. Instead, the two spent the next hour filling in the blanks of the past week.

Rosie drove back to her place after dinner with visions of Libby happily twirling pasta on her fork and cleaning the last dregs of Alfredo sauce from her plate with the crusty bread. Love that girl, but her relationship with Fingers is just plain destructive. Wonder how she'd do with Arnold. Hmm . . . not a bad idea, except . . . As she drove home, Rosie tried to imagine the combination of chubby Arnold atop plump Libby. (I just don't want to know about it.)

And then she got a flash: *You looked, but you did not see.* Well, something else to ponder.

★ ★ ★

It was all over the news. After a long and frustrating day with the mystery of Grace's disappearance following her everywhere, FOX News was repeating what Rosie already knew: . . . *and as of eight o'clock this evening, the police still had no motive or suspects,* the broadcaster was saying, while a photo of Grace popped up on the screen. *The blond, five-foot-five-inch-tall attorney was last seen this past Friday in her office on Court Street in Brooklyn. Those who know her say Grace Osborne is a respected professional without any known enemies. Interviews conducted so far have not shed any light on her mysterious disappearance. The FBI as well as detectives from the Eighty-fourth Precinct in Brooklyn continue to question Ms. Osborne's neighbors and acquaintances.*

Rosie switched stations. CNN was broadcasting along similar lines. She watched another few minutes, then turned off the set, shaking her head in bewilderment. Who had a reason to do such a thing? Grace had no enemies that she knew of. Rosie thought of Chandra Levy, the Washington intern whose body was not discovered until almost a year after she disappeared, and suddenly felt closer to the pain her family must have endured. But bad new sometimes erupts in clusters. Rosie's intuition begged for attention.

Don't ever take your life for granted. There was nothing specific, only a sick sensation that left a trail of bad vibes. Her stomach fluttered like a young bird who is unsure of where to land. But this dread had nothing to do with Grace. *Something's wrong at home.* Then the phone rang; it was almost eleven at night.

Her mother's voice was on the edge of panic. "Na-ta-lie—thank God you're home!"

"What happened?"

"It's your father. I don't know. He's . . . he wasn't feeling good, so I called Dr. Schoenberger, and he told me to meet him here."

Rosie subscribed to Caller ID and noted the location. "You're at the hospital, Mom, right?"

"Yes, and I . . ."

"I'll be right over. It'll be okay. I'll see you in ten minutes. And tell the doctor I'm coming. I want to speak with him."

"Okay, dolling."

Rosie was climbing into a pair of cotton slacks even before she hung up. She pulled a T-shirt over her head, grabbed her purse and was out the door in less than a minute.

"Could be a simple case of indigestion," Dr. Schoenberger was saying as Rosie joined her mother and sister. The others had arrived in the emergency room only minutes before.

The sisters signaled each other as only siblings who are truly close can, and Rosie observed that Julie's lovely eyes conveyed both fear and strength. A head taller than their mother, Rosie's older sister supported the frightened woman who appeared uncharacteristically subdued. Ida Rosenstein was experiencing the rare taste of depending upon her daughters for a change. Now it was Julie's turn, as the mother of two young ones, who took charge.

"Can you tell us what will be done for our dad?" she asked.

"I've ordered some tests," the doctor said, "and we should keep him at least overnight." To both daughters, he added, "I've warned him about overindulging his appetite with spicy foods. Seems he went overboard tonight, but we'll get him straightened out." He was smiling a little too broadly, perhaps in an effort to keep their panic down.

Dr. George Schoenberger was a rarity, a throwback to an extinct breed known as the good county doctor. Sixtyish, with a slight build, a head of gray hair and an athletic stride, he'd taken care of all the family members at one time or another. During his years in practice, he'd handled everything from sore throats to birthing.

Rosie turned to her mother after finding out she'd served stuffed peppers for their dinner tonight. "Didn't Dad have bad heartburn when he ate that the last time?"

"Yes, and tonight I tried to hold him to one small portion, but you know your father. He helped himself to a second."

"It's very likely that Joe's having a reaction to your wonderful cooking," the doctor said good-naturedly. "Go home. Get a good night's sleep. Your husband's going to be fine. I'll call you first thing in the morning."

Her mother was smiling with relief. "You think that was all it was?—the stuffed peppers?"

The doctor put on his everything's-going-to-be-all-right face. "All of you should go home. Get a good night's rest, and leave the patient in our good care. Think I've got a trick or two left up my sleeve."

Rosie drove home with her mother and went directly into the kitchen and put a kettle of water on the stove. Second only to chicken soup, tea was also a good soother.

"You're a good girl, Na-ta-lie. You know I don't like to bother you." She looked as if she wanted to say something more, but held her peace until she and Rosie sat down to a cup of tea a few minutes later. "You know I was really upset earlier when I heard the news."

"The news . . ."

"Your boss—she's *still* missing and you don't even call?"

"I didn't want to worry you." A lame excuse that still had the magic to defuse.

They sat up talking for about an hour, then went upstairs. Rosie grabbed an extra blanket from the linen closet and plopped down on the chaise lounge in her mother's room. By that time, it was a quarter to one in the morning. She knew her mother wouldn't sleep past six. Oh, what the hell! Five hours were better than none.

Rosie readjusted her position several times on her makeshift bed, but sleep did not come easily. She felt guilty about standing up Mike. Other emotions vied for attention as well, not the least of which was regret. What's his story? she wondered. Good-looking smart-ass like him must have lots of women. Forget about it. The last thing I want is to be just a number in the harem. Another half hour of restless tossing about, and Rosie finally fell asleep—at least she thought it was sleep—until she heard the woman's voice call out, *Please help me!*

The scene revealed itself as in a play: An overgrown lawn dominated the front of an old, boarded-up redbrick house on a breezy, drizzly evening. While standing in the weed-infested backyard near the basement, one could hear muffled banging against an old pipe from within. Perhaps it was the wind, which picked up from time to time. Accompanying noises were so indistinct as to make Rosie wonder what kind of illusion she was witnessing. But inside, the darkened old cellar told another story:

A shadowy figure was barely discernible in the dim light. Upon closer inspection, however, one could see that it was a woman, bound at the ankles and wrists and tied to an old furnace. One hand had been worked free, but at what cost? From wrist to fingertips, it was red and swollen. Her head hung over her chest from exhaustion. She was a slight woman with hair as pale as new corn. Of her face, nothing could be seen, but her chest rose and fell, so she was certainly alive. A crack in the ill-fitting window pushed in some outside air as well as rain, which licked across a rusted pipe on the ceiling and dripped onto the concrete floor. The woman stretched out her free arm and cupped her swollen hand under the drip, bringing a few drops to her parched lips. She moistened her tongue, then held out her palm for more. In between sips, she rubbed her moistened hand across her forehead and cheeks. Her body begged for sleep, but she reckoned that she didn't have the time for such luxury. She was weary, but conscious and determined.

Rosie struggled to attain a wakeful state like someone who'd fallen into deep water and was scrambling to get to the surface. What a nightmare! Or was that a nightmare? She shivered, pushing aside the haze and wondered who to talk with. Mike? Yeah, he'd laugh me right out of the club. Nikki? Nah, don't know him well enough to divulge the extent of my insanity. Who then? Carolyn perhaps? Definitely not. When Grace returns, she'll certainly want to recover as much dignity as possible. Should Carolyn have a vision of her colleague held captive in a—what? A basement? I don't think so. Then there's always the chance it was only a bad dream after all.

Madame Volante would argue that everything had meaning. Give yourself some credit. Your special gift is trying to tell you something. Okay, but in this case—what? Rosie could almost hear the dear woman cautioning her protégée to have patience. *Don't worry, chérie. In time you will learn the truth.* Yes, but does Grace have time to spare?

Rosie finally decided to tell both Mike and Nikki about her dream/vision and risk their ridicule. The clock on her mother's bedside table read 3:25 A.M. Well, this was not the best time for sharing. She turned over, expecting to toss and turn for at least another hour. Instead, she fell asleep almost immediately.

Dad is out of danger. That was the first thought that came to her as Rosie pulled herself into the new day. Rosie was pleased to see that her mother was still sleeping. She listened to the rain slapping against the window and noted that it sounded the same as in her dream. And without a doubt, that woman was Grace!

Now her mother moaned softly, and Rosie whispered a silent prayer to the Powers Above: *Please let Dad be okay.*

When they arrived at the hospital at seven, her father was sitting up in bed and eating oatmeal. Later, the doctor would explain about GERD (gastro-esophageal reflux disease) and that a sudden attack can mimic angina. Her dad grinned sheepishly and announced that he was ready to go home as soon as the discharge nonsense was attended to. Rosie watched her parents embrace, and wondered if she would ever find a really great guy with whom she'd want to spend the rest of her life. *You already have!* came the return message from "Information Central," but Rosie was not quite ready to sign for the package.

She took her folks home and promised to call them later, assured that her sister Julie would now take over. Then she drove back to Oceanside to shower and dress for the city. No reason not to go into the office; she'd just be a little late, that's all. And what difference would that make? Her life was one big mess again anyway. *Do I even have a job anymore?* A lot of questions. What she needed was answers. So while the hot water cascaded over her, Rosie zoomed in on all the players.

Hans Schreiber was Rosie's top choice for Bastard of the Year award. He surely knew that Grace Osborne would go after his ass. Stood to reason that eliminating his ex-wife's attorney from the equation would be a plus for his side. Hmm . . . motive, but opportunity? Supposedly, he had his son with him all weekend. Okay, who else?

Arnold Feltman. Rosie considered him nothing more than a big damn pest, but Mike insisted he was a stalker. That's sick enough, but what would Arnold gain by making Grace disappear? She took it a step further. *Like, he wanted me to become more dependent on him? My savior? And my mother would be relentless in her campaign to see me married. Yucch! The idea of that beer belly bearing down on me is beyond depressing, but perverted as his constant shadowing has become, I just don't think he has the brains or chutzpah to engineer Grace's disappearance. Next?*

Nikki Marcos. She was confident that Grace's Greek friend had nothing to do with her disappearance, but he was certainly a distraction. *Is he hot or what? This is definitely not someone my mother would go for.* One did not have to be clairvoyant to imagine the dialogue:

He doesn't even have a steady job, she'd argue.

Yeah, Mom, but—

But nothing, missy. Not Jewish, no job, no good. And that's final!

Rosie could only wonder what her mother would have said about that smoothie, Jean Marc, an adventure she never saw fit to share.

Now something else picked at her brain, something obvious that she was not recognizing. Distracted when the telephone rang, she grabbed at it, neglecting to check the Caller ID.

"Getting up this morning? Or you just gonna hang out for a while?"

There was no mistaking that gruff voice. "Mike!" She flicked eyes toward the nearest clock. (*Oh, shit! It's after nine.*) Then she remembered she'd stood him up the previous evening. "Uh . . . sorry about last night, really."

"Don't give it a second thought."

His cavalier attitude surprised her and left a bad taste. He's not even annoyed? Well, that shows he doesn't care. And if he doesn't care, why should I? She was wallowing in a snit, but Mike had already moved on.

"Give me an idea when you'll be in."

See? He doesn't care! "Definitely before noon," she said, in what she hoped sounded like a bored voice.

"Well, don't rush yourself." There was no mistaking the acid.

She was on the verge of a smart comeback, but he clicked off and that caused Rosie to blow. "I swear I'm gonna smack him!" she said, but Gabby was the only living creature to hear her. And here she'd been on the verge of telling him about her father going to the hospital. Hmpf! From now on I'm keeping this strictly on a business basis.

Chapter 8

Take care. You're not alone. Indeed, Rosie sensed another presence as soon as she stepped out of the elevator. She glanced around suspiciously and was getting ready to insert her key into the office door when the stench of overripe fruit engulfed her. A familiar voice said, "Okay, my little won ton, maybe now you could give me a moment."

"Arnold!"

"One and the same." He emerged from the door frame of the office next to hers and grinned a lopsided leer.

"Arnold, I don't know what I'm going to do with you."

"Well, for starters, you can go out with me instead of treating me like someone who has the bubonic plague."

"How many times do I have to say this? I'm not interested in starting a relationship with you."

"Look, I'm not proposing marriage here—at least not yet. I'm only asking that you give nature a chance."

"Nature? Is that what you call it? What part of 'not interested' don't you understand? Please, Arnold, for both of our sakes, take a breather."

The elevator doors opened at that moment and Mike joined them in the hall. He took in the scene, glanced at

Arnold and zeroed in on Rosie. "Good morning." He sounded annoyed. Then his eyebrows began climbing as if to say, *How desperate can you get?*

"Hi." She flicked her eyes from Mike to Arnold. If her mother were here, she'd say, *Take the lawyer, he's Jewish.* "Uh, Mike Bartel, Arnold Feltman."

The two shook hands as if each had a contagious disease, appraising each other at the same time like secondhand cars they had no use for. The office phone was ringing as Rosie pushed open the door, so she took the opportunity to step away from the battlefield. When she turned back, Arnold was just leaving.

"I'll call you," he mouthed at her, and spun away.

Rosie set to work fixing the coffee, but she could feel Mike's eyes on her back as well as his irritation. By the time she turned around, he was staring hard.

"What?" she challenged.

"Y'know," he began, "for a smart girl, you sometimes don't use any brains at all."

"What do you mean?" She was thoroughly annoyed now. He didn't have to insult her. And what was he getting all hot about anyway?

"What was this Arnold guy doing here so early anyhow?"

"How should I know? And who are you to talk to me like that?" Damn, she thought, they're as territorial as wild animals.

"First you stand me up—and for who?"

"—That's *whom.*"

He ignored her. "None other than that greasy Greek. Now you're playing footsie with a stalker? Where in the hell are your brains?"

Rosie was unhappily impressed that he knew of her visit from Nikki Marcos. "How did you know about Nikki?"

"Oh, is it *Nikki* now?"

She blew out an angry breath. "Do you think I really need an ex-policeman tailing me?"

"What I really think you need is a frontal lobotomy."

The two stood glowering at each other. Mike's eyes pierced the distance between them like two laser beams. Rosie's chest was heaving. She clenched her fists, then took a step forward, opening her right hand. But the office door was still ajar, and Rosie froze when she heard the ding of the elevator as the doors opened.

Carolyn Hughs knocked on the open door and swept in with a big smile, while the two combatants strived to look as though everything was normal.

"Hi, Carolyn, come on in." Rosie called, with as much cheerfulness as she could muster, but she was thinking, *Damn! I wasted precious time fighting with Mike when I should have been telling him about my vision of Grace.* Meantime, Carolyn was doing her version of the Queen: *"Charmed,* I'm sure."

After the introductions, Mike offered a general wave to no one in particular. "I'll catch up with you later," he tossed in Rosie's general direction.

"Yeah, right!"

"Coffee?" Rosie pointed to the pot after Mike left.

"Why not? Say, he's *rahther* cute."

"You're welcome to him, the hard-ass," Rosie said glumly, wondering why she had such an empty feeling.

"Oh? Sounds like a story."

The other immediately regretted her indiscretion. "Forget it. Think it's me. I woke up on the wrong side of something this morning."

And even though Carolyn tried to pry more out of her, Rosie stayed firm, beginning to feel the pangs of contrition and self-doubt. Again, it's my heritage, she finally conceded to herself. We're bred for this shit. Naturally, her mother perpetuated the myth. Now she thought about Mike's description of Arnold as a stalker. Hah! He should know how *he* comes off, the overbearing, controlling, possessive prick!

Carolyn glanced at the clock and picked up her briefcase. "Sorry. Really have to get going. Let me know if there's anything I can do."

Thinking of Mike after Carolyn left, Rosie reminded herself that her mother had programmed her to find the perfect man. It was more than likely that, in spite of all her protests, she was still on the hunt. But that stuff would have to wait. Her first priority was to locate Grace, a wonderful advocate in court but one who'd drawn a curtain around her personal life. Rosie only knew that she came from a modest background, and that she was bright and well educated. Probably could have had her pick of jobs: six-figure income with a prestigious Manhattan firm, but she chose a modest family law practice. So who or what would want to harm this paradigm of goodness?

As soon as the question loomed, Rosie thought she heard a voice. She glanced around quickly, but she was all alone. And then came a kind of rushing sound, like waves at the ocean, a whispering that formed the plea, *Help me. . . .*

Huh? That was not her imagination. The call for help was the same one she'd heard last night. It was Grace, definitely. Now she had no choice. Rosie pulled the phone close and dialed Mike's pager. Ten minutes passed before he called her back.

He was curt. "Yeah?"

"We need to talk."

"Why? The stalker giving you trouble?"

Rosie inhaled deeply. She had the urge to slam down the phone and wished he were close enough to smack. But her

mother's teachings included the caveat that any girl who
would slap a man was no lady, whatever the hell that meant.
Be that as it may, she'd get great pleasure from circumcising
him without anesthesia. With a mighty effort, she managed,
"This has to do with Grace, but I'd rather not go into it over
the phone."

"Okay. I'm actually on my way back. See you at about a
quarter of."

She spent the next few minutes trying to decide the best
way to tell Mike that Grace was calling from a basement.
Sure, that would give him enough ammunition to have her
certified. But when he walked in a few minutes later, Rosie
was more annoyed with herself than anyone else because her
heart rhythm had skipped to a mambo beat.

Mike slumped down on the couch. "Yeah?"

Rosie struggled to assume a neutral tone. "You're not making this any easier."

The other threw open his hands and dropped his shoulders—a gesture she took for *I'm listening.*

"Look, this has to do with finding Grace. I'm going to try
to explain something. This is kind of personal. I only ask that
you hear me out and . . . well, try to leave room for something that isn't in your inventory."

He hadn't changed his expression, but she knew he was
curious.

"Ever since I can remember, I've had the ability to know
certain things, many in advance. Well, nothing was ever clear.
I'd get a strong feeling about something that was about to
happen, like a premonition, or remember a dream that contained a message." She kept her eyes on Mike, who hardly
blinked throughout her explanation. "Then I met someone
while I was living in Paris." (Mike's eyes narrowed, but Rosie
raised her chin, rebuking his doubt.) "A very astute *woman*

who had powers of her own. I didn't have to tell her anything. She knew about me the first time we met."

"Where did you meet her—at a circus or something?"

"I knew you'd react this way."

Mike threw open his hands. "Sorry. This is just a little out of my field, but I'm listening."

She pressed her lips together for just a moment, then set her face. "I don't expect you to understand this," she said, stretching out her words, "but try to expand your horizons." Her sarcasm sliced through the air like a hedge clipper.

"Touché."

Then Rosie told him about her recurring vision.

"Sounds like you're saying that Grace is being held prisoner in a confined area of some sort."

She took a chance. "More like a basement."

"Hmm . . . who's on our list that goes for that kind of kitsch. Well, we've got the wife beater, Hans Schreiber, who could have it in for Grace since she's doing all she can to queer his case. Then there's the maintenance man in Grace's building, with a record, by the way, *and* easy access. And let's not forget good old Arnold. Of course, he's only a stalker." He followed this last salvo with undulating eyebrows.

Shit! This guy is so irritating! Rosie began drumming her fingers. After a minute, she smiled coldly. "I'm sharing this personal stuff with you in an effort to save Grace. Are you in or out?"

He knew he'd reached her but nodded innocently. "Okay," he sang out. "I'll try to focus on the goal. But I'm not sorry about the Arnold thing. Stay vigilant. Now, getting back to your, uh, dream. You see Grace in this, uh, dark place?"

"Not clearly. It's more that I know she's . . . being restrained or something, and I get the impression of an underground place . . . like a basement." Rosie was also getting the message that Mike was not a devotee of ESP.

He appeared to digest her explanation but didn't try to hide the smirk. "I see . . ."

Who was he kidding? "Look, I know this is out of your sphere. If you don't want to talk about it . . ."

"No, no. That's fine." But he answered a little too quickly.

"Real brave of you."

"Thanks," he said wickedly. "A basement . . . like maybe a prison cell?"

"A cell? It never occurred to me. Just can't pin it down. I only know that Grace is calling for help. If anything becomes clearer, you'll be the first to know."

"That's a deal. By the way, your Greek tycoon is not on the 'A' list of suspects; he was out of the country from Thursday of last week till Monday. Whatever happened to Grace occurred sometime between Friday evening and Sunday night, so consider Marcos off the hook."

Rosie thought he sounded disappointed. She decided now was not the time to offer any explanation regarding her visit with Nikki Marcos, but Mike had other thoughts.

"Care to share what transpired on your date with the big guy?"

"Date? We didn't go out on a date!" Was that what he was thinking?

Mike didn't try to hide the smile that said *gotcha!*

Yes I am gonna smack him, she thought. The palm of her right hand tingled in joyful anticipation.

But Mike was sprouting his I'm-just-an-innocent-boy grin. "So, okay," he conceded, "probably Marcos is just as anxious to find Grace as we are."

"Right. But *we're* not finding her."

That reached him. He stood up and headed toward the door.

"Where are you going?"

"Out—to look for Grace."

"But . . ."

"But what? Make up your mind. Are we gonna sit around and talk all day, or should I hustle my ass off to look for her?"

"But . . ." Even to her own ears, she was beginning to sound like a flat tire riding on the rim.

He swung around before stepping out of the office. "Oh, and I'll meet you at Casey's around five for a drink. That is, if you and *Nikki* aren't driving up to Maine for lobster."

Rosie started sputtering.

"It's all right. You don't have to thank me. See you at Casey's around five."

"How much of her story is made up, do you think?" asked Marino, when Mike called him from his cell phone a few minutes later.

"Can't answer that. From what I gather, though, she's supposed to have some ability in the woo-woo area. 'Course, I don't particularly believe in that stuff, but that doesn't mean anything. Got any ideas?"

Marino let some twenty seconds go by. "You remember that case we worked where the witness was so traumatized, he'd blocked out the identity of the intruder who turned out to be the killer?"

"Yeah, I was thinking of that. The skel was Jackson Pearce. Turned out he was wanted in two or three other cases. Anyhow, the woman who helped us was a hypnotist—Mary . . . Mary something-or-other. Think we got her from Al Corcoran in the Fifteenth."

"Mary DeWitt. Yeah, she was pretty good. Called her back on another one last year. Maybe we should get her in to see if she can clear the fog off Rosenstein."

"Yeah, let's do that. And—just in case Rosie is onto something, maybe we shouldn't wait on this."

"Okay. Let me make some calls. I'll get back to you."

"Good." Mike felt hopeful when he hung up. Whatever works, even something offbeat, like this hypnotism shit.

Rosie argued mightily with herself after Mike left: *Why,* she pressed, do you always fall for the unconventional? (Because that's the only kind that interest me.) Maybe Mom is right. Maybe you should settle for a dentist. (Right. And maybe I should just talk to Schwartz's Funeral Home about preneed.) Thereupon she put the subject out of her mind and began to busy herself with routine paperwork in preparation for the eventuality of the transfer of Grace's cases to Carolyn. When the phone rang in Grace's private office an hour later, Rosie felt the swoosh that comes with the gift of clairvoyance. *That will be Nikki.*

"Hello?"

"Yes, Rosie, you know who this is."

"Yes."

"I thought we might be able to talk . . . in the same manner we did the last time."

Two things struck Rosie. The first, that the detectives might have already put a tap on the phones. And second, that the last time she agreed to meet Nikki Marcos, she wound up standing up Mike.

"That would be okay, but . . . I have plans for later."

"Would you be able to meet me before then—perhaps within the next half hour?"

He certainly was persistent. She glanced at her watch—
almost two o'clock. She had worked right through lunch and
never realized it. Leave the office in the middle of the day?
Yes, whatever it took to bring Grace back. "I suppose I could
do that."

"Good. I will look for you."

After running a comb through her hair, Rosie locked up
the office and went downstairs. When she exited the building, a light drizzle began to fall. Damn! She'd left her umbrella upstairs. She started walking toward the corner, but
before she got there, the long black limousine pulled up
alongside, and Nikki Marcos once more stepped out of the
rear door and beckoned.

"I can't stay long," Rosie forewarned him.

Marcos nodded. "I understand. But you have something
you wish to share with me?" It was a question, but also a conclusion.

Maybe Nikki Marcos had powers of his own? "Actually, a
couple of things." She felt a little like Tokyo Rose, telling him
about the phone taps, but she didn't want to get caught in the
middle of the detectives' logs, which she was sure they'd be
keeping on all incoming calls. Then she told him about her
dream that Grace was somehow confined and calling for
help. He questioned her carefully, but she couldn't tell him
any more than she'd told Mike. Nikki's reaction was far more
immediate.

"Confined? You mean imprisoned?" His next words were
spoken in his own tongue, but Rosie didn't need an inter-
preter. His eyes narrowed in anger, black pupils riveted on her
in disbelief, then he reverted to English. "No . . . no! I cannot
accept that!"

"Please . . . don't take this as absolute fact. It doesn't mean
anything—like a dream, you know. A bad dream on my part."

She immediately regretted her indiscretion in sharing this with him.

"Don't be afraid that you told me," he said, as if he could read her mind. "This is something I need to know." He stared out of the window for a few minutes, then turned to face her. "And did you see this more than once?"

She was startled. "Yes," she answered quietly.

He put his hands to his head and began to massage his temples. "That case she was supposed to begin Monday, that Schrei—Schrei—Schreiber, that's it, Hans Schreiber!"

Now Rosie was paying attention. Grace *never* discussed her cases with anyone out of the office, at least that was what she believed up till now. If her boss mentioned Hans Schreiber to Nikki Marcos, they must be even tighter than she thought. Talk about significant other, this was definitely pillow talk. No wonder Nikki was so stressed. Now I've so much as told him that someone is holding his beloved prisoner. What could get a macho guy like him more infuriated?

"Please, Rosie, try to imagine who could be doing such a thing." As he spoke, the rain increased in its intensity, drumming on the car's roof like background music in a thriller film.

She hesitated. There was no way she was going to hazzard a guess. She had an idea there was another side to the suave Nikki Marcos, and she didn't want to be responsible for unleashing the beast. "At this time, I don't," she said in earnest.

"You know how to get in touch with me."

She nodded. Nikki directed his driver to return Rosie to her office building. The rain was bouncing off the sidewalks by now, and she held out little hope for her hair, but when the car pulled up in front of Rosie's office building, Theo, the driver, slipped out quickly and swung an umbrella over her head. Six or seven steps to the building entrance, and she was safely inside the lobby. Rosie had to wonder what she'd been doing wrong her whole life up to now. *I'll bet my mother would forget about the "nice Jewish" part if I ever fell into this kind of life.*

Seconds later, the limousine rolled away. Neither she nor Nikki were aware of the dark blue Ford Escort that rolled out from around the corner to follow.

Rosie barely had time to unlock the office door before she heard the phone. She snatched up the receiver before the answering machine clicked in.

"Law Office of . . ."

"Yes, my apple strudel, I know whose number this is."

"What do you want, Arnold?"

"Do I have to spell it out?"

"Agrrrrrrh . . ."

"Let me tell you something, *Natalie.* According to what I hear, you may not have a job soon. Maybe then you won't be so high and mighty."

"Are you threatening me?"

"Of course not, my little knish," his voice softened noticeably, "but you should be realistic. Word has it that Grace may not be resuming her practice."

"Oh? And just where did you hear that?"

"Never mind. The point I'm trying to make is maybe you should soften your tone with me. Take a step back!" Arnold's voice took on an unfamiliar edge. "Think through the situation, my little dumpling! Reevaluate your situation." You have no reason whatsoever to be so goddamned independent!"

She took a moment. "If I didn't know better, Arnold, I'd say you were threatening me."

"You've got that wrong, my angel. I only want the best for you."

★ ★ ★

Lesnick and Masterson had been beeped earlier after the FBI
intercepted the call from Marcos to Grace's private line,
which was being tapped. Agents driving a dark blue Ford
Escort were dispatched to the area in time to observe Rosie
entering and departing the limo. In view of this interesting
development, an interview with Ms. Osborne's assistant was
certainly indicated. The sooner the better.

Chapter 9

Here comes trouble. Icicles began trailing down the back of Rosie's neck a full five minutes before the knock on the office door. *Now what?* The two well-dressed gentlemen who entered shortly after seemed polite enough, but their good manners did not disguise the threat of their presence. They flashed badges yet—FBI badges. *Gotteniu!* she could hear her mother scream, *this is no place for a Jewish girl!*

"Would you mind telling me where you were this afternoon at two o'clock?" the taller of the two inquired.

"At two?" she repeated like a dummy, and her stomach flopped over. Ohmygod—*Nikki!* They must've followed me. "Well, uh, that is . . ." Rosie felt as guilty as a six-year-old caught playing doctor. How would she get out of this one? *Quick!* Think of something that might explain what you thought was a private meeting but instead turned out to be enough evidence to send you to Sing Sing. "I . . . met with a friend—actually, a friend of a friend." She was certain her nose was growing by the minute. After a few more minutes of feeling stupid, she finally acknowledged what they already knew—that she'd met with Nikki Marcos—"WHO," she'd stressed, "IS JUST AS CONCERNED AS I AM ABOUT GRACE OSBORNE'S DISAPPEARANCE!"

Another fifteen minutes of questioning and they finally left, after what Rosie interpreted as a temporary reprieve from serving time in the penitentiary. Her desk clock read four-fifty. Her stomach had been growling during the entire interview, and it dawned on her that she had not had anything to eat since her morning bagel. Even if she considered meeting Mike, she couldn't drink on an empty stomach. Certainly not. I'll stop by Casey's, bring him up to snuff on Arnold and head for home. He doesn't need to know about my session with the FBI. It's been a long and very interesting day, and I'm beat. Oh, what the hell! Shouldn't be a total loss. Rosie applied some lip gloss and added a dash of blush to her cheeks. She glanced outside, pleased to see that the rain had stopped.

Mike sat at the bar, eyeing the clock and nibbling on peanuts. The cubes in his glass looked fresh, and the golden liquid was still at the same mark. Casey eyeballed him from the other side and raised an eyebrow. He might have just as well posed the question.

"I'm holding off till five."

Casey shrugged his shoulders and moved on. At five precisely, Mike took a healthy swig. At two minutes past, Rosie pushed open the door. It took her a couple of seconds to adapt to the darkened interior. Of course, Mike spotted her right away, but stayed put. She's feisty, all right, he thought. A little insecurity never hurt. As her eyes adjusted, she scanned the place quickly, finally lighting on Mike at the bar. He timed it so that as she sighted him, he could pretend he was just noticing her, too.

He waved halfheartedly. "Come on over." And as she popped atop the stool next to him, he added, "What are you drinking?"

"Um . . . don't think I should have anything. Haven't had a chance to eat today, and my empty stomach wouldn't know how to process the stuff."

He shook his head. "You're a sad case. Y'know that?"

"Why? Because I can't drink on an empty stomach?"

"No. Because you have a problem keeping to the plan."

"The plan?"

Mike gulped some more of his drink, and Casey appeared out of nowhere. "Tell you what," Mike said to the latter, "bring the lady some of those little hot dog thingies and—" He turned to Rosie. "Glass of wine?"

"Is that what your *ladies* drink?" She swivelled in Casey's direction. "I'll have whatever the *gentleman* is drinking."

Casey nodded at Rosie, swung his eyes at Mike and disappeared. When he returned a few minutes later, he placed a plate of pastry-wrapped cocktail franks and a Chivas Regal on the rocks in front of Rosie. She picked up her glass. "Cheers!"

"Yeah, cheers."

The drink felt good, Rosie had to admit. She knew it was scotch, the good stuff—very potent, but what the hell, she deserved it after the day she put in. "So," she turned to Mike. "How was *your* day?"

He laughed. "You should loosen up a little more often." He was also checking her out: pretty face; sexy hair; intelligent eyes; the full, eminently kissable lips—*yesss!* "Another drink?"

"Haven't finished this yet, thanks."

He pushed the plate of franks toward her. "Eat."

She giggled. "You sound like my mother."

"I like your laugh."

She felt guilty. He was actually being nice. "Listen. I spoke with the Greek today," she offered, hoping it sounded less challenging than if she said she'd talked to "Nikki."

"Oh, yeah?" But he had a flash of guilt, like he was getting her boozed up so he could extract information.

"Yeah," she mimicked, dragging out the sound. "I told him about the, ah . . . dream."

Mike held up two fingers toward Casey, who returned a minute later with two fresh drinks.

In the next minutes, Rosie managed to relate Nikki's emotional reaction to her dream before realizing that the first drink had hit her hard. She pushed the second glass away. "Sorry. Don't think I can go another."

Mike smiled charmingly. "Whatever you say." But he made no effort to move it farther. He then introduced the subject of helping her unblock via a hypnotist. "This is someone on the up and up. Used her before on a case."

Rosie was moving the glass around on the polished bar and studying the wet rings. Mike prodded. "Are you up for something like that?"

She looked up at him, noting that the color of his eyes appeared to change with his mood. They ranged in tone from there's-a-fog-rolling-in gray to deep-sea-fishing blue. But he was waiting for an answer. "If it will help find Grace—yes."

"Good."

Someone turned up the volume on the music—an old Gershwin song, "They Can't Take That Away from Me," and Rosie got a faraway look in her eyes and started humming and nodding to the beat.

"You like the oldies?" Mike asked, unsure.

She turned to him. "And if I say yes are you gonna give me some smart wisecrack?"

"Actually, if you say yes I'm liable to forget myself and kiss you right here."

She felt a blip in her heart rhythm and looked at him curiously. "You know, you're a complicated man."

He looked down at his drink and didn't answer. He didn't have to. Rosie studied him for a minute and knew. He's got a story, she decided. We all do. They sat in silence a little while longer, made small talk, then Rosie swivelled around in her seat. "Gotta get going," she announced suddenly, but her legs felt a little unsteady. "Thanks for the drink."

"How about I see you home?"

Another polite gesture—or was he pushing for the bedroom scene? "Thanks. I'll settle for the Atlantic Avenue station, if that's not out of your way."

"Deal."

They didn't talk much in the taxi, but Rosie had the feeling she'd touched on a nerve—the music. What's up with that?

Chapter 10

Am I nuts? The next morning Rosie found herself fighting off her attraction to Mike. The idea of getting involved with him was dangerous. Sure he was good-looking; sure he was probably great in bed; and last but not least: sure he'll break your heart like that other rat, Jean Marc. *Am I looking for more of the same?* Still, that look on his face when she'd hummed along with Diana Krall (like that kind of music actually means something to him). If her mother were here, she'd say, *Well, there's more to a relationship than music, missy!* And she'd be right, of course. Her mother needed to be right, and tomorrow night she'll have another chance. It's *shabbes*.

The Friday menu was always the same: chopped liver, challah, soup with *k'naidlech* and chicken. And for dessert, she could expect more stories about the dentist, no doubt. *Agrrrrrh!* As if to comfort her, Gabby jumped up on the bed and began purring softly. She pushed her head up against Rosie's arm looking for attention. Her mistress petted her absentmindedly, stretched and rolled out of bed.

A slight drizzle scratched against the windows as Rosie fixed some food for Gabby and made coffee for herself. An hour later, she was on her way to the station ready to catch the eight-ten. It was a gray morning with a hint of possible clearing later on. As the train approached, Rosie clutched her umbrella and maneuvered to the spot where, if she were on target, she'd be among the lucky ones to grab a seat. The doors opened, and Rosie moved quickly toward her quarry. She settled onto the well-worn leather, shoved her monthly ticket in the slot of the seat back in front and took out her book. Across the aisle, four men were engaged in their daily gin rummy contest. She tuned out their early morning antics and tried to read. But after a couple of pages, her thoughts turned once again to Grace's mysterious disappearance. I can't sit idly by, she concluded, and determined that today was the day she'd take a more active role.

There were three messages on the answering machine when Rosie arrived at the office: Arnold, Mike, and Carolyn, in that order.

"Good morning, my little prune danish. Didn't want you to think I'd forgotten you. I was hoping we might have a drink together tonight. Noticed you last night at Casey's, and think I should be entitled to equal time. Call me, sugarplum."

Maybe this bastard really is a stalker as Mike says, but was he capable of something as grotesque as a kidnaping to gain her attention? At one time, she had played with the idea of introducing him to Libby. Obviously, that was out of the question now, and who knows but that it was for the better.

The message Mike left was brief: He had to take care of something and would get in touch later. The last call was from Carolyn. "Please page me if there's any news of Grace." She added that something unexpected had come up and she would not be in until late in the day. A sudden draft of cold air grabbed Rosie. She glanced up at the air-conditioning duct, frowned, then went to check the thermostat. But as soon as she moved away from the phone, the temperature in

the room returned to normal. She made a face—*early menopause?*
Then she poured herself a cup of coffee, went over to the filing cabinet and returned to her desk with several folders. Almost
immediately, Rosie began shivering again. *What's going on?*
Madame Volante's words came back to her: *Let the power in.*
She guessed someone or something was trying to communi-
cate with her, so she turned off the ringer (let the answering
machine pick up), locked the door, sat on the couch and closed
her eyes. *Let the visions come to you.*

Silence surrounded her like a blanket of cashmere. Within
minutes she reached a deep, meditative level, and felt a great
calm wash over her. The concept of a woman restrained appeared, and Rosie thought she detected the sound of moan-
ing. It was Grace crying out for help. Rosie's eyes flew open,
and she grabbed onto the side of the couch. There wasn't a
doubt in her mind that it was Grace. She was being held prisoner somewhere—but where? Rosie needed help in figuring
out the location. Her powers didn't include a zip code. But
assistance from whom? She grabbed a legal pad and started
making lists of all the people she knew who had any contact
with Grace and/or might have a grievance with their office. *I
can't depend on the police, or Mike, or anyone else for that
matter. This is something I have to figure out for myself.*

She decided to start with Hans Schreiber. From the little
that Grace had shared, Rosie knew the big man had a temper.
It's not a stretch to imagine that he'd do whatever it took to
obtain custody of his son. Kidnap Grace? Hell, why not remove the obvious obstacle? Rosie went into her boss's office,
opened the Fisher/Schreiber file and started leafing through
the pages. Some of this was familiar, particularly the domestic
violence reports and, eventually, a restraining order. Rosie recalled Grace's remarks regarding the latter:

"You see," she'd said, "at the beginning, the abused is

made to feel like it's her fault. And that kind of thinking con-
tinues even as bruises and pain escalate. The victim begins to
believe that if she'd only have done right in the first place: not
argued, for instance, when the big man says it's night, even
though the sun is shining; had apologized to him for breaking
her nose when he was the one who slammed his elbow into
her face; or even had not overcooked the steak, 'when you
know Goddamned well I like it rare!' "

Rosie had been shocked. "Oh, come on. You're telling me
women can let themselves get caught up in this kind of stuff
in today's world? In Afghanistan, maybe, but here? In the
good old U.S. of A.?"

Grace had assured her that domestic violence was far
more common than most people would think. "And it has
nothing to do with income level, either."

"Well, what gets these women past it?"

"Glad you asked—devoted psychologists, social workers
and volunteers who can listen, guide and find ways to show
victims that they do have a choice. Difficulties occur when
women refuse to acknowledge a problem exists. There is a
tendency to rationalize called the *it-must-be-my-fault* syndrome.
You'd be surprised how much abuse people are willing to accept before they get up the courage to do something about
it."

The discussion impressed Rosie, but it wasn't until several
hours later that she reminded herself of her own gullibility
some years before. Abuse comes in many forms, and even
though he wasn't physically violent, Jean Marc still took her
for a good, long ride.

His city was Paris. Rosie couldn't take it in fast enough. Of
course she was the perfect patsy, something like a sucker at a

carnival for the first time, and Jean Marc was the huckster. Rosie was buying the charm of the city, its ancient cathedrals, the renowned museums, cobblestone streets, outdoor cafés, the whole bit. But mostly, Rosie was buying Jean Marc, his gorgeous accent, the way he looked at her through half-lidded eyes, his gentle hands that honed in on her erogenous zones like well-trained missiles, his tongue, his ever-ready phallus. Within a week, she moved into his place on Rue Boulle, what one might call a workingman's district, except that Jean Marc had a conflict with that particular occupation.

"Guess what, *ma chérie?* I think it's possible to find you some work!" was his enthusiastic surprise for her one evening.

"What?—uh—*quoi?*" Her French would eventually expand to include full sentences, but for now, she was only able to reach for the abbreviated version.

"I think you will be very comfortable there—it's the district known as *Le Marais—trés charmant.*"

"Oh, I see." But she didn't, really. Putting it together later on, Rosie could understand why Jean Marc would assume she'd feel more comfortable there. *Le Marais* was charming all right; it was also known as the Jewish quarter where the more Orthodox men wore long black coats, black hats, and long, curly sideburns. And the restaurant where Rosie would work was strictly kosher.

She didn't mind the drudgery. What disturbed her, though, was Jean Marc's aversion to joining her in the process—work, that is. He talked grandiosely about various moneymaking schemes and interesting-sounding propositions, but except for his occasional calls to help on documentary filming, he seldom, if ever, held a real job for more than two days. Meantime, Rosie was scrubbing the skin off her hands, literally. Whenever she'd try to take a firmer stand, Jean Marc found a way to schmooze her right back into bed. He was a

gorgeous lover, she'd give him that, and the greatest guide a
newcomer to Paris could wish for (on her money). But it
would take two years until she finally got fed up with his
leeching and homesick enough to leave. Her disappointment
in him followed her all the way back to America.

Rosie wrestled herself back to the present and the task at
hand. So, Schreiber's got her vote. She was loath to look further, but good sense dictated she clear all possibilities.

Arnold Feltman. She thought back over the past couple
of years, and the many occasions when she'd turned him
down. "I just happen to have tickets to *The Producers,*" he'd
boasted, shortly after the show opened. "Oh, gee, how nice of
you, Arnold. Did you say they were for this Friday? So sorry,
but I have plans." His persistence under even the most trying
of circumstances was exasperating. He just happened to have
tickets to just about every first-run Broadway production,
Lincoln Center special, symphony or opera currently being
performed in the Big Apple. Rosie was sure any right-
minded girl would jump at the chance to attend these pricey
performances, but Arnold seemed disinterested in exploring a
relationship with anyone else but her. Nothing discouraged
him—neither her turn-downs, nor her negative banter. There
was a time when she felt guilty, but after a while, as Arnold
became more and more obnoxious, she grew immune to his
feelings. One time, when she was celebrating the end of the
workweek with some of her friends from the courthouse, he
came up behind her and placed his hand on the back of her
neck. While it wasn't rape, it was unexpected, and the shock
of such an unsolicited intimate gesture made her angry. She
didn't disguise the fact. Since then, communication between
them usually required a third party.

The idea of spending any time with Arnold made Rosie gag, but she acknowledged that he was someone she could no longer ignore. Was it possible that her refusal to see him socially had warped his mind to such an extent that he would take it out on Grace? With that jerk, anything was possible. She had to find out. So, okay, she'd fight through the nausea. Rosie didn't have long to wait. When the phone rang, she picked it up on the second ring.

"Did you get my message, my little kugel?"

"Arnold—what a surprise!" So, okay, she couldn't entirely erase the sarcasm.

"So, what do you say, Natalie. A drink tonight?"

"Not if you continue to call me 'Natalie.' "

"Oh? Do I hear a possible thaw in the Cold War?"

She bit down on her lip and could feel her mother hovering near, reciting her favorite spiel: almost thirty-four, not getting any younger, and he's Jewish! She knew Arnold was about to pin her down to a time and place. She had her answer prepared.

"So, *Rosie,* a drink—tonight?"

"Um . . ." She had already decided to avoid being out with Arnold at night. "Tonight's not good for me. How about coffee—um, later this afternoon?"

"Coffee," he repeated, sounding annoyed. "Well, all right, sweet thang. If that's best for you. I'll pick you up around four?"

She could imagine Mike being at the office and seeing Arnold arrive for their "date." "Why don't I meet you at Freddie's?" This was a luncheonette in the general area of the courthouse.

"Freddie's it is!" Arnold sounded as though he had all six numbers in the lottery.

Rosie tried to put the impending date out of her mind

and went about the business of the day. Mike called in around eleven. Said he'd be tied up with something this morning. If he didn't get over to the office today, he'd see her tomorrow. She thought that was strange, but decided not to question the circumstances, which at least prevented Mike from observing the afternoon fiasco.

Chapter 11

Mike had been standing across the street from Hans Schreiber's Fine Watch Repair for twenty minutes. According to his observation, Schreiber wasn't doing a raging business. It must be his winning personality, Mike thought wryly. He kept his eye on a customer who had just exited the shop and waited until the man was a quarter of a block away. Then Mike crossed over and approached him.

"Excuse me, sir, but I couldn't help noticing that you were just at the watch repair shop."

The guy looked up suspiciously, so Mike smiled and spoke quickly, pointing at his own watch. "This thing is on the bum, and I'm really up the creek until it's fixed." He adopted a helpless look. "Did you just have something repaired there?"

When the man saw that Mike was not looking to rob him, he appeared to relax. "Yeah. Left my Rolex there a week ago. The guy told me he'd have it fixed in two days, then gave me a hard time when I came to pick it up. Shit like 'yours is not my only job,' and 'I only have two hands.' Finally told him fix it or fuggedaboutit. Picked it up today."

"And is it fixed?"

The man shrugged. "Time will tell." He laughed at his own joke, and Mike grinned along and gave him the elbow.

The next customer was a little more difficult. She clutched her purse with both hands and glanced around, looking for an escape. "Don't touch me! I have Mace."

Mike backed off and softened his voice. "No, ma'am. I just need to ask you a question." He held out his arm and pointed to his watch, giving the same speech as before.

"Well, maybe you can deal with him better than I can," she huffed. "The man is rude, short-tempered and a crook! Wanted to charge me seventy-five dollars to replace something I'm sure isn't worth more than seventy-five cents. I took my watch back and told him in no uncertain terms that I would call the Better Business Bureau."

Out of the mouths of babes, Mike thought, watching her stamp away. He went into a nearby luncheonette and helped himself to the telephone book. The Better Business Bureau turned out to be a good lead. There had been several complaints about Schreiber, including unusual delays in processing, price gouging and rude behavior. One customer said she thought Schreiber was going to strike her when she protested that he'd scratched her gold Geneve. This definitely warranted a closer look.

Small bells attached to the inside of the door vibrated when Mike entered the shop, but there was no one at the counter. "Hello," he called out.

A heavily accented voice from the rear shouted back, *"Ja,* I'm coming," and a large, big-shouldered man soon appeared, filling the curtained doorframe.

"So? Vat can I do for you?" His face was red, as though he'd been exerting a lot of physical effort.

Mike took in the overdeveloped shoulders, heavy jowls and hard stare and established that he would not want to be taken unawares by the guy in a dark alley. Still, he smiled easily and held out his watch. "This thing seems to be running slow. I can't afford to be late for my appointments. Can you fix it?"

"Give it here!"

Mike thought it sounded like an order from the commander of a tank corps, but he held out his watch anyhow. Schreiber took it behind the counter, donned a pair of eye-glasses and snapped on a lamp. "Not a very good vatch," he announced.

"Maybe not, but it works for me—or at least, it did."

Schreiber handed back the watch. "Forty dollars. No guarantee."

"Wait a minute." Mike allowed an edge to creep into his response. "You're saying you'll charge me forty bucks and won't even guarantee the job?"

Schreiber stared back. "Cheap vatch. You bring me decent timepiece, I say different."

"Oh," Mike goaded, "you sing a different tune for more expensive watches. Well, isn't that nice? Listen, this is the only watch I have. Fix it or forget about it."

Schreiber's complexion took on a deeper crimson, and his eyes flashed. "Take back your vatch, mister, and get out of my store!" He stepped out from behind the counter with clenched fists.

For one wild moment, Mike had the urge to take on the giant, but in this instance, allowed his brain to control his actions. He backed out the door with the satisfaction that he'd accomplished his goal. This guy was capable of violence. If Grace stood in the way of his gaining custody of his son, what wouldn't he do to circumvent that?

For Rosie, the day sped by more rapidly than she would have wanted. As four o'clock approached, she started having second thoughts about meeting Arnold as well as a distinctly sour taste in her mouth. But she reminded herself that if her meeting with him led to finding Grace, it would be worth it.

The rain had stopped by the time Rosie left the building and headed toward the luncheonette. The skies remained overcast, however, draping a foggy quilt over the streets. The scene portended what she knew would be a depressing encounter. When she arrived at Freddie's, Arnold was waiting, a shine of nervous sweat glistening on his upper lip.

"So, Nat—Rosie, together at last!"

She strived to substitute a smile for the grimace that itched at the corners of her mouth. "Arnold."

"Come." He led her by the elbow. "A booth, I think."

With an effort, she withheld her comment. *Like, this is the Plaza?*

"So," he continued after Rosie slid onto the bench opposite, "what's new?"

He sounded just like her mother. Actually, the two would probably get along just fine—but not in this life, she swore. Just managing the thirty minutes she'd allotted for this fiasco would be a major feat on her part. Rosie figured the safest bet would be to get him to talk about himself, so she asked about his family.

"My parents divide their time between Great Neck and Florida," he recited. "My father's retired, advertising. My brother, Sam, who's married—got one boy, one on the way—took over the business. My mother's launched her second coming. She's into Oprah. Now she wants to be a famous writer, so she made Dad buy her a computer." He rolled his eyes. "She meets with a writer's group once a month." He shook his head. "She's off and running. Oh, well, it ought to keep her out of mischief."

Rosie cringed.

Now he was asking about her family. She bit back the sharp retort that came to mind. "Not too much to tell. My folks live on Long Island (she thought it best to skip the exact location) and seem very content." Quickly, she smiled, widened her eyes with phony interest and gushed, "But I think what your mother is doing sounds absolutely FABULOUS!"

Arnold puffed himself up like it was all his idea, but since he was out of shape, he couldn't hold the pose for long. "Yeah, but what does she need that for? She's better off sticking to what she does best—like cooking and canasta." He smiled, like Rosie should appreciate the alliteration.

Listening to the condescending bastard without exploding was not easy, and Rosie thought time never moved so slowly. While flicking her eyes at the clock on the wall behind Arnold, she twisted the ring on her finger to keep from screaming. After half an hour, she made a show of gathering her things together.

"Where are you going?"

"Home. It's been an exhausting day, Arnold."

"We're all tired, Rosie, but I don't like being polished off."

Something in his tone struck her as un-Arnold-ish. Every once in a while, he rears his ugly head, she thought, and shows me another side of himself. Dull, love-hungry, yet the shlump has a nasty side.

"I want our friendship to *go* somewhere!" he emphasized, "and so does your mother, my little chicken leg."

(Now you've gone and done it—spoken the magic words that will guarantee we'll never have a relationship—*my mother*.) She stared him down, completely ignoring his outburst, and after a few more minutes, begged off with a headache and made for the trains, declining Arnold's offer of a ride home.

After she finally got away, Rosie went back over the part of their conversation that concerned Grace. Arnold had seemed sincere in his regret over whatever misfortune might have befallen her. She'd watched him carefully, as Grace had taught her. He didn't blink or look away.

Rosie was deep in thought when, as she neared the subway, a flash of blond hair the color of new corn moved past her in the opposite direction, setting off an electric response. *Grace!* Heart pounding, Rosie wheeled around and ran to catch up. "Wait!" she yelled. The figure halted and turned to face her.

"Oh . . . Carolyn!"

"Hi, Rosie!"

"For a minute there, I thought . . ."

"Yes?"

"For just a second, I thought . . . Your hair—it's just like . . . It's different," Rosie stammered.

Carolyn beamed. "Why, thank you! I've just had it done— a little lighter than usual. Don't you like it?"

(Lighter, all right, but that's not all.) "Yes, it's fine. You've cut it, too. It looks very smart."

Carolyn launched a lawyerly missile, designed to reject any further arguments: "It's the hair, I suppose—Somewhat like Grace's."

Rosie gulped. (Exactly what I was thinking.)

"Grace was fortunate to have inherited good genes," Carolyn added.

Rosie briefly noted the use of the past tense, then shrugged it off. Just a slip of the tongue, she concluded.

"Are you headed home?" Carolyn asked, adding that she'd cleared her desk and was ready to take over the Schreiber case.

"I'll be in tomorrow around nine. If you like, I could bring the file over to your office."

"Splendid. That way we can go over some other issues I've been meaning to talk with you about." Rosie was curious, but Carolyn said it could all wait until morning. She smiled mysteriously. "You'll see."

Mike saw his answering machine flashing when he arrived home at eleven that night. Among the several messages, was one from Marino informing him that Mary DeWitt was out of town, but expected back sometime tomorrow. He'd left a message on her answering machine and would get back to Mike as soon as she returned his call.

Chapter 12

The familiar hubbub washed over Mike as he entered the Eighty-fourth Street Precinct the next morning. Since retiring after Monica's death, he hadn't seen some of these faces in four years. At that time, he thought he'd just take some time off, but when weeks lapsed into months, he realized he wasn't being fair to the squad. They'd been scrambling for temporary coverage, awaiting his return. As time went on, he realized it wasn't just some time off that would make things better. He needed a whole new scene. After a lot of soul-searching and counseling (yes, in desperation he'd even gone that route), Mike realized he wanted out of the Eighty-fourth altogether. But entering the squad room now, nostalgia wrapped around him like a favorite old sweater. Former colleagues clapped him on the back or shook his hand as he made his way across to his old desk.

Chris Marino shot him a wide smile. "Just can't stay away, huh?" He punched him playfully in the shoulder.

Mike nodded to Adella Parsons. "How're you doing?"

"Can't complain." Her warm smile showed genuine respect. "And why do I have the feeling that you're bringing us something for the missing lawyer case."

The other gave a thumbs-up. "Let me lay it out for you; then you can tell me if it's something."

Adella set aside her paperwork and Marino gestured toward an empty chair. "Let's hear it."

Mike perched on the edge of the seat as though he was afraid of becoming too comfortable in his former digs and told them about his visits to Schreiber's store on Canal Street and the latter's home near Bedford Stuyvesant. "He's a mean guy with a short fuse, and it blows when things don't go his way. I like him for this case, but I'd appreciate any information you might have on some of the others."

Adella said, "The others . . . meaning?"

"Why don't you tell me?"

She turned to Marino. "Yeah, you sure must've missed this guy after he retired."

"Nah," he said good-naturedly, "got me a better partner."

Adella nodded. "That and a quarter won't get you on the subway." She swivelled back in Mike's direction. "Sure, we're looking at Schreiber—and you're right, he is a nasty guy, but Nikki Marcos can't be ruled out either. He claims to be in love with Grace Osborne, but who knows? Even if he was not in town, he's still got a long reach. And FYI, we haven't eliminated Natalie Rosenstein."

Mike showed surprise at this last. "You got something on Rosie?"

Marino picked up on the shortened "Rosie" for Rosenstein. He leaned back in his chair, stretched his arms overhead and said gently, "Did you know she's met with Marcos a couple of times?"

"I know about one of them. When was the last?"

"Yesterday."

Mike gave this some thought. "Motive?"

"Haven't figured it out yet."

"That's because she doesn't have one."

Marino took in the protective tone. "And Marcos?"

"Looked into it. The relationship he and Grace have seems real enough. The guy's really going crazy since she vanished. Besides the fact that he was not even in the vicinity when she went missing, what's his motive?"

Adella took note of the dialogue between the former partners and elected to stay out of it. She observed Marino as he shot forward in his chair, opened his mouth as if to speak, then closed it again as another thought had struck him.

"I should let you know a body was fished out of the East River near Seventy-second Street. Unidentified female, age uncertain. We checked it out. Not your client—missing pross—reported ten days ago. Looked like a suicide. The M.E. is working on it, but there doesn't appear to be any connection to your Grace Osborne." He shrugged his shoulders. "Maybe you're right, Schreiber looks best overall. We've got a tail on him, and we're monitoring his home and business phones. As far as motive is concerned . . ." He looked up at Mike.

"Yeah, I know, with Grace out of the way, a new lawyer would have to take over. He might figure he'd have a better chance of winning custody of his son."

"Anyhow," Marino continued, "we plan on bringing him in for questioning. Interested?"

"Why not?"

Marino checked his watch. "Say around eleven."

On the way out Mike chatted up some of his former buddies. An hour later, after taking care of some personal errands, he returned to the precinct and waited for Marino, his partner and Hans Schreiber, which took longer than expected because the scene on Canal Street was not going smoothly.

★ ★ ★

The detectives had parked their car in the No Parking Zone in front of Hans Schreiber's store on Canal Street, flipped on their rotary dashboard lights and moved inside. They approached the counter and held up their badges.

Adella Parsons said, "Hans Schreiber?"

"*Ja?*"

"Detectives Parsons and Marino. We'd like you to come with us."

"Vot iss?"

"We need to ask you some questions," said Marino. "We'll explain when we get to the precinct."

"Questions about vot?"

Adella reached for Schreiber's arm. "Come on."

"*Nein!* I don't go!"

"Listen, fella," Marino began, shoving his face over the counter, "you don't got a choice. You're coming with us nice or the other way. Your decision." He pulled out his cuffs and dangled them in the air.

Schreiber's eyes closed in on the cuffs and his jaw tightened. He hesitated a few seconds, but when Adella's hand went to her gun, Schreiber relented. "I have to lock up first!"

"Of course," said Marino, who stayed close to the watchmaker while the latter turned off lights, set the alarm and switched the front door sign from OPEN to CLOSED.

With their catch firmly settled in the backseat, the detectives drove to the precinct where Mike waited. The private detective caught the wild-eyed expression on Schreiber's face as he was led down the hall toward the interrogation room. Mike moved to the one-way observation glass and turned on the sound.

"So," Adella began, "I understand you're looking to take your son and move out of the area." Schreiber stared straight ahead, but didn't answer. She pressed him again, adding, "I know you speak English."

"SO?"

Marino inched forward. "SO," he mimicked, "maybe someone's standing in your way of gaining custody."

"I got a good lawyer."

"Maybe your wife does, too," Adella said.

"Vot do I care?"

"Because her lawyer's gone missing."

Schreiber pushed his bulging forearms onto the table. He looked straight at Adella and sneered, "SO? Maybe there is no more case?"

Marino interjected, "Yes, asshole, there's still a case!"

The subject smirked, sat back and folded his arms across his chest.

Adella frowned. "Seems to me you'd have a lot to gain with your ex-wife's lawyer out of the way."

Schreiber didn't rise to the bait or change his expression.

"The timing's awfully convenient," she pressed.

"I vant to get back to vork now." He started to rise up from his chair, but Marino pushed him back.

"We're not done yet."

"So, okay, then I vant my lawyer."

Marino asked him why he thought he might need a lawyer. "Maybe there's something you want to get off your chest?"

"I don't know vot you're talking about. I don't know vot you vant from me. Is not right—you take a man from his business. I'm angry about this. I vant my lawyer."

He's not stupid, Mike thought, as he observed from the other side of the wall. Either he's an awfully cool character, or he's got nothing to hide. Marino came out after a while and spoke to Mike.

"Whaddya think?"

"Think he's a dickhead, and the perfect candidate behind Grace's disappearance, but he's cool. . . . I'm not sure."

"Yeah. So far he didn't give up anything. I'll probably spend a little more time making him miserable before we turn him loose with the usual warnings. We know where to grab him up if we need him."

Mike agreed. The interview dragged on another ten minutes. When Marino came out next, the two talked about getting together soon, but both of them knew it wasn't likely. Their reunions had gotten fewer and farther apart in the last year. They had different agendas now. Mike thought about how close they were at one time. Nothing ever stays the same, he reminded himself, aware that he'd become more philosophical since Monica was out of his life.

She'd held their lives together. No two ways. When he'd return from a shift, tense from confronting the lowlifes of their city, she was always there to massage the misery out of his day. Monica was a good listener, and her sense of humor saw them through a lot of difficulties—especially at the end. He could never have that kind of relationship with anybody else. Then why was he spending so much time thinking about that broad at Grace's office? Shove that!

Chapter 13

The week was drawing to an end, and there was still no word on Grace's whereabouts although Rosie sensed she was nearby. It was frustrating that the exact location could not be pinpointed. At the moment, she was giving her boss's desk a light dusting when she heard tapping on the door and a voice she'd known all her life called out.

"Yoo-hoo!"

Rosie moved through the reception area and whipped open the door, where her mother stood beaming. "Mom! What are you doing here?"

"You're not happy to see me?"

"Well, sure . . . I'm just surprised, that's all. Come on in."

Her mother pointed toward the other office and barely voiced a question. "Is that Grace's office?"

(Oh, shit—she knows.) "Sit down, Mom. Would you like some coffee?"

"So, if I hadn't seen this on TV, you were planning on keeping this a secret?"

(Damned if I do and damned if I don't.) "It's just that I didn't want to worry you." She said this last with a smile, like maybe that would make up for the deceit. But after thirty-

three-plus years, she should know better. Her mother kept her
eyes on her, pressed her lips together in a thin line, and Rosie
knew she had a lot to make up for. It reminded her of when
she was six and decided she was going to surprise her mother
with a cake. She'd dragged all the fixings out of the pantry
and started mixing the flour and shortening. Only problem
was there was more flour on the walls, the floor and her hair
than there was in the bowl. *It's a mistake,* she'd cried out when
her mother discovered the mess, *just a mistake.* Not a good
defense, but she'd give it another shot.

Before she had a chance, Ida Rosenstein asked, "Have you
heard anything? The police—they found her?"

(This would be Agatha Christie on the scent.) "No, Mom,
not yet."

"So? What will happen next?" She eyed Rosie suspiciously. "You're looking for another job of course."

"No. I'm sure the police will find Grace." She wasn't sure
at all, but didn't want to give her mother any more reason to
push the dentist.

"So maybe I made a mistake," she offered now, stealing a
glance at her mother. Not surprisingly, her mother was wearing *the stare.* No, it was not a good defense. To add to her
woes, the office door opened (she'd forgotten to lock it), and
hell came calling.

"Is my little macaroon hard at work?" The familiar voice
slithered around the door like the snake he was.

"Arnold!" (Well, at least he'll provide a distraction.) "Do
come in."

Unaccustomed to such pleasantry, Arnold bounded around
the door, then froze when he saw Rosie's mother. Initial surprise segued into knowledge as the resemblance between the
older woman and Rosie registered.

"Ah . . ."

"Arnold, I'd like you to meet my mother. Mom, this is Arnold Feltman." (Now, if I can just fall off a cliff or something.)

Ida and Arnold were smiling and shaking hands and giving each other the once-over. "I can see where Rosie gets her good looks from," he oozed.

But Ida's smile paled a bit. *"Na-ta-lie,"* she corrected him.

Arnold didn't miss a beat. "Natalie, to be sure."

The older woman relaxed. "So, Arnold. What do you do?"

"I'm a lawyer."

"Aha!" Ida's smile would have lit up London during the Blitz. She turned to her daughter. "So this is your lawyer!"

(Just stomp on me and roll me up in a rug.) She pressed her mother's arm and said, "Mom, please don't get carried away. Arnold and I are just friends." She followed this up with a hard stare of her own.

"Of course." But her mother's expression seemed to be saying: *The rabbi can be ready on a moment's notice, and I have a wonderful caterer.*

Rosie could read it all, and wondered what terrible sin she'd committed in her previous life that she deserved this. She began fussing over the papers on her desk. "I really have a lot of work to do and wonder if . . ."

But her audience wasn't listening. The two were communicating volumes with their eyes. Now *there's* a match. She couldn't determine which of them was happier at their imagined good fortune. And where were the interruptions when you needed them? She stared at the phone, willing it to ring, but silence prevailed. Then she glanced down at the Schreiber file, held it up and tapped on it for additional effect.

"Sorry to break in on you two, but I'm leaving in a few minutes to run an errand and will have to lock up."

But the others were in a world of their own. "Won't you join me for a cup of coffee?" Arnold was asking her mother.

"Why, how very nice! I'd love to, but I don't have too much time. I have to go home and finish cooking for *shabbes.*" She watched his reaction carefully.

Panic overcame Rosie. *No! Do not invite this opportunist to join us for dinner.* She begged her brain, Quick! think of something, but Arnold himself saved the day.

"I know. That's just what my mother is doing as we speak. I'm due there at six-thirty."

"Perhaps you'll join us another time."

"I'd love to, Mrs. Rosenstein," he said, turning sideways toward Rosie with an expression that said, *see?*

"Call me Ida . . ."

This whole conversation was making Rosie nauseous, but Arnold threw an I-told-you-so look at her and held out his arm to her mother, who said, "And maybe *you* can tell me what's going on with Grace Osborne." She nodded at her daughter meaningfully and held out her cheek for a good-bye kiss.

Behind her back, Arnold blew a kiss of his own through the air. Then the two waved cheerfully and were out the door, leaving Rosie to ponder her fate. (Might as well end it all here.)

A little while later, Rosie walked the half block to Carolyn's office, trying to sort out her mixed emotions—not about Arnold. She was clear on that. But hefting the Schreiber file in her hands, she was feeling like a traitor to Grace. Nevertheless, what choice did she have? The judge had decided that, due to the circumstances, continuing the case was unfair to the plaintiff; therefore, Grace's designated substitute should step into the breach. That meant Carolyn. Rosie offered up a silent apology to her boss as she strode through the lobby of Carolyn's building toward the elevators.

Carolyn's suite was on the fifth floor, and Rosie noticed the empty chair in the reception area. She called out, and Carolyn came out of her office. "Welcome!" she called cheerfully. "Really appreciate you bringing over the file."

Rosie was once again taken aback at Carolyn's transformation. Her hair, carefully layered down the sides and back was attractive but so similar to Grace's. And the color—just about identical. "Not to worry. Should I just set it down here?" She gestured to the receptionist's desk.

"Oh, that's all right. I'll take it. Stephanie's out with a cold. Would you care for some coffee, or tea, perhaps?" Carolyn's British ways were thoroughly rehearsed.

"No, thanks. Gotta get back."

"What's your hurry? Mightn't we talk a few minutes?"

"Well . . . just a few. I don't like to stay away long. Guess I'm always hoping when the phone rings it will be Grace, or some good news about her."

Carolyn looked amused but said she understood. "Just a couple of minutes, then. There's something rahther important I wanted to speak with you about."

Rosie was getting a clear picture of what that was. They sat facing each other in the reception area, and she heard her stomach grinding nervously. (What's wrong with me? A couple of minutes is not going to change anything.) "Go ahead," she said, but she already knew: Carolyn was about to ask her to come to work at her office.

"To be blunt, Stephanie's been out quite a lot lately, and I have to think she might be looking for another job, sooo . . ."

(Here it comes.) Rosie held up a hand. "Carolyn, I don't want to be rude, but before you say anything else, I'm really in a flux right now. My head isn't on straight. I'm worried about Grace and can hardly keep up with the phone calls, the police department and the like. I have a pretty good idea of what you want to talk about, but I don't think I could accept any more responsibility or commitment at the moment. I hope you'll understand."

"Of course. And may I say you're amazing. This job is yours any time you're ready for it. Now go ahead and take care of what's on your plate."

When Rosie left a few minutes later, she was grateful for Carolyn's understanding, but also relieved—and she didn't want to pinpoint why. Then she reminded herself that it was Friday. The end of the week was the good part, but dinner at her folks' held other problems, especially because her mother had now met Arnold. She groaned at the impact of that knowledge on tonight's conversation.

Chapter 14

When Rosie returned home at five, the skies hung over the buildings like heavy curtains, barely disguising the impending rain. She dialed Libby, but the answering machine kicked in. (Well, either she's already left for dinner with her folks—the two friends had the same Friday night routine—or Dr. Fingers kept her late. Yeah!) Rosie was due at her parents' by six-thirty and needed half an hour to shower and change and fifteen minutes more to get there. But if she couldn't find time to calm down, she'd be doomed before the evening began. Her concern about Grace filled almost every waking moment. Where is she? Who is responsible? Will the police find her in time?

After showering, Rosie lay down on top of her bed and attempted to relieve her mind of everything stressful, but thoughts of Arnold and his behind-the-scenes maneuvering with her mother were too distracting. What a putz! He's got this grandiose idea of a match. Now there's a sentence, all right! Being attached to him is about the worst fate she could wish on anybody, especially herself. She had a mental picture of the two of them standing under the *chupeh,* the rabbi sealing her fate, Arnold stomping down on the wineglass, relatives and friends yelling *mazeltov!,* her mother glowing with accomplishment. *Oy.* The food and wine would be flowing. Everybody would be *chmalling* it in, but she'd have absolutely no appetite. The next thing you know, they'd be at the hotel (probably Kutsher's or some such Catskill retreat) and Arnold would be lusting after her. She could see herself at that point, running down the hall in her bra and panties shouting, "It's a mistake! A mistake I tell you!"

Now her pulse was racing, and she realized how much damage that jerk could actually do. Just thinking about him made her ill, and she jumped when the phone rang.

"How's your headache?" Mike inquired.

"Who told you I had a headache?"

"A question for a question? Maybe you're the lawyer. Okay, it was the stalker. Guess he wants the world to know you went out with him."

Take a deep breath, she warned herself, before you say something you'll be sorry for. "I didn't go *out* with him, for God's sake. It was coffee. Anyway, why is it any of your business?"

"Think you need a keeper. I told you to watch out for that guy. He's possessed."

"He's harmless."

"Yeah, that's what they said about Son of Sam."

Rosie inhaled deeply. "What did you call for anyway?"

"Wanted to know if Grace ever discussed Hans Schreiber with you—besides what you may know about the custody case, I mean."

It was obvious that Mike was through with his irritating opening gambit and was attempting to get back to business, so she thought about his question for a minute. "I got the impression that Grace disliked the man—he's an abuser, of course—and she has little patience for his kind."

"And?"

"And what?" she countered.

"That's it?"

"Can't think of anything else." She tried to change the subject. "Sounds like you had a busy day."

"Tell you about it next time. Gotta go."

"—Wait a minute!" But it was too late. He'd already hung up, confirming in her own mind what her mother would say: *What kind of job is that?—a private investigator!*

Uh-oh, the clock was running. Rosie was glad she'd taken her shower earlier. Now there was just enough time to change into something her mother would consider appropriate. T-shirt and shorts didn't cut it for Friday nights. Twenty-five minutes later, she pulled up to her folks' house wearing a flower print, mid-calf length cotton dress and it was equally as comfortable as her shorts, she thought. The familiar car parked in front indicated that her sister and brother-in-law were inside with the children. Please, she prayed, let Mom be distracted with her grandchildren. I'm not in the mood for dentists.

Gut Shabbes greetings rang out as she came through the front hallway. The house smelled of chicken soup, and her niece and nephew were chasing each other around the living room. Rosie pushed out a wide smile and returned the greetings, kneeling and gathering the children in her arms. When she stood up, her mother was glowing.

"See what a wonderful future you could look forward to? Such a nice man, your Arnold!"

She was on the verge of a panic attack but couldn't escape the big hug nor her mother's next words of wisdom: "Don't wait too long, dolling. Mother Nature doesn't stand idle, you know."

Rosie managed a smile despite her cringing. She reached out to embrace her father, who was talking baseball to his son-in-law. He stopped long enough to give her a kiss and a warm hug before her mother called her to the kitchen, ostensibly for some assistance in getting dinner to the table, but when she entered, Ida Rosenstein had *that look.*

And her sister confirmed her suspicions, flicking her lovely brown eyes from their mother and back to Rosie, conveying sympathy. Fortunately for Julie, she'd never been put through the trials she knew her sister now faced. She'd not only met her husband-to-be in college, her mother had stamped him *kosher for Passover* even before she'd considered the idea of spending the rest of her life with him. But there you go! That was Ida Rosenstein.

Rosie took in Julie's contented expression and had to admit that in this instance, their mother had not done any damage, and her sister, older by three years, was none the worse for the arrangement. Despite managing a household with two children, she'd managed to acquire her master's in social work and now worked part-time at a rape crisis center. It was evident her busy schedule suited her. Julie's lovely face, framed by dark, shoulder-length waves the color of rich earth, exhibited no conflict.

"*Nu?* How is your lawyer?"

Rosie gripped the platter that had been abruptly shoved into her hands. "Fine," she managed.

"So? Fine? Is that it? Arnold is very nice, but you were always picky. Never mind. You remember I told you that I had a dentist?"

Rosie inhaled deeply. "Mom, listen . . ."

"I'm listening."

"It's just that . . . look, can't we just give this a rest?" Oh, God! Her mother's hopeful smile had changed to an icy stare. "Um, let me take this stuff inside."

When the family sat down to dinner a few minutes later,

it didn't take long to realize that Rosie was on her mother's shit list. That was clear to the rest of the family as well. Her sister eyed her sympathetically and tried to introduce another topic, not realizing she was stepping even further into the doo-doo.

"So, any news about finding your boss?"

Rosie kept her eyes in her soup plate. "Nothing I can discuss at the moment."

"Your sister's life is a secret," her mother intoned.

When Mom talked about her in the third person, Rosie knew she was in the worst possible trouble. Julie's face wore an apology, but at this point nothing helped.

Her mother gestured grandly around the table, bypassing Rosie as though she wasn't even present. She smiled and addressed the others: "Once a week our family meets for dinner. Isn't it wonderful that we can catch up with what's *new?*" She was nodding her head for emphasis. "For example, my friend, Thelma, the dentist's mother—did I tell you that her son is not only a *dentist*—he's *single?* Imagine, he could have his pick of any girl he wants." Her eyes went around the table like a searchlight and stopped on everyone's face but Rosie's. "Imagine!" she repeated, finally turning to Julie.

Rosie recalled how her mother had always played one against the other when they were growing up. (Let's face it, she wrote the book on manipulation.)

Her mother, who was now on a roll and enunciating each word as though her speech was being recorded, continued to hold sway: "How many Jewish dentists or Jewish *lawyers,* for that matter, are legitimate marriage material?"

Recognizing that Ida Rosenstein had now entered the no-fly zone, no one dared respond. They'd been on the receiving end of her tirades before and tried to remember that every storm had an ending. For Rosie's mother, that ending did not occur until after dessert. Rosie helped clear the table but deferred to Julie to assist with the last course: baked apples for the adults and cookies for the children, who dashed out to watch television as soon as they were finished.

Julie took a cue from the Geneva Convention and tried to bring their mother back to the bargaining table: "Mom, we all know you mean well and we respect your opinion, but . . . well, sometimes we have to work out things by ourselves."

Rosie thought her sister generous in using the plural, since there was no doubt she was the only criminal at the table. The point was, Julie was trying to open the door for negotiations, so now it was Rosie's turn (God help her!). "Mom, I know how much you want me to be married and settled, but . . ."

Her mother opened her mouth to speak, but her father suddenly burst forth, "Ida, *shveig!*" The room was immediately stilled, and everyone turned in his direction. Joseph Rosenstein didn't assert himself often, but when he did, the shock was too much to ignore.

"Listen to her!" he continued. "She's got a life of her own. Stop pushing the girl to get married. You've got a married daughter; you've got grandchildren; let Natalie live her own life. Enough already!" He turned to Rosie. "Your mother told me about a lawyer—Arnold, schmarnold—something like that. So? Are you interested in this person? Yes or no."

The moment of truth had arrived. "Uh, no, Pop. I'm sorry."

"Don't apologize." He turned to his wife. "Ida, you heard? She's not interested in the lawyer."

"I heard."

"Then the subject is closed. I don't want to hear another word. Rosie, give your mother a kiss, and let that be the end of it."

Like a dutiful child, Rosie went over to her mother and

embraced her. "I'm sorry it couldn't work out, Mom." She kissed her.

Ida Rosenstein's eyes were moist, but she kept the tears in and patted her daughter's shoulder. "Okay, we'll say no more about it."

The only thing Rosie felt bad about was that her father's rare outburst demoted her mother from her accustomed spot on the podium, but in truth, Rosie knew her mother had more than enough ability to climb back up. (She guessed the dentist would still be on the agenda.)

It was not quite ten when Rosie returned to Oceanside. She hung up her clothes, brushed her teeth and pulled on a cotton nightie. Just as she was about to pick up the latest Susan Isaacs novel from her night table, the phone rang. It's *him*—Nikki Marcos. She was right, of course.

"I was hoping you had some good news for me," the man himself was saying. "Perhaps you wanted to tell me something?"

Rosie thought his bent for turning a statement into a question sounded so . . . so continental. Jean Marc came to mind, but she didn't give him much airtime. "Yes," she said, compelled to relate her recurring vision of Grace. "I have no way of knowing if the dream or the experience, or whatever you want to call it, is true," she cautioned. "And I have no sense of the geographical location."

"Is Grace . . . still alive?"

"I believe so."

Rosie was becoming increasingly apprehensive. In fact, the whole conversation made her nervous, and she was beginning to have misgivings about sharing these details with

Nikki in the first place. The silence on the other end made her wonder if she'd overstepped the bounds of good fellowship. She recalled Mike sketching the mysterious Greek's background and his warning: *He's got friends!* So she quickly added, "Surely you know I would do almost anything to find Grace. I promise to think harder about this experience—maybe even figure out the location. In which case, I will certainly call you back."

"Soon, please."

She agreed, but as soon as she got off the phone, Rosie knew she was getting herself in deeper and deeper. She wished she could hash this out with Mike. Personal feelings aside, he was a damned good detective, and they both wanted to locate Grace. It made sense to speak with him. He might have some constructive thoughts. At ten-thirty at night? Not a good idea. But she couldn't stop thinking of him and figured out later that she must have sent off some signals because a minute later, ten-thirty or not, the phone rang and it was Mike.

"You're not sleeping yet, I hope," he began.

"Guess not, if I'm talking to you."

He let that one go. "Do you think you could meet me tomorrow?"

Her center of gravity leaped out of bounds and she almost didn't hear him add, "I've lined up a person who'll try to help you pinpoint Grace's location."

Her balloon deflated. "A person who will . . . what?"

"She's someone I've worked with before. Name's Mary DeWitt. You'll like her."

"Oh. Mary DeWitt . . . Is this the hypnotist?"

"That's the one."

"Uh, okay." In an effort to sound composed, Rosie was coming across as bored.

Mike didn't try to hide his annoyance. "Last I heard, you were willing to do anything to find Grace."

The hackles on the back of her neck were beginning to rise, and she upped the volume. "What makes you think I've changed my mind?"

Here was Mike's opening: "So, shall I pick you up or what?"

"Fine!"

"Address please."

This is like chess, she thought, acknowledging she'd made the wrong move, but also realizing she still had options. "Shouldn't we set up an appointment with Ms. DeWitt first?" *Gotcha!*

A flicker of space passed. "Call you back in a few." Typically, Mike hung up without waiting for an answer.

Five minutes later, he called back. "Twelve-thirty tomorrow at her office. She's on East Seventy-second, between Park and Madison, so I should pick you up no later than eleven-fifty."

"Wouldn't it make more sense for me to meet you in the city?"

"More sense for who?"

"That's *whom.*"

"And that's eleven-fifty. Address?"

Rosie gave Mike the information with the same enthusiasm as she would if she were filling out a tax form, adding, "I'll wait for you out front." She heard his grunt just before he hung up.

Chapter 15

The truth sometimes eludes even the most honorable. Gabby jumped on the bed and began pushing up against Rosie's hip, almost as if she knew her mistress had an appointment with Mike. Rosie squinted through sleepy eyes. The window blinds were not completely closed, and she could see that sunlight had replaced yesterday's rain. That was the good news, but she could still not get the picture of the trapped woman, who was surely Grace, out of her mind. And she was praying the meeting with Mary DeWitt would penetrate the mystery. Not even Grace, who was a fighter, could last much longer without food. But if Rosie's visions were on target, it would appear that Grace had found a way to avoid dehydration altogether. Even still, sipping from a limited supply of untrustworthy water could not contain her indefinitely. Rosie had to find a way to pinpoint Grace's location soonest. Today's session with the hypnotist held out high hopes.

The coffee had barely started dripping in the coffeemaker when the telephone rang. She hesitated. If it's Mom, I'll have to suffer an instant replay of last night. If it's Nikki, he'll want an answer. If it's—and she started a rundown of some of her friends when the caller's identity suddenly became clear. Oh, hell! I'm gonna buy a gun and shoot myself.

"Good morning, my little *schnecken*."

"Arnold!"

"Who else?"

"How did you—?"

"Get your number?"

(Hate to admit it, but Mike's right. The sonofabitch is a stalker.) "I do not appreciate this at all, Arnold."

"Before you say another word, Natalie, it was your mother who gave me your number."

Rosie couldn't contain herself. "You're a liar! And stop calling me Natalie!"

"Am not. Ask her, sugarplum. She's worried about you. So am I. And your mother prefers 'Natalie.' "

"I can worry about myself, thank you. Now get off this damned phone before I call the police!"

Arnold made a gurgling sound. Maybe it was his version of a chuckle. Well, Rosie didn't give a shit if his tongue had gotten caught in his windpipe. She slammed down the phone in a fury.

Coffee and a shower helped bring back some perspective; Antonio Carlos Jobim's soft Brazilian music filled in the rest. She shifted through her clothes closet, trying to decide what was suitable for the occasion, finally opting for a casual cotton dress of mid-calf length, low-heeled sandals without hose. She went easy on the makeup, too, telling herself that she was not out to impress either the hypnotist or Mike Bartel. This was Saturday, after all, supposedly her day off. Rosie suspected that Mike would arrive early. She didn't intend to give him an excuse to come upstairs, so she was standing in front of her building at twenty minutes to twelve. She was early; but she was right. Mike came rolling down the street only minutes later. (Ha! Had you figured correctly.)

If Mike was disappointed by her one-upmanship, he never let on. "Hi!" he said easily, leaning over and pushing open the door on the passenger side. Now if Arnold had this opportunity, she thought, he'd have waddled around and opened the door for me. Some inner voice cautioned her to quit while she was ahead, so she slipped into the seat and buckled her seat belt, murmuring something about his nice car, a late model Toyota Camry.

"Borrowed it from a friend."

(It's probably a rental. Living in the city, what use would he have for a car?)

They rode in silence for the first few minutes.

"Nervous?" asked Mike.

Rosie didn't answer right away. "Well, I'm not exactly a pro at this sort of thing."

Mike bit back a snappy wisecrack and offered some solace instead. "I'm sure it'll work out just fine."

Now it was Rosie who held her tongue. She let a beat or two pass and then inquired about his previous experience with Mary DeWitt.

"We were working on this case, Marino and I, and an important witness who wanted to cooperate was too traumatized by his experience to give us much help. Mary was able to get him to recall details that enabled us to arrest the bad guy. The D. A.'s office took it from there. Now that piece of trash is serving his time in Ossining, and everybody's happy—except the deceased, of course."

Rosie was listening carefully, trying to imagine how Mary DeWitt's expertise would help her hone in on Grace's whereabouts. She had no doubt that Mike and the rest of the department would take it from there. For the hundredth time, she wondered who in the world had it in for Grace. She voiced this aloud to Mike.

"Believe me, that's what we intend to find out."

Mike had elected to take the Triborough Bridge into Manhattan. He figured the extra few miles more than made up for an uninterrupted drive. To that end, he took the Van Wyck Expressway, which melded into Grand Central Parkway and onto the bridge. The traffic on the expressway was moving along pretty steadily this morning, and Rosie admired Mike's smooth handling of the car. He drove with the confidence of someone who was looking to arrive in good time but in one piece. None of this weaving in and out of lanes, trying to beat every other car on the road; yet, he didn't let anyone shove him about either. The way a person drives tells a lot about his personality, she decided. Mike pushed a button, activating the music system, and the soft sounds of John Coltrane's jazz slid smoothly from the speakers. A peace settled over the occupants.

Rosie found the music soothing, like a promise that somehow everything would be okay. Overall, she trusted Mike, but if you tried to pin her down, she'd be hard-pressed to put it into words. Had something to do with authenticity. This was no Jean Marc. No empty promises, no grandstanding, no power plays. As the saying goes: What you see is what you get. And, yes, that led into another area. She wondered what kind of lover he might be.

Mike liked Rosie's presence next to him in the car. She smelled clean and fresh, he thought—from soap, not perfume, which he despised. Even the way she was dressed today—plain and simple, not all frilled up. He hadn't exactly been celibate the last four years, but the women he'd slept with were nameless, faceless. This one, he thought, he'd really like to know better. He fell asleep last night, anticipating today's meeting, and his imagination had suddenly taken off. He could see the two of them standing in front of a mirror, his hands following the arch of her back, the curve of her hips, sliding up and cupping her breasts. She'd lean back against him and—oh, shit!—he'd felt himself getting harder with each imagined trespass of her body. Now in the broad daylight, with her looking so innocent in that plain little dress and sandals, he felt like a dirty old man. But, no, he wouldn't stop dreaming.

They rode in silence, content with their thoughts, but as they made their approach to the Triborough, the reality of what she was about to experience erased all romantic notions from Rosie's priority list, and she suddenly broke the silence. "What kind of person is Mary DeWitt?"

"What kind of person . . . ?" Mike repeated. "Nice. And don't get the wrong idea. She's normal."

"As opposed to?"

He kept his eyes on the traffic flow in front of him. "Not nice. I don't know how else to put it. If you had a cousin, aunt or friend that was easy to get along with, and someone asked you what kind of person she was, you'd probably say, 'nice.' "

She digested this and followed it up with, "You ever been hypnotized?"

"Me? Nope."

Another lump of silence. (Sure, why should he give this a second thought. It's like a father-to-be who accompanies the mother-to-be to the hospital. The guy can afford to whistle. He's not doubled over with labor pains, but he sure as hell has no trouble taking credit for the accomplishment after its debut. The operative word here is *after.*)

As they maneuvered across the bridge, Rosie tried to an-

alyze her apprehensions. Of course I want to help locate
Grace. That's not in question. It's someone playing with my
mind that disturbs me. The hidden therapist in her suggested
the problem lay in the sub-basement of previous experience,
and she gave herself a free session: Sure, certain people took
advantage of you in the past, but you're levels beyond those
times. Lay it out: Grace Osborne, the person who is your
friend and employer, is in trouble. How, what, why—will be
determined later. Maybe, because of some special talent, you're
the only one who can help the police find her before it's too
late. What's the problem? Stop thinking about yourself; start
concentrating on helping Grace. It's the old adage: Keep it
simple, stupid.

She turned to Mike. "I'm ready."

If someone had wakened him from a deep sleep, Mike
couldn't have been more surprised. His mind had drifted back
to imagined sexual encounters with Rosie and he was caught
off guard. Her remark set off a chain reaction in the barracks:
a sudden surging in his testicles began loading the ammunition, the corporal came to attention—No! Stop! Hold your
fire! "Huh?" he managed.

"I think I'll be all right with this hypnosis stuff."

"Oh, the *hypnosis*. Sure." But silently, he admonished himself. *Get a life!*

Half an hour later, they were across the bridge and gliding
south down the FDR Drive, which was surprisingly clear this
morning. Mike exited at Seventy-second Street and headed
west, slowing down after he passed Lexington. It was Saturday,
and he hoped he might get lucky. If not, there was always a
garage. He finally opted for a parking lot between Lexington
and Park, and the two walked the remaining block and a half
toward Madison Avenue. Rosie took note of the address. Pretty
neat. She must be making bucks up the ying-yang.

The doorman looked them over and decided they deserved to have the door opened for them. Rosie smiled back her thanks, and Mike noticed that she had the whitest teeth. He didn't know that she was gritting those same teeth as they rode up in the elevator to the seventh floor where Mary DeWitt was waiting for them.

A pleasant-looking woman in her sixties, the hypnotist invited them into her living room and bade them sit down. If furnishings reflected the personality of their owner, Rosie would guess Mary was comfortable with herself and enjoyed a pleasant, cheerful existence. A chintz-covered couch and two sturdy-looking armchairs covered in the same fabric beckoned. Off to one side stood a large, overstuffed easy chair with a matching hassock. Rosie noted a music center stocked with CD's and a closed cabinet, which she figured held a television set. The coffee table and several small side tables were of a vintage mahogany that reminded Rosie of her grandmother's darkly polished heirlooms inherited by her mother. Their hostess offered coffee and, upon receiving a positive response, excused herself, saying she would not be more than a minute. Rosie cast her eyes about, intending to learn as much as she could about the person who would be putting her into a potentially fragile state.

Built-in bookcases lined one wall and were filled with volumes of various sizes. Rosie wandered over to check the titles and was surprised to see not only texts but old masters like Dickens, D.H. Lawrence and Jane Austen among the lovingly worn tomes. *Interesting.* You can tell a lot about a person by the kind of stuff she collects, and her eyes swept the room, taking in the various knickknacks that were scattered about. She was just beginning to relax when Mary returned with a tray of coffee and what turned out to be homemade butter cookies.

Mike took the tray from her and placed it on the coffee table. Their hostess sat down next to Rosie and suggested that Mike pull up one of the side chairs. Rosie was getting ready for a barrage of questions, but Mary only poured coffee, offered cookies and smiled.

After a while, she gestured around the room. "I've been living in this same apartment for twenty-two years, and every time I think of moving, I start to feel sad, like I'm giving up on an old friend."

Rosie nodded sympathetically. "Guess I can't blame you. It's a great location."

They talked easily for another ten minutes, then Mike unfolded his long legs from the chair and announced that he was walking over to the park. "I'll let myself out," he announced. "Back in—an hour?"

Mary smiled at his delicacy.

As Rosie followed the hypnotist toward the study, she looked back at Mike, who tried to buoy her spirits with a thumbs-up motion. She imagined him in the hallway, striding happily (freely) toward the elevator, then out to the fresh air and a pleasant stroll. Sure! Don't give me a second thought.

Rosie studied the woman as they settled into comfortable chairs, then allowed her eyes to roam the room. It seemed a peaceful space with pleasant, pastel-printed drapes and slip-covers—about as Martha Stewart as it could be. Her host chatted amicably enough, but soon Rosie became aware that the room's illumination was changing. She knew the hypnotist hadn't adjusted a dimmer switch, yet, to Rosie, the light around them had begun to take on a soft, pink glow. At the same time, the air-conditioner motor reduced its volume to a whisper. *What's going on?* From somewhere deep inside, Rosie's powers were rising, resisting a force that threatened to take her over. She knew instantly that Mary, as expert as she was, would not be able to hypnotize her, and this made her mad enough to spit.

Dammit! I'd finally accepted this as a route to discovering Grace's whereabouts, and what happens? My own energy is overriding the circuit!

"Whaddya mean, you don't want to talk about it?"

Rosie refused to discuss the experience with Mike. She wanted to go home, be by herself—not think about the matter for a good, long while. Running away? Sure. It was the Scarlett O'Hara thing; she'd "think about it tomorrow." Something happened in Mary's study, something neither one of them was prepared for. And she just didn't want to talk about it. Mike hadn't been too happy.

Driving home, she'd sat with her arms crossed over her chest like a stubborn child who refuses to divulge some secret thing. "I don't want to talk about it," she repeated.

Jeeze. This broad is a pisser!

"Just take me home—please." She'd added the last because she reminded herself she was supposed to be a grown-up now.

"Home it is!"

They didn't speak until they'd crossed the Triborough and were once more on the Long Island Expressway.

"It was a bust," Rosie blurted.

"A bust," he repeated.

They traveled another quarter of a mile before she elaborated. "I told you I had some special *energy.*"

"Yeah?" He waited for the rest, but again they rode in silence.

"So?" he urged.

"So . . . nothing. Your Mary DeWitt, Houdini's cousin, is a nice lady but she couldn't override my circuit."

"Are you saying that she couldn't put you under?"

Rosie grunted and allowed her pent-up frustration to stream forth. "That's what I'm saying. All that hype, and she couldn't do it. I mean, this was not a pleasant experience. I was up half the night with nervousness, and it was all for nothing. And on top of it, we're no closer to finding Grace. What are we going to do?"

"My turn?" he cracked, not waiting for a comeback. "Okay, I hear what you're saying. Mary couldn't get you hypnotized. Disappointing, but it's not the end of the world. We'll have to go at this through another door."

"Like what? You have some other weird thing in mind?"

He really wanted to answer that, but held himself in check. "Okay, without a dramatic Broadway performance, can you give me—in two or three sentences—why Mary couldn't get you hypnotized?"

"Apparently, my special abilities blocked the process—and if you say anything smart, I'll smack you, I swear. So, because of whatever you want to call it, there's a wall, a resistance, that she cannot penetrate."

Mike was on a Freudian roll. The word *penetrate* started action in the camp below. Christ! Couldn't she choose her words more carefully? He adjusted his position and made an attempt to appear normal. "Okay, so Mary couldn't, uh, get through. (That's not a terrific substitute either.) Really? That's surprising, but it's not the be all and end all. We'll have to think of another plan."

"Like what?"

"Hey. Give me a few minutes. On second thought, maybe I should ask you, the gifted one, to come up with an alternative plan."

"Like maybe you think I can just snap my fingers or push a button?"

He was on the verge of saying something harsh but stopped. What's to be gained? At the same time Rosie heard the echo of her own smart-ass wisecracks and realized she sounded defensive.

"Let's—"

"Hold on—"

They were both talking at once, trying to hose down the irritation. Then they did it again.

"GO ON," they said, at the same exact moment, and laughed.

"You go first," Mike offered.

"I guess I feel like a failure. As much as I dreaded today's experience, I also anticipated gaining some solid information on Grace's location. I was disappointed. Now I'm scared—not for me, for Grace."

"Yeah, me, too—on both counts. So, where do we go from here?"

"How about my place?" she offered. "I'll make a pot of coffee."

The telephone rang in Mike's basement.

Chapter 16

Fortune is smiling on you today. Take advantage. Rosie drove out to Long Beach on Sunday humming along with Rosemary Clooney. The humid conditions of the past week had evaporated, leaving behind a Walt Disney sky and temperatures in the low seventies. Life could be wonderful if only she could seal up the memories of Jean Marc in a carton, bury it (and him) at sea and start over.

Mike had shown another side of himself yesterday when they returned to her place after the fiasco at Mary DeWitt's. Of course she knew he was looking for more than a cup of coffee, but she wasn't ready to go down that road yet. Poor guy. She almost felt sorry for him when, after an hour or so, he saw that she was not going to strip down to the bare facts. He seemed to expect such a scenario—duh! Well, later for that. Mike did have a few nice things to say about her apartment, though, and he was impressed with her music collection. It was eclectic and featured everything from light classical to salsa. But it was the old jazz part that got his attention. It was evident they shared an appreciation for that particular genre. He browsed through some of her old records and found the same artists he also collected, like John Lewis,

Milt "Bags" Jackson and the Duke. Yes, the music part was fine, and the apartment comfy. But his years in law enforcement had nurtured a bad habit: He always had to poke a little deeper. And now the thing that was bothering him was the building itself. It posed a security problem.

"What do you call that stuff on the side of the house? Stairway to heaven?"

"You might say that," Rosie responded impatiently.

The original design called for a balcony, which, for some unknown reason was never completed. Broad plateaus of now moss-covered stone rose to an ill-defined ledge along the side of the building. When Rosie saw the house for the first time, she dubbed the vision as *the unfinished symphony*. But over a period of time, she'd stopped noticing it altogether. Now, he was explaining it might be a security risk. Of course, Rosie pooh-poohed this, and that got them going. Then an unexpected guest interrupted their debate.

Rosie heard the clomping of heavy shoes on the stairs and wondered who would be visiting as she wasn't expecting anyone. She was twice as surprised to hear Libby's voice: "Hey, Rosie, open the door. It's me." Libby breezed in seconds later and threw herself into the nearest chair, declaring, "Whew! those stairs. How do you do it?" It was only then she noticed her friend had company. "Oh, Rosie. I'm sorry. Didn't know . . ."

"That's okay. Libby Goldfarb . . . Mike Bartel."

While the two acknowledged the introductions, Rosie sized up her friend, who was struggling to recover from climbing one flight of stairs, and then it hit her. *Why am I so stupid?* Libby was not only bigger than life, she was supporting life—a new one. Sonofabitch! That bastard, Dr. Fingers, knocked up my best friend. There wasn't a doubt in Rosie's mind. She sensed the new life clearly. Only, why hadn't Libby said anything? Oh, later for that. I'll have a good talk with her. In the meantime, Rosie's shock had created an awkward moment, also known as a *pregnant pause.*

The other two were studying each other. Rosie was the only thing they had in common. She stepped into the breach and played hostess for the next half hour until Libby rose to go with some story about having to visit family. The interruption put a damper on anything Rosie and Mike might have been leading up to, as well. Downstairs, Mike offered a casual good-bye to Rosie and walked slowly toward his car, which happened to be parked right in front of Libby's.

Rosie whispered to her friend, "We have to talk."

"God, yes, he's really a hunk."

"Not about Mike—about you." She stared at her friend and nodded meaningfully, reminding herself of her own mother.

"Rosie , I, uh—" Libby looked embarrassed.

(Like, how long had she expected to keep this a secret?) "Hush, now. We'll talk later."

Rosie was ripping mad after Libby left, mostly at herself for not having diagnosed her friend's condition sooner. *Sheesh!* Libby could have done something about it months ago. Now she's too far along. Also wonder what Dr. Fingers is planning to do about it. Sonofabitch! He should be strung up by the balls. Yeah, that would be perfect. Maybe then his wonker wouldn't work so good anymore. What to do about this? I have to think.

In retrospect, Rosie's mood this morning tempted her along healthy pathways, so she directed her car down Lincoln Road toward the beach, parked, and went up on the boardwalk for a look-see. Dynamite! She inhaled the fresh salty air and

blinked at the diamonds on the water. Lazy waves rolled onto
a pristine beach with only a few noisy seagulls circling overhead. What better way to salute this perfect day than a run on
the beach? She'd have to keep a rein on the time and effort,
though. Can't get too sweaty before visiting her folks, but a
short jog wouldn't hurt, and off she went. She did her best
thinking when running. After only fifteen minutes, she'd resolved some strategy regarding Libby, also Arnold, and neatly
secured Mike in an indefinite holding pattern.

Arnold's just a sad case—a dork, really, looking to fill a
gap in his life. He's got a law degree and nothing else. The
problem is, he's latched on to me. So what I have to do is find
a substitute. Yeah, that's it—a substitute. Unfortunately, it's too
late for Libby. Rosie couldn't see her and Arnold pushing Dr.
Finger's baby down the aisle toward the rabbi—not Arnold's
style, so Libby's out on this one. Rosie then reviewed a roster
of all the single women she knew: relatives, girlfriends and
coworkers. Out of the whole bunch, only one fit the bill: her
cousin Amy. Yeah—Amy! (Not very pretty, but a good soul.)
A *mieskeit,* her mother would say. So? Arnold's a bargain?
Okay, now I have something to work with.

That solved, she figured this was the morning she might
resolve some other lingering problems. Hans Schreiber, for
instance. Mike had insisted that he and his buddies at the
Eighty-fourth were keeping close tabs on the guy, but what
did that mean? If Schreiber was behind Grace's disappearance, Rosie didn't expect he'd advertise. But something else
was nagging at her, another issue she'd been overlooking, but
what?

She was walking back to her car when her ESP kicked in:
The missing piece of the puzzle may not be related to Schreiber.
Huh? Rosie stopped in mid-stride and waited for a follow-
up bulletin, but none was forthcoming. She slid behind the

wheel to drive to her parents' house, wishing she could tap into her source as she would the Internet. I've got to find a way to make this work better!

Her father was sitting on the small porch reading the Sunday newspaper. He looked up and waved when she pulled up in front. Then his smile expanded as she came up the walkway, holding aloft a paper bag. "Stopped off for your favorites at Chalet Bakery," she called. "Mom inside?"

"She's on the phone with your sister."

"Good. Maybe we could talk for a couple of minutes?"

"Nu? Talk." Joseph Rosenstein was, for the most part, a gentle man with a lifetime of experience in dealing with people. A former restaurateur, he'd learned early on that a good listener was as much appreciated as good food. And if the latter was consistent, success was guaranteed. Since retiring eight years before, Joseph had been happy to catch up on his reading and immerse himself in sports, while his wife, who loved talking more than life itself, kept him abreast of all the family doings. He also enjoyed a weekly poker game and playing with his two grandchildren. His younger daughter visited once or twice each week, but Ida always managed to monopolize. Rarely did he have Natalie to himself. He smiled at her now, gesturing to the chair next to him. "Sit."

In as few sentences as possible, Rosie reviewed the strange story of Grace's disappearance, including some facts the newspapers weren't privy to. Her father listened without changing his expression. When she had finished, he asked only one question: "Still no leads?"

She shook her head. "But . . ."

Joseph knew something about his daughter's special powers. "But you've had some inkling of where she is."

"Yes, but nothing so definite that the location can be pinpointed." She explained about her vision of the woman in the basement. "There's something else—I saw a hypnotist." And Rosie described the abortive session with Mary DeWitt.

Joseph Rosenstein was thoughtful. "Who is this Mike person?"

Her father was also intuitive. Rosie suspected that whatever talent she had in the ESP area, she'd inherited from him.

"He's a private investigator that Grace hired about four months ago."

Her explanation was straight out, but her father detected a note of conflict that Rosie had not been able to disguise. "But maybe right now, he's become something more?" he prodded.

Color warmed her cheeks. He smiled and rolled his eyes toward the house. "It's okay. I won't tell your mother."

"The important thing here," she said, trying to refocus the conversation, "is that he's a former NYPD detective and he's got a lot of connections. If anyone's going to find Grace, he will." She spoke of Hans Schreiber, whom she'd originally thought was the culprit but, in view of her recent "flash," was no longer certain that was true. "He's nasty and quite capable, I believe, but I can't block out the possibility it could be someone else."

Her father listened attentively, encouraging her to think of anyone else who had recent dealings with Grace or herself. Rosie thought the part about herself was strange.

"Something to do with me?" she repeated. "Gosh. Well, of course there's *Arnold*." She didn't disguise her contempt. "And Grace's good friend, Mr. Marcos, and various attorneys who know her well, including Carolyn Hughs—who, if we can't find Grace, will probably cover at least the Schreiber case."

"Why is that?"

Rosie explained about malpractice insurance and the accord Grace and Carolyn had reached a few years back. While her father was digesting this, she added, "Actually, they had a falling out but never changed the beneficiary on their policies. Now that I think about it, it is a little strange."

Now Joseph Rosenstein was even more interested. "Tell me about Ms. Hughs."

"What's to tell? She's been very nice to me—actually offered me a job working for her if this situation ends in the worst scenario." As soon as she said this, Rosie felt chills, but as she turned toward her father with a questioning look, her mother came bursting out onto the porch.

"Na-ta-lie! When did you come? Joseph!" she admonished her husband. "Why didn't you tell me Na-ta-lie was here?" She held out her arms to her daughter for an embrace.

Rosie looked over her mother's head toward her father, who shrugged his shoulders as if to say, *Why should today be different than any other day?* His wife had an uncanny talent for bad timing. But his eyes were sympathetic, and Rosie interpreted his expression: *I'm here for you if you want to talk more.*

A little while later, her mother turned up the volume on the living room TV, and the latest on Grace's disappearance blared forth: . . . *The FBI confirmed today they have no new leads in the Grace Osborne case.* . . . That was the problem, Rosie thought. There was nothing new, but the networks were keeping the story alive because people were ghoulishly fascinated with *the mystery of the missing attorney.*

Along with some iced tea and unimportant family gossip, Ida Rosenstein brought up her favorite topic—her daughter's failure to connect with a future husband—and the afternoon went downhill after that. Her father offered some sympathetic glances, but Rosie could see he was disconnecting from the rest of the conversation.

Her dad dealt in peaks and valleys, she thought, as she

drove back to Oceanside an hour later with a lingering vision of him planted in front of his television set watching his beloved Yankees. His "war" stories concerned his many years in the restaurant business and his show business friends who dropped in for lunch or dinner. Outside of the pleasure he derived from watching the sports programs on TV, he lived mostly in the past. So, am I any different? she wondered, as she pulled into her block, vowing to eliminate Jean Marc from her life once and for all.

But the impact of their two-year relationship was not so easily dismissed. He'd caught her at a vulnerable age—twenty-three—the time of life when a young woman believes that love is real and to be in Paris with Jean Marc was her destiny. To fall off that mountain hurt more than she could ever admit. And to acknowledge that she'd been wrong had shaken her confidence. *Okay, but even criminals go free after they've done their time. Haven't you been punished long enough? Here's your card: GET OUT OF JAIL—NOW!*

Coincidentally, her ESP chose this moment to make an announcement: *Watch for new developments.* Rosie knew that whatever was about to happen had nothing to do with Paris.

Rosie parked her car and headed upstairs to her apartment. Inside, she set her bag down and pushed the button on her answering machine. Nikki Marcos's voice rolled out: "Please contact me soonest. You know who this is."

What now?

She returned his call and agreed to meet him at the Green Acres Shopping Center in Valley Stream. The last thing Rosie needed was a mile-long limo pulling into her block, giving the neighbors even more to gossip about. Once at Green Acres, she didn't have to search long. Marcos's car stood out in the parking lot like a helium-filled cartoon in the Macy's Day Thanksgiving Parade. Ignoring the gawking crowd, Marcos himself opened the door and gestured her inside.

"I am sorry to bother you on a Sunday," he began, "but I am deeply troubled."

Always intimidated by the Greek's imposing presence, Rosie decided to keep her smart-ass comments to herself. She also commanded her face to remain blank while waiting for him to continue.

"It's been one week." He stared at her—almost accusingly.

"I know, but the police are doing all they can."

"What about your *special powers?*"

"Mr. Marcos—"

"Nikki," he corrected her.

"Right . . . Nikki, please understand that I'd do anything to find out where Grace is, but I haven't a clue. All right, that's not quite true. I've seen some kind of scene, but I have no idea where the location is."

"And the hypnotist could not help you?"

Rosie was stunned. She could feel her heart accelerate and imagined anyone within listening distance could time the pace. "How did you . . . ?"

"I have my ways. Please don't be upset about it." His handsome face sought to calm, but Rosie felt even more vulnerable.

She inched away from him. "How can I not be?"

"Please believe me. I will not let any harm come to you."

Her response escaped before she could stop herself. "You couldn't stop the harm that came to Grace." (Oh, God! Why can't I keep my big mouth shut?) Rosie wanted to sink through the floorboards.

Nikki wasn't smiling. The silence lasted for a full minute before he spoke. "Touché."

"I'm so sorry. I didn't mean . . ."

He held up his hand. "Not your doing. Or mine. But it is necessary that we find out who's behind this—now." His eyes pleaded urgency. On this, she was on his side.

They talked about the possible culprit, and Rosie told him what she'd heard about Hans Schreiber. "A nasty guy."

Nikki was thoughtful. "Do you speak with Ms. Carolyn Hughs?"

"You know Carolyn?"

He paused before answering. "Oh, yes."

Something about his tone closed off any further comment on her part. They spent a few minutes going over the vague images Rosie had discerned during her meditation, and again, she promised to concentrate on those scraps.

Sleep would not come easily this night, and Rosie knew the reason: I'm blocking out my session with Mary DeWitt, just as I prevented her from penetrating my defenses this afternoon. *So take a look at it. Can't do any harm.* Easier said than done.

Rosie threw back the covers after twenty more minutes of the same and headed into the other room to read, but she couldn't shake off the afternoon's fiasco. Mary had put her at ease, all right, but the wall came up anyhow.

"Try to relax," she'd begun.

"I'm trying."

"Think of something pleasant—like colors. Your outfit, for example, is a soft peach. Very becoming."

"Thanks."

"Sunsets have many colors, sometimes they're peach or orange with yellow or red."

"Uh-huh."

"Do you ever have a chance to watch the sun set?"

"My parents don't live too far from the beach. Sometimes, before a visit, I'll go for a run. Yes—I've seen the sun sink into the Atlantic Ocean."

"Good. Maybe you can remember the last time you watched."

"I'll try."

"Good. I'd like you to concentrate on the lovely colors as the sun moves down—sinking, sinking, lower in the sky."

Rosie closed her eyes, recalling the beauty of the sun setting over the ocean: As it dropped lower, streaks of apricots and plums danced astride a lemon globe that seemed to expand as it sank lower in the horizon. A rainbow shimmered on the undulating waves. She focused on the moving sun but began to experience a sinking feeling of her own. Descending lower, a panic grabbed hold without warning. Rosie had to save herself before she, too, dropped into the ocean. With a mighty effort, she opened her eyes and leaped from the chair. "I can't do this."

"Can you tell me what's happening?"

"I only know I will get lost if I continue."

"Lost? How?"

But Rosie had started for the door. "Please excuse me. You're a nice person, Mary, but I can't do this." And that was the end of the session.

Replaying the scene turned out to be a healthy thing for her. Even though she had no further explanation, Rosie could almost hear Madame Volante's reassuring words: *People may not always understand,* chérie, *but they do not have your powers.*

Chapter 17

You have to take an active part. "Okay," Rosie said aloud to her reflection when she finished brushing her teeth the next morning. "This is the day I'm taking a hands-on approach." She wanted to ensure that whoever was responsible got punished—certainly put away so he couldn't commit any more harm. She felt buoyed by her decision and wasted little time with the rest of her morning routine. She was anxious to get to the city and examine the contents of a carton in the closet of Grace's private office, particularly anything related to Hans Schreiber. Even Grace had not had the time to go through it all.

The answering machine was blinking when she arrived, but Rosie passed by without even so much as a moment's curiosity. "No, Arnold," she flipped over her shoulder, "I have no intention to start my day with any of your shtick."

In Grace's office, she dragged out the carton from the back of the closet, but something flew out when she lifted the top flap. *Jeeze! What the hell was that?* Another quick flash turned out to be a moth diving back into the dark, seeking immunity. *It's a warning. I need to remain on guard.* As soon as her heartbeat returned to normal, Rosie squatted down on the floor beside the box. At first, she started rifling through loose papers, then she picked out one or two folders. But her back ached after five minutes and her thighs began to cramp. Finally realizing the folly of her approach, she dumped out the entire contents and plopped down next to the mess. The commercial Berber carpet was not that tushy-friendly, but Rosie found it the lesser of the two evils and stayed with it. "No sacrifice is too great if I can get that sonofabitch," she muttered aloud. A half hour later, she reread a stapled clump of papers for the third time and felt like she'd won the lottery. "Hello!" she called out to the empty office, pulled herself up from the floor and sat down at Grace's desk to record her find.

Her boss had painstakingly recorded the journey of German citizen Hans Schreiber who, in nineteen-ninety-eight, met an American woman, married her in record time, applied for a visa and a green card and immigrated to the U.S. They began married life together in Chicago, but after only three months, Hans left her there and moved to New York by himself. Rosie flipped the page, noting that a copy of his marriage certificate to Jane Fisher, wife number two, was dated a month after he arrived in New York. That's only four months after his marriage to the one who opened the door to the land of milk and honey. Only four months? Fast worker. Okay, so at what point did the bastard cut the bond with wife number one? Rosie spent the next half hour going back through the mountain of papers to no avail. Come on! she exhorted herself. Haven't got all day. Must've missed it some-where. But repeating the search again turned up no clues. What's the mystery about *when* he divorced wife number one, the lucky woman? Then it dawned on her. Ohmygod! There's no copy of the divorce papers here because the sonofabitch never bothered to *get* a divorce. This bastard's a—a—bigamist! And what does that make his marriage to Jane Fisher? God-damned illegal, that's what. And if it's not legal, how does that affect his petition for custody? Never mind that—if he married his first wife in order to gain entry into the U.S., then deserted her, married another, what the hell is his *status?* Gotta be illegal something-or-other. AND, if Grace found out about it, isn't that enough motive to kidnap and imprison her long enough to keep her out of the picture until his motion for custody is granted? You betcha! Rosie couldn't get to the phone fast enough.

Mike called her back within ten minutes: "Whazzup?"

"Get over here quick. I have news!"

"On my way . . . ten minutes."

Rosie's pulse was racing so fast she thought she'd have a stroke before Mike arrived, but he showed up even sooner than expected. She was trying to get the news out so fast he finally held up his hand.

"Whoa. Take a breath and start from the beginning—and slowly this time."

Rosie pushed papers at Mike, describing their significance. When she finished, she all but crowed. "See? Sometimes I'm ambivalent about whether or not he's the one, but Schreiber has a big motive for getting rid of Grace, or anyone else who stands in his way. Guess he figured she was getting closer to the truth. Actually, he doesn't have too much support for his case altogether, unless maybe if he could prove Jane Fisher was an unfit mother."

Mike was happy with Rosie's enthusiasm, but she wasn't getting the whole picture. "Let me give you the other side. What makes you think Schreiber did not divorce his first wife?"

"Because there was no—"

Mike held up a hand. "The fact that *you* didn't find a copy of the divorce papers doesn't mean there isn't one."

"But—"

"Now wait. I grant you the guy's an S.O.B. And I'd be pleased to haul him off to jail myself, but . . ." Mike hesitated. Struck by the excitement in Rosie's face, he softened his tone. "Actually, the detectives questioned him once before, but I'm sure they'd be glad to grab him up for another session. And when they hear what you've got to say, they probably will. What you did here was good."

Rosie tipped her head to one side. "Am I hearing right? Did you actually pay me a compliment?" She could almost hear her mother prodding her to do the right thing, so she added, "Thank you."

"You're welcome."

The two were just holding each other's faces in the mirrors of their eyes and probably would have continued to stare back at one another if they hadn't been interrupted by the phone.

"I'd better take that," Rosie said, reaching for the instrument. "Law Offices of— Oh, it's you."

Mike's face split into a not-very-nice smile, one that showed teeth, and he mouthed the word, *stalker?* She grimaced, nodded and rolled her eyes. Mike stood and started to move away, but Rosie reached out a hand to stop him.

"Excuse me," she said into the phone, "but I have someone here. Can we continue this later?" It was not so much a question—but more like a signing off. She wasn't offering a choice. "Right!" she concluded and replaced the receiver, then looked up at Mike. "All kidding aside, Arnold's turned it up a notch lately."

"Turned it up like how?"

"Like, maybe coming on a little too strong." She told him about their recent encounter, and how Arnold protested he didn't want to be treated like a pet—'like a cat,' is what he actually said."

"So?"

"So I *have* a cat— Do you think it was just a coincidence?"

Mike was headed toward the door, but he stopped and turned around. "I told you at the beginning what I thought. Guy's a stalker. Don't encourage him." He paused, as though he were going to add something else, then shook it off. "I'm going to talk with Marino now about the information you found in Grace's closet. Then I'm going to see what I can dig up on Schreiber and his first marriage. Don't do anything stupid." He swung open the door and was gone within seconds.

Marino and Adella were waiting for Mike, who'd called ahead. On his way to their corner, he stopped a few times to chat with former buddies and helped himself to some coffee. As he finally neared his former partner, he took in the clutter on top of their desks and remarked, "Ah, yes, seems like only yesterday . . ."

Marino shook his head and waggled a finger. "Besides coming here to gloat, you got some information?"

"Yeah—some interesting stuff about Schreiber." Mike told them about Rosie's discovery.

"Pretty smart on her part," said Adella with a wink. "Think she's a keeper."

Her partner and Mike exchanged looks, but neither

spoke. Mike, however, felt a surge in his belly. *Shit! I gotta stop acting like a teenager.* "By the way, can you give me a few minutes with your computer? I want to check something."

Marino swivelled around to check where his lieutenant was. He looked uncomfortable. "If it were up to me . . ."

"Yeah, yeah, I understand."

"Tell me what you're looking for, and let me give it a shot."

"Deal. I want to do a background check on a guy—a lawyer."

Marino rolled his chair to a computer on the table behind him. "Name?"

"Arnold Feltman."

"Isn't he one of the—?"

"Yeah."

Mike left fifteen minutes later and patted his back pocket where he'd shoved the computer printout Marino had made for him. His cell phone rang just as he reached the street. Rain had begun to fall, so he ducked into a doorway for better reception. He spoke in monosyllables, snapped the phone shut and hailed a cab.

Upstairs, meanwhile, their lieutenant was instructing Marino and Parsons to bring back Schreiber for questioning.

Chapter 18

Mike walked around the corner after exiting the taxi and headed toward the newsstand. He pulled out a twenty-dollar bill from his wallet and slapped it down on top of a stack of *Wall Street Journals*. "Thanks," he said, but didn't take a paper or magazine. The woman inside reached out a leathery hand, palmed the bill and grunted. Mike donned a pair of wire-rimmed glasses and moved on toward the building directly across the street. He was carrying a well-worn briefcase. As he approached the entrance, he made a show of frowning and looking at his watch. "Excuse me," he said to the doorman, tapping his briefcase, "I've got a depo in here that needs signing, and I'm late."

"A depo?"

"You know—a deposition." He held out his wallet, flipped it open, then shut it, all in less than a millisecond, too quickly for even the most alert eyes to catch the word *retired* that appeared on his old NYPD identification card.

"Oh, yeah. Sure." The doorman held the door, and Mike disappeared inside and made for the elevator. He stepped out on the ninth floor and, after carefully scrutinizing the empty hallway, strode down to apartment nine-twenty-four. As expected, the door was locked. Mike glanced around, pulled out a slim leather case from his breast pocket and extracted his favorite lock-pick. A swift, silent insertion, and it slipped in just like his other favorite tool. *Gotta get my mind off that stuff.* He closed the door swiftly and made for the desk in the study. All the drawers were unlocked except the wide center drawer. Mike sighed briefly (they'll never learn), selected something shiny from his tool case and made some more magic. Gingerly, he sifted through the papers inside, but discovered nothing more incriminating than boring personal letters. When he tried to shove the drawer back, however, something caught, so he removed it completely, slid his hand toward the rear and brought forth the prize. Uh-huh . . . there's always a little something extra for services rendered.

The envelope was expensive—thin parchment. The handwriting was masculine and strong. It was addressed to Ms. Carolyn Hughs. He knew who the sender was even before he flipped it over and saw the gold-embossed shield supported by two Olympic goddesses. The single sheet slid out easily.

Ms. Hughs,

I do not mean to embarrass you and I hope you will understand when I state firmly that I am not interested in a deceitful friendship with you. I was pleased that you could join us for dinner last night, and you are welcome to do so in the future. But do not again take advantage of Grace's good nature by putting yourself forward as a substitute "should Grace not be completely satisfying," as you put it, when she was not present. This offends my sensibilities and is extremely disloyal to Grace, whom you profess is your good friend.

Nicholas Marcos

Well, well, well . . . what a stand-up person Carolyn Hughs must be to hit on her friend's boyfriend when Grace's back was turned. With friends like these . . .

Mike folded the letter carefully and pushed it to the rear of the desk. Then he replaced the drawer, glanced around quickly, retrieved his "prop"—the old briefcase—and let himself out of the apartment.

An hour later, he was back at the precinct, sharing it all with Chris Marino and Adella Parsons: "So, here's another one with an agenda," he finished.

"In theory anyway," said Adella

"Well at least it explains what happened to the close friendship she and Grace Osborne once shared," said Mike. "Rosie couldn't figure it out, but the letter clears it up for me."

After tossing it around for a while, Adella asked, "Yes, but how does that translate into a motive? Maybe we ought to just pay her a visit."

Her partner was looking at his watch. "Let's try to squeeze in some lunch first. My stomach's complaining." He turned toward Mike. "Join us?"

But Mike had started for the elevators. "Why don't I check with you later? Got something I need to take care of."

He had that I've-got-an-agenda look on his face that his former partner instantly recognized.

Mike's expression wreaked of confusion as he approached the court officer in the lobby of the courthouse. "Excuse me, but I could use some help."

"What kind of help?"

"My sister . . . *sheesh!*" He shook his head. "My sister's looking for a lawyer and doesn't know who to see." He lowered his voice. "Y'see, my brother-in-law's an S.O.B. Slaps her around, y'know? She's got two kids and, well, she's looking to get out of a bad situation, but doesn't have much money. Told her I'd help. For starters, I guess I'm looking for a lawyer who does divorces but doesn't charge up the ying-yang. Know what I mean? I thought maybe there was a list or something here in the courthouse."

"You can go up to the second floor—Records. Tell 'em what you want. They got a list. I can tell you none of these guys are giving a free ride. Some charge less than others though. The one you would've wanted is . . . well, she's not around just now, but there are others." He offered up a couple of names, one of which was Arnold Feltman.

"A stand-up guy, is he?"

"I wouldn't exactly call him stand-up. He does a lot of divorces and such. Maybe you can give him a sob story, like you ain't got too much money and all that stuff. If he's in a good mood, maybe he'll take you on where you don't got to rob a bank."

"So, you're saying he's a good guy?"

"I guess—except for . . ."

Mike looked up, his face a big question mark.

"Well, the guy's got the hots for some dame who works near here. Everyone talks about it. He can't keep his eyes off her."

Mike chucked the other playfully in the shoulder. "Hey, I've chased a few myself, don'tcha know?"

"Yeah. Guess we've all had our moments, but this guy's kinda over the top. Know what I mean? Anyway, you give him a call. Maybe he'll help you out with your sister."

"Thanks. I will."

★   ★   ★

Mike booted up the computer as soon as he returned to his office. The search engine processed his request, and he was soon browsing through a list of Feltmans in Great Neck. There were fifteen viable possibilities. He took a long gulp from the iced cappuccino he'd picked up on his way in and studied the list. "No shortcuts," he mumbled aloud as he pulled the phone closer to dial the first number. "Yes, hi," he said to the woman who answered, "I'm trying to locate an old college buddy of mine—Arnold Feltman. By any chance, is he related to you?"

"No," came the suspicious reply.

"Sorry to bother you."

Mike went down the list, repeating the same speech. There were ten negative responses, three answering machine machines (he left no messages) and two where nobody answered. He made a note to try these last five later in the day or early this evening.

When Carolyn's assistant told her that two detectives were waiting to talk with her, she came out of her office smiling. "Detectives Marino and Parsons, I believe." She gestured toward her private office. "Please do come in." And to her assistant, she added, "Please hold all calls." The other two followed her in, and Carolyn closed the door and indicated two chairs.

"So, what can I do for you?"

"Our visit concerns Grace Osborne," announced Adella Parsons.

"Is there any news?"

"We're questioning everyone in the hopes of throwing some light on her disappearance. Perhaps you have some thoughts to contribute?"

"Really, no. I just think the whole situation is *utterly* unthinkable," she said, her British inflection settling in.

Marino leaned forward, catching Carolyn's attention. "What it amounts to is that the chances of finding Ms. Osborne alive lessen with every passing day. Maybe *you* know something that will help us find who did this?"

"I *cahn't* imagine!" she responded, a little agitated as the conversation was taking on the flavor of an interrogation.

Marino was not put off. "Nobody that might have had an agenda?—like an angry loser or an unhappy client?"

Carolyn was shaking her head from side to side. "I wouldn't know." She inhaled deeply as her voice took on a dramatic, musical quality. "Grace is admired by *so* many, I couldn't *begin* to imagine who would want to hurt her." She divided her gaze equally between both detectives.

"Would you mind telling us where you were last Saturday night?" asked Adella.

Carolyn tapped her chest with a carefully manicured forefinger and repeated the question. "Where *I* was?"

A lyrical laugh preceded her statement of how she spent her time, the gist of which was titillating to be sure. "I was with a very dear, very close friend, and I can say we were quite occupied the entire night!"

As they headed back to their car, Marino elbowed his partner. "Do you buy that she was having a private evening with Sam Pixel, the writer?"

"I buy that she's got hot pants. Maybe Nikki Marcos wasn't up for that, but evidently it fit well with Pixel's plans. She's gotta know we're gonna check. Meantime, let's just keep her on the 'maybe' list."

"Yeah. That should make my day."

On their way back to the precinct, they discussed the latest character in the case of the missing lawyer:

Sam Pixel was a popular British novelist whose works included the *Royal Crown* mysteries, a string of detective stories featuring protagonist Grant Hill. Pixel's ascerbic tongue and rugged, chisled features were well known to viewers of the late-night shows. And stories of his ex-wives (there were six so far) were familiar fodder for the gossip columists. Marino and Parsons were taking bets that Carolyn Hughs was angling for the lucky seven spot.

Chapter 19

Rosie turned up the volume on the small television set next to the copier. CNN was giving what she had now come to think of as a non-update on Grace. There wasn't anything new happening, she knew that, but along with the rest of the city, she couldn't stay away from the news stations. Rosie lived in the hope that just as she'd turn on the TV, a "breaking news" sign would flash on the screen and a wonderful announcement would be forthcoming. If she could just find a way to relax, maybe her ESP would kick in. But even that seemed to have become numb of late. As if to contradict that very thought, she began experiencing familiar shivers. *I know this has nothing to do with Grace! It's* him*—Arnold, and he's getting closer. Quick! Think of some excuse of why you have no time to gossip—or why you can't go out with him, or, or . . .* She heard the ding of the elevator doors opening. Too late.

"Hello, my little ball of gefilte fish." The familiar pudgy body appeared around the office door, which, unfortunately she'd forgotten to lock. (*Why don't I just wear a sign that says* Kick Me*? And couldn't he at least think of some nonethnic food-inspired greeting for a change?*)

"What is it, Arnold?"

"Not very friendly, Natalie."

"I'm really very busy now. And please stop calling me Natalie."

"Number one: How can you be busy when your boss isn't even here to give you the work? Number two: I believe one should honor one's parents. They named you Natalie. That's good enough for me. And incidently"—he was grinning—"what are you doing tonight, my little angel?"

Rosie sucked in a measure of air. Easy does it, she cautioned herself. "Honestly, Arnold . . ."

He looked at her hopefully. "Yes?" he began, but then his tone became warlike: "You were saying?"

The hackles on the back of her neck tickled unpleasantly. "You know—we've been through this before. Nothing can come of it."

"How do you know when you won't even try? You won't even give me a chance. *I* think we can hit it off."

(Yeah, just like George Bush and Osama Bin Laden.)

"And furthermore," he continued, "this whole business with Grace—"

"What about it?"

"I'm just saying that you should be more . . . more appreciative of all the help I've offered. And I can do a lot *more,* if you'll let me."

Rosie thought the remark strange. "More? Like, what do you mean?"

His eyes flicked quickly toward her breasts, and Rosie thought she detected some spittle glistening in the corners of his mouth. Again the back of her neck prickled. (He's even weirder than I thought. And what does he mean by "a lot more?" Isn't his drool disgusting enough?)

With her stomach now on the verge of rebellion, she

tried to think of ways to distract him and still remain on his good side. "Arnold, you're smart." (Yes, his chest expanded ever so slightly—keep going.) "Would you have any idea where to look for Grace? I'd be ever so grateful if we could find her." Rosie struck a vulnerable pose and hoped she didn't sound too much like Melanie in *Gone with the Wind*.

She caught him appraising her like a slice of rare beef. (Uh-oh, think I went a little overboard just now.) "What I mean is, I'd count you as a really good friend if you can help us find her."

"Who is the *us* you're referring to?"

(Oy. Don't even breathe Mike's name.) "Um, why the police—and, uh, the FBI, of course."

"I see."

She thought she detected a wise-ass smirk, but he took his time responding. "Don't you think I'd be forthcoming if I knew Grace's whereabouts?" He widened his eyes for emphasis.

"Of course. All of us would." Rosie was beginning to think the entire exchange had gotten way out of hand. (He's just pulling my string—anything to find a way in. Well, he'll have to come up with something more creative.) Still, she was beginning to get the creepiest feeling. The telephone startled them both.

"Law offices of— Oh, yes . . . Mr. ah, Prenstick."

Mike laughed loudly on the other end. "Let me guess— Arnold?"

"That's correct. I haven't been able to process your request, but I'm working on it."

"I'm on my way."

"That's really not necessary."

"Yes it is. I'm two blocks away, and I'm coming in. Uh, do you think he'll keep his fly zipped till I get there?"

"Most likely." There was an abrupt click and a dial tone, Mike's signature sign-off. "And thank you for your call, sir," Rosie said to the empty line.

Arnold was looking at her questioningly. "New case?"

"Could be. Obviously this person is in need of a lawyer, but I have no idea when Grace will be able to . . ."

"Well, you could show your friendship by passing along some of this flotsam and jetsam to me."

Rosie appeared to be considering his request. "Tell you what. Why don't you give me some cards? If he shows up, I'll pass one over to him."

"You will? See? That's why I think we'd make a good team."

"Don't push your luck, Arnold." Once again, she saw his hard stare and took the warning. "On second thought—let's take this one day at a time. Now, will you please let me finish up here?"

He didn't budge, continuing to fill the time with idle chit-chat, but they both looked up when Mike came bustling into the office. "Hello there," he called out, acting surprised when he spotted Arnold. "Oh. It's Feltman, right?"

"Arnold Feltman."

"Right." He looked from one to the other, then took a step back. "Not interrupting anything *personal,* I hope."

"No," Rosie said quickly.

But Arnold looked over at Rosie intimately and shrugged his shoulders. "I'm not so sure about that." He grinned hopefully.

Mike walked over to the coffee machine, grabbed a Styrofoam cup and filled it halfway. "Okay?" he tossed over his shoulder at Rosie.

"Feel free."

Then he draped his jacket over the back of a chair, sat down and threw out his long legs. "I'm telling you, it's a killer today. Heat index must be over a hundred."

Rosie murmured something sympathetic. Arnold said nothing.

"So, Arnold. How're things going with you?" Mike inclined his head like he was really interested.

The other seemed surprised. "Oh, not too bad. Y'know . . ."

"Catch that Yankee game last night? Unbelievable! Don't think any other team will come close."

"Yeah, well, I'm not that much into baseball."

"Oh, football your game? Or is it golf?"

"I like to watch the golf sometimes."

Stimulating dialogue, Rosie thought. Hope I don't fall asleep before the exciting conclusion. And speaking of sports, with her eyes swinging back and forth from Mike to Arnold, she could have been watching a tennis match; however, she jerked to attention with Mike's next salvo:

"They say kids follow in their parents footsteps when it comes to sports. Your Dad play golf? Oh, I'm sorry. Are your folks still . . . still okay?"

"My parents are just fine!" But there was something in Arnold's tone that sounded more like *my parents are none of your business.*

Rosie was trying to figure out where this conversation was going. When Arnold finally left a little while later, she asked Mike what he had in mind.

"Just tracing the pedigree, is all."

"Pedigree. I wouldn't attach that term to Arnold. From what he told me, his background is ho-hum, middle-class Jewish."

"Oh, and that interests you?"

"Not me—my mother." She let out a deep sigh.

Mike started to say something, then changed his mind. Rosie noticed.

After he left, she wondered if maybe Mike was developing sensitivity. She looked around the office, aware that she was running out of legitimate chores. If Grace wasn't found soon, there'd be no reason for her to come to work here, in which case, she'd have to find another job. Carolyn? Working for her would be really strange after the mysterious break between her and Grace.

After dusting the tops of tables and desks, Rosie turned on the small TV set, knowing it was useless. If anything new had developed, she'd have heard about it firsthand. Captions running across the bottom of the screen repeated the same information that everybody already knew: *Lawyer still missing; no new clues in the case, but police and the FBI are following all leads.*

There must be a way to provide more of these.

"Please *do* help me out, Rosie," Carolyn's crisp tones crooned over the phone. "I'd be *ever* so grateful."

"Um, I don't know what to say. Things are so up in the air right now."

"I realize that fully but I'm *desperate.* Stephanie's out again—her cold returned, she *says.* Honestly, I don't know what I'm going to do with that girl. Oh, *please,* do come for just an hour this afternoon."

"Well . . ."

"I'd *so* appreciate whatever time you can give me."

"Okay. Somewhere around four okay?"

"Perfect!"

Rosie was feeling somewhat disloyal to Grace when she showed up at Carolyn's office. Then a surge in general discomfort took over. Why? It was something she just couldn't put her finger on. *Pay attention,* she reminded herself. Her eyes swept the scene, a professionally decorated job, to be sure. The furniture in the waiting area where Stephanie's desk was located boasted an African motif and harmonized with the same color scheme as the carpet and drapes. *Expensive, but not my taste.* Carolyn, who was on the phone, waved a greeting and lowered her voice to a husky, seductive level, but her door remained ajar, and one could see her perched comfortably behind a huge antique cherrywood table. Rosie moved over to Stephanie's desk, but the other's provocative dialogue floated out toward her.

"But, *dahling,* of course!" (a pause) "Oh, you *bad boy!*" (more laughter).

Well, that couldn't be a client. Guess she's got a good one on the hook. But not wanting to waste any time, Rosie scanned the notes on top of the folder Carolyn had prepared and booted up the computer. There were two letters and a motion. *This shouldn't take long.*

Carolyn joined her after a few minutes. Her face was flushed, and her eyes gleamed with triumph. "I have an appointment, luv, so I'll leave the key. Would appreciate it if you locked up."

"Sure. But this will not take even one hour."

"I knew you'd be fast *and* efficient. Thanks *ever* so much!" She was already walking toward the door. "Ta-ta!" a phrase Rosie repeated after the door closed.

"Yeah, and a *ta-ta* to you, too!" Rosie realized she didn't much care for Carolyn. *Influenced by Grace? I don't think so. It's just easy to get turned off. She's a phony, and who knows?—maybe something more besides.*

There was an envelope under the key with her name on it. The check inside was overly much, but that still didn't endear her to Carolyn. *I know I'm going to watch my step with her.*

★ ★ ★

As Rosie locked Carolyn's office door behind her, she knew she wouldn't be returning for any more of these sessions. No matter how she pleads, *I'm not going back. Let her replace Stephanie if she's not happy, but count me out.* As the elevator descended to the lobby, she put her negative feelings about Carolyn aside, more concerned about a sudden forewarning: *Pay attention—there's more trouble ahead.*

Rosie took a careful look through the glass exit doors before stepping out onto the sidewalk. Passersby appeared to represent the usual five o'clock working crowd emptying out of their offices at the end of the day. *So, she wondered, where and what is the problem?* She wouldn't have long to wait.

"Hey, lady! *Ja,* you there!"

Jeeze. It's Schreiber! As he approached, she could sense his anger spilling over. *What does he want from me?* She looked around, but like typical New Yorkers, everyone was doing a fine imitation of the blind. She felt really afraid.

"You!" he screamed. "I vant to tell you something. You listen to me!"

The angry presence was heading directly toward her, clenching his fists and babbling in unintelligible German. Rosie could feel the pulse in her neck exploding. *Quick! Think of something.* But help arrived with the sudden screech of a car's brakes, and everyone on the scene froze.

A long, dark limousine slammed to a stop against the curb. The passenger and driver doors opened simultaneously, dispatching Nikki Marcos and his driver/bodyguard, Theo. The two quickly edged themselves in between Schreiber and Rosie. The whole event took only seconds. Rosie allowed herself to be guided by Nikki back to the limo, while his driver muscled Schreiber down the block and out of sight. Theo returned shortly and took his place behind the wheel, easing away from the gawking crowd. Nikki had already reached for his magic decanter of ouzo and was pushing a glass at Rosie, instructing her to "drink deeply." This time, she didn't demure. Within moments, warmth filled her chest, and she could feel her shoulders dropping down from her ears.

"Thank you," she managed.

"I told you that I would protect you from harm."

Rosie didn't want to think he'd been following her all this time just waiting to fulfill his promise, but she didn't want to appear ungrateful either. "I appreciate your help."

The other nodded and the same procedure as before ensued: Nikki left the car a few blocks later, and Rosie was told that Theo would be driving her home. As the saying goes: Her mother didn't raise a fool. She knew enough not to argue.

As soon as she was safely inside her own place, Rosie dialed Mike's cell.

"Go ahead," came his gruff reply.

"Whatever happened to 'hello'?"

"Who are you—Dorothy Manners, or something?"

Her chest was heaving. "See? This is what gets me. I call you—and maybe I have good reason—and then you start to dish it out. That's when I want to reach out and smack you."

On the other end, Mike was grinning. I love it when she lets her temper show. The troops below were starting to get excited, too, but he managed to sound placid. "Any particular reason you called? Or were you just lonely?" He knew she'd get even more bent out about that, but guilt spread over him like oleo when he found out the real reason she called.

"You mean the bastard came at you?"

"I was scared. If not for Ni—Mr. Marcos, I don't know what I would have done."

"Sonofabitch!"

"He's crazy!"

"Yeah. What did he say exactly?"

Rosie went over the scene. "Basically, he was threatening, mumbling stuff in German. Bizarre. But even worse were those big, meaty fists coming at me. I didn't know if he was gonna hit me or what. The guy's certifiable."

Mike's jaw was working on the other end of the phone, but he turned his anger to action. "I'll talk to Chris. You're gonna file a complaint, and that jerk will be arrested. The courts can take it from there." Now Mike was feeling bad that he'd given her such grief when she first called. "Sorry if I gave you a hard time before."

Was she hearing right? The big tough detective apologizing? A lot of smart-ass cracks came to mind, but common sense told her to quit while she was ahead. Besides, she knew: *They were now moving toward each other like stars in the galaxy.*

Chapter 20

The detectives from the Eighty-fourth were on their way down to Canal Street. When they stopped for a red light, Chris Marino turned to his partner. "Whaddya think of this jerk?"

"Oh, I have a special place in my book for spouse abusers who think the whole world's their personal target," said Adella. "Let's just say I'd like to pin him up—and I don't mean by the shoulders."

"I'm also beginning to like him for the Osborne disappearance."

"I'm right with you."

"Let's really turn him over when we get him back to the house."

Her grin was wide now. They were speaking in the code of partners who worked really well together. "Are you thinking what I think you're thinking?"

His grunt was assent enough. How long she'd waited for that. Chris Marino and his former partner, Mike Bartel, had been together for eight years. Chris did not take Mike's departure gracefully. When Adella had been assigned to partner up with him, the wall surrounding Chris Marino might just as well have been made of stone. Oh, he was polite enough—

even respectful, but the camaraderie that NYPD detectives normally share was limited. Now he was opening the door wide. "Guess Schreiber's in for it now," she said. "We'll turn him over so's he'll give up his mother."

Without taking his eyes off the road, Marino stuck out his hand for a high five. A few blocks later, he pulled up behind the fire hydrant in front of Schreiber's Fine Watch Repair.

"Hello and good-bye, Schreiber," said Marino as they entered.

The watchmaker looked surprised. "Vot iss?"

Adella pushed forward. "I'll tell you vot iss, mister. Lock up. We're going down to the station."

"No. I don't go. I have vork—"

But Marino already had the cuffs out. "You have nothing, asshole. You're coming with us. You want to lock up your shop or not? Up to you."

"Not right," Schreiber was mumbling as Marino moved in. "Is wrong."

"Yeah," Adella agreed. "Life is cruel."

He looked at her, his eyes raised in surprise. "Vot did I do that you treat me this vay?"

Adella jangled her own handcuffs in his face. "Do you want me to tell you now or when we get to the station?"

"Now. I should know now."

"How about, you attacked a young lady on the street yesterday afternoon."

"Attacked?" He puffed himself up in mock surprise, but Schreiber wasn't good at acting. His face flushed as he recalled his anger during the incident. Nevertheless, he made a stab at self-righteous denial. "Vot? I didn't do nothing!"

"Sure!" Adella said, "and a crocodile has no teeth." She grabbed one of his wrists and snapped on the cuffs.

"Vait! I must lock my shop."

"So? What are you waiting for?"

The detectives each grabbed an arm and walked him to the door. As soon as he turned the key, they snapped on the other cuff and marched him to their car, settled him in the rear seat and headed back to the station.

Their boss, Lieutenant Ed Grosky, waited for Marino and Parsons to fill him in on just where Schreiber fit in on this high-profile missing person's case. As soon as the detectives secured the watchmaker in an interview room, Grosky waved them into his office.

"What've you got?"

Adella said, "A very nervous suspect."

"Tell me about it."

Marino described the scene the previous day when Schreiber approached Rosie as she was leaving Carolyn Hughs' office building. "He must've followed her there and was just laying in wait."

"If not for some action by a witness . . ." Adella interjected, "who knows?"

"How are you tying this to Grace Osborne's disappearance?"

"Osborne's the ex-wife's lawyer in Schreiber's custody case," Marino offered. "Maybe he figured on removing the opposition. And Rosie—Natalie Rosenstein—is Osborne's assistant. She's a smart gal who's been asking a lot of questions. Oh, and one more thing: This Schreiber's got a watch repair place on Canal Street. According to some very dissatisfied customers Mike Bartel talked to, he's got a temper. Put that together with him going after Ros—the Rosenstein gal, and we could like him for the lawyer's disappearance."

"Okay, go ahead with the interview and let me know what happens."

Rosie was aware the detectives would be pulling Schreiber in for questioning. There wasn't one nice thing anyone could say about the guy. He was mean-tempered, plus, he had a motive for getting rid of Grace. Mike had indicated that Marino could be plenty tough. Good. She only wished she could be there when he and his partner put the screws to the bastard. If her spirit could fly through the air, settle into a corner of the interrogation room, and enjoy Schreiber's misery, it would make her day—especially if he gave up Grace's location. Rosie closed her eyes, trying to imagine the scene, while pleading with whatever power she might have to allow her just one peek:

Minutes passed, with Schreiber shifting his weight about on the hard wooden chair while Marino and Parsons made a show of leafing through some papers. Their subject was getting more and more antsy as the silence dragged on. The detectives planned it that way. Then, without warning, Marino shot out the first question:

"What did you have in mind when you attacked Ms. Rosenstein yesterday?"

"Attacked? No! I didn't attack."

In her strange in-between state, Rosie choked back her anger. *Liar!*

"We have witnesses that say you approached her in a threatening manner," continued Marino.

"Ach! That's nonsense!" He slapped at the air with his

open palm, dismissing the accusation, but couldn't disguise the anger that flooded his cheeks.

The energy that was Rosie said, *It's not going to be nonsense when I kick you silly.*

"So," Adella challenged, "you're saying these witnesses are lying?"

He shrugged his shoulders, and Rosie imagined his mental Rolodex spinning through the section labeled "excuses."

"It wasn't nothing. I just wanted to talk."

"Do you usually scream at someone when you just want to *talk*?" Adella prodded.

Schreiber folded his arms across his chest. "I don't say more."

Marino leaned forward. "*I'll* say when this interview is over." Sparks flew from his eyes like electric currents.

Yeah, let him have it, Marino. Show me what Mike was talking about.

"I think you have the wrong idea, Schreiber. You're in *my* cage now. When *I* ask a question, *you* answer. Got that?"

The subject blinked and glanced first at the other detective, who showed no sympathy, and then toward the exit. But Marino, still standing, smiled. "You weren't thinking of leaving us just yet, were you?" He allowed a few seconds of silence to elapse before continuing. "So, what did you want to talk with Ms. Rosenstein about?"

Schreiber's collar had darkened with sweat. His eyes kept flicking toward the door, then he dropped his shoulders. "Okay," he conceded, "the lawyer lady she vorks for is the one who tries to keep me from getting my son—*my* boy. So, she's gone now. I don't know vhere and I don't care. But this *Rosenstein bitch,* she don't let go. If the lawyer lady is gone, that's good for me. Now, the other one should mind her own business, this Rosenstein, and clean a house or cook—vot a girl is supposed to do. I just vanted to ask her vhy she does not let go. Vhy she still talks to lawyers? Vhy she still talks to judges? She should mind her own goddamned business is vot she should do!"

With a half smile, Marino deferred to his partner.

"So," Adella jumped in, "you're saying women belong at home. Is that right?"

"Right!"

The detective could read right through to the other's brain. (No doubt he's thinking, with my black skin, *I* should be attached to a mop and pail.) It was all she could do to keep her nine millimeter in its holster. "Is that why you beat your ex-wife and now try to take her son away? Because she wouldn't stay at home?"

Schreiber was so flustered, he spit when he spoke. "Is *my* son, and she can go to hell!"

"No, *you're* the one who's going to hell, mister," Adella said evenly, but anyone witnessing the scene would know that Schreiber had already ordered his own coffin.

Imagining the details of this interview empowered Rosie. Suddenly she knew she would be able to locate Grace, whether Schreiber was the guilty party or not. Madame Volante was right. I do have power!

"Now," Adella Parsons continued, "let's talk about what you did with Grace Osborne." Schreiber's eyes went wide.

"Vot *I* did?" He appeared truly shocked. "I do nothing!"

The detective asked, "Where were you last weekend?"

"Last veekend?" It became apparent that Schreiber couldn't find an answer unless he repeated the last part of every question.

"Yeah," prompted Marino, "last weekend."

The subject's eyes gazed upward and off to one side, search-

ing. "Okay—I vorked on Saturday until six o'clock." Then,"
he stated emphatically, "I took my son home vith me where
he belongs!"

That was simple enough to check. Rosie didn't like the
man. It would have been the easiest thing in the world to dis-
believe him. Nevertheless, her highly attuned instincts confirmed that the bastard was telling the truth.

After they finished their questioning, the detectives con-
ferred with their boss. "As good as he looks for this job,"
Marino began, "if his alibi pans out, we're back at square
one."

Adella agreed. "Based on what he's told us, there doesn't
seem to be enough to hold him."

"Okay," the lieutenant said, "you can let him go. Remind
him we may call him back in for more questioning."

Chapter 21

Your life will take a downward turn, but often these times are temporary. By Friday, Rosie was doubtful that life would ever return to normal. How could she believe that Grace would ever be found when there were no encouraging signs? No new leads from the police, none from the FBI, nothing from any source to indicate that Grace was even still alive. She was looking around the office and wondering if she should make this her last day when the doorknob rattled and someone knocked on the door. She'd finally followed Mike's advice and was keeping it locked.

"Who is it, please?" (Like she didn't know. The aftershave pushed through the small space under the door like fumes from a leaking exhaust.)

"It's me, my little kreplach."

"Arnold . . ." She didn't want to admit him, but what excuse could she offer? She flipped the lock and opened the door a few inches, braving the overdose. Rosie tried holding her breath and speaking at the same time, but she sounded like an over-the-hill actress with a cold: "I really cad spare too buch tibe right dow. Is it sobthig that could wait till later?"

"Later . . ." His smile faded and was replaced by a frown and a hard stare. "I don't appreciate that. You never seem to have time for me, Natalie."

"Really!" She wanted to add, *and why should I?* But that would only lead to more games. "Arnold, this is just not a convenient time for me."

"And what time would be convenient, Natalie?"

She was thinking, *never, you jerk,* but decided to take a page from her mother's book instead. Placing one hand on her chest in the general vicinity of her heart, she made a long, funereal face and whispered hoarsely, "My life is in such turmoil right now." She lowered her chin, shook her head and shrugged her shoulders. "I know you'll understand. . . ." She dipped her chin and allowed her voice to trail away like she'd observed her mother doing most of her life. Guilt—that tried and true Jewish weapon—appeared to reach the would-be seducer.

"I understand. But will you remember that I'm here for you should you need anything—anything at all?"

A sigh. "Of course." Act two: Rosie raised her chin and smiled bravely while inching the door closed. When she heard the elevator doors close, she punched the air in celebration. Yesss! (But how long will that be good for?)

Rosie began organizing files in preparation for the worst scenario. If, for whatever reason, Grace would not be returning, the legal material would have to be sorted, labeled and packed in cartons. The idea was disheartening and made her angry, and she was determined to find out who or what was responsible for the outrage. Once again, she went over the list: Schreiber? He's still the most likely. Carolyn? She's hiding something, and I just don't trust her, but what's her motive? Arnold? He's a jerk, but he and Grace never had much contact outside of professionally. What would he have to gain? But supposing Grace's fate was dictated by someone other than characters I'm familiar with. Then I'm out of luck. *Oh, Grace, if you could only tell me where you are!* That's it! I've got to penetrate the fog. Why, it's even possible that Grace is trying to send out signals. Why didn't I think of that before? I'll pack it in early, she thought, and head on back to Oceanside where I can concentrate—and not be a moving target for Arnold.

No one has the power to stop Time. This was true, and it was a sure bet that Grace couldn't last much longer. Rosie could almost hear Madame Volante scolding her: *Be bold, ma petite, you have a gift.* She knew the pieces were there—hers to fit into the right places—she had no choice. So she sat in a quiet corner of her living room and prepared to meditate. This time she would succeed; her friend's life depended on it. Indeed, a few minutes later, she felt herself sinking into a state of calm.

The outside of the house with its boarded-up windows was familiar, and so was the block. She'd been here before. Rosie zoomed in on the rear of the house. Focusing with all her might, she moved through the back door, which led directly into the kitchen, and then down the back stairs into the basement. And there was Grace! Still bound to the old furnace, her head hung down and, for one shocking instant, Rosie could not tell if she were alive or dead. Finally, a slight movement. So—now Rosie knew what to do. She retraced her route, mentally transferring her energies to the front of the house where she started looking for landmarks. Why was the

street so familiar? Think! she exhorted herself. Look around;
find something that makes sense.

*Hey dummy move your ass to the corner and check out the street
sign there you go now pull it into focus and read it*

The corner sign says—no it's too blurry

No excuses read it

One side says ohmygod it says Hicks Street

Okay now what does the cross street sign read

Gr—Gr—something

*Not good enough hone in concentrate take a deep breath blink
your eyes a few times and read the damn sign*

*It says shit I don't believe this someone's playing a joke it says
Grace Court*

Rosie vaulted out of the chair and went to the side table
and pulled out a map. Sure enough, there really is a Grace
Court. I gotta get over there!

She called Mike, intending to ask him to meet her there,
but he was not home. She tried his cell but could not get
through, and there was no time to leave a voice mail. She'd
keep trying him on her way over.

The roads into Brooklyn had already transported most of
its beach traffic home by this hour, as folks prepared for another workweek in Gotham. Rosie drove her Honda Civic
along Sunrise Highway, trying not to go more than five miles
over the speed limit. She activated the recall button on her
hands-free cell phone and got Mike's voice mail.

"Hi, it's me. I'm on my way into the city. Tried to call you
before I left my place, but your line was busy. Listen . . ." She
paused—how to briefly explain she was about to put her
own head on the chopping block. "I think I've targeted
Grace's location." (Oh, what the hell . . . here goes nothing.)
". . . She's in the basement of an old house on Hicks Street.

The nearest corner is Grace Court. You heard right—I said *Grace* Court. That's Brooklyn Heights. Let's coordinate: It's about seven forty-five now. I'm about twenty-something minutes away, but I'm planning to shut off my phone before I go in. Just come, or call the SWAT team, whichever comes first."

The target house was located only ten minutes from the office. That figures. Anyone who knows Grace's habits wouldn't have to travel far. And who is the culprit, anyway? The whole scenario comes across like an old Frankenstein film.

Turning onto Atlantic Avenue, Rosie was surprised she hadn't heard back from Mike. Probably out screwing. What can you expect? Even so, I'd feel more secure if I knew Mr. Macho was on his way. What bothers me now is, who's responsible for this mess? Schreiber, the wife beater? Arnold, the jerk? Nikki, the mystery man? The only other guy who was connected to this was Mike. Mike? Nah! He's a lot of things but not a suspect. Okay, smart-ass, put your shoulder to it and come up with someone better.

The car was on the outskirts of the Brooklyn Heights division now, and Rosie put aside all thoughts in order to concentrate on finding *the* house. As soon as she turned onto Hicks, she began to get chills. This is crazy. I should wait for Mike or the police. But an invisible gremlin sitting on her shoulder argued that every minute counted.

Slowly . . . slowly, her car crawled down the block, her eyes seeking the vision that had shown itself to her during her meditation. Could I be wrong? Madame Volante's words came back like a mantra: *Trust your instinct. Believe in yourself.*

There! There it is. Her pulse raced like a shuttle about to leap off the launching pad. She parked her car down the street and tried to compose herself. Okay, okay, I'm going to do this just as I did when I was zonked out on Zen. If memory serves, there's an entrance at the rear of the house through the kitchen door. Well, most of these houses have that feature.

Rosie surveyed the scene. The dusk of a summer's day settled quietly over the neighborhood. Not much action except for some children playing down at the end of the block. *Daylight saving time—yeah, I remember.* Although it was hard to put those long-ago carefree days in the same context as her present mission. In the midst of reminiscing, Rosie suddenly felt cold. Chills traced the vertebrae along the back of her neck, and a clear warning rolled over her. *Take care; there is an evil spirit nearby.* Yet except for the silhouette of a lone pedestrian across the street, nothing appeared out of place. Rosie stepped out of her car, took a deep breath and headed toward the house. *Hold everything!*

Out of the corner of her eye, she noticed the figure on the other side had crossed over and was now headed toward her. A surge of adrenaline, and Rosie's body sprang to the classic "fight or flight" mode: "Carolyn! What are you doing here?"

The other's smile was cold, and she stared back a full six seconds before answering. "I have an appointment nearby, but *you* . . . Isn't this a *little* out of your way?"

What's going on here? Carolyn's not what she seemed, but I can't believe . . . Rosie got a bad feeling—like she'd been outmaneuvered at chess, but this was no game. *Think! This is the time for you to come up with the biggest lie in your repertoire.* And she went for it. "Well, you know . . . I've been looking to move closer to work for some time now, and, uh . . . someone was telling me there are some possible rentals in the vicinity."

"Really!" But disbelief was plainly etched in the other's

face. No one needed special powers to see that Carolyn wasn't buying what Rosie was selling. "Maybe you were spying on me? Do you think I had something to do with Grace's disappearance?"

"Of course not. . . ." Rosie's weak reply lay on the deepening dusk like a spent phallus. (Okay, smart-ass, now you've gone and done it. Got any other brilliant tricks up your sleeve?)

"So," the other continued, "if Grace were someplace in this vicinity, would that interest you?"

(What's up with that?) "Well, sure," Rosie replied, with what she hoped sounded like confidence despite the quaking voice.

Now Carolyn was smirking. "Shall we have a look around—together?" Her tone was scary.

(She's playing with me. If she gets me anywhere near the house, I'll probably never see the light of day again.) Rosie said the first thing that came to mind. "Actually, I'm expecting Mike Bartel." She made an exaggerated gesture of checking her watch.

"He's supposed to have been here five minutes ago. Guys! Can't imagine what's holding him up." She tried sounding annoyed, but her voice was thin.

Carolyn's eyes narrowed. "Mike Bartel?"

"Yes." (Good! Keep going). "Well, I guess it won't be a secret for too much longer. Mike and I are . . . thinking of moving in together."

The other digested this tidbit. "You and Mike?"

"Yeah." Rosie tried to sound casual while she stemmed her fear, but her stomach was churning. She turned her palms out and shrugged her shoulders as if to suggest it was up for grabs what living with Mike Bartel might be like.

Now Carolyn hesitated.

(Good! She's buying it. Now pray. *Yis-ga-dal v'yis-ka-dash*—No, not that one. That's the prayer for the dead, and I'm not ready for that!)

The screech of tires alerted them both, and Rosie strained in the direction of the noise and caught headlights rounding the far corner. Tell me it's him, she beseeched the One Above.

Mike didn't bother to park. He just pulled up even with Rosie, jumped out of his car and grabbed her by the shoulders. "Are you all right?"

"Yes, but I can't believe you're actually here." She wanted to fall into his arms, but held back.

"Okay, you want to tell me what the fuck you're doing?"

What a miserable contrast! Here I thought he was playing loving hero, and he winds up blasting me. "Let's step right into it, shall we?—I did try to call you, you know."

"Never mind that shit. What are you doing here?"

"I'm trying to rescue Grace."

"Rescue . . . Do you want to explain that?"

"Carolyn Hughs—ohmygod, where is she?"

"Who?"

"Carolyn."

"Have you been taking funny pills lately?"

Rosie looked up and down the block. "She was just here a minute ago. Mike, she scared me." Rosie went on to describe their exchange. "Her behavior was definitely not normal."

"Whoa—let's go back to the beginning. What are we doing here in the first place?"

"This is the place—the location where Grace is being held prisoner. The vision that I told you about, that I couldn't pinpoint? Well, this is it. I finally reasoned it out. Grace is inside—in the basement to be exact. But, Carolyn said—"

"Never mind about Carolyn. We'll get to that later. First,

I'm calling for backup, the thing you should have done before you waltzed yourself out here." He pulled out his cell phone and dialed a number.

"Well, Mr. Big Shot, I certainly did try to inform you of my plans. Can't help it if you're too busy to answer."

"Did you ever hear of voice mail? Or even just a little patience?" He held up his hand for her to be quiet. "Yeah, Chris, it's me. . . ." In just a few words, Mike conveyed their location and told him he was planning to start without him. "Yeah, right."

Rosie hoped his former partner had told him to exercise caution. Even if he did, that would not stop her from going down to the basement as well.

"You stay here."

"No way."

"Do I have to handcuff you to the tree?" He knew this was not the time or place, but why did the idea of handcuffing Rosie to anything start his juices going?

"I'm coming in and that's final!"

"When this is over, you and I are going to have a strong talk. Get that?"

She didn't answer him.

Resigned, he pushed her to one side. "Stay behind me," he ordered.

The tree-lined block was now shrouded in dusk. Mike grabbed a flashlight from the glove compartment of his car and checked his weapon, a Sig Sauer nine millimeter, and moved toward the rear of the house.

"There's an entrance by the kitchen," she confided.

A low grunt was his only reply.

They came upon the back door, and Mike turned the handle, but the door wouldn't budge. He reached into his back pocket and Rosie saw the glint of something metal in the light of a thin moon. Mike inserted the piece in the door lock and, after a few seconds of twisting, the handle turned. She admired that, thinking, I'm actually casting my lot with a professional lock-picker.

Mike shone the flashlight around a fifty-something styled kitchen with color-faded appliances from that vintage. A tiny shadow dashed across the checkered linoleum and skittered under an old wooden kitchen table. Rosie jumped and grabbed on to Mike's shirt. Facing away from her, he smiled. Never thought I'd owe our first physical contact to a mouse, he thought, then turned serious when he spied the door that could only lead to the basement.

At the same time, Rosie whispered, "That's the door to the basement."

He spun around for an instant and touched a forefinger to his mouth. *Jeeze*, she thought, I'm only trying to help. Holding the flashlight in one hand and his weapon in the other, Mike led the way down the narrow wooden stairs. Rosie held on to the banister with one hand and Mike's shirt with the other. Ever since their initial contact a few minutes earlier, her fingers had clutched his shirt like a security blanket. When they reached the bottom of the stairs, Rosie received a most welcomed signal from her unknown source. *No need to fear; the coast is clear.*

"It's all right, now," she mumbled hoarsely.

Mike swung around and placed his entire hand over her mouth. "Shut up!" he breathed back at her, flashing his light around the room.

Rosie broke away and gasped. "There she is!"

Indeed, the beam of Mike's flashlight illuminated the center of the room like spotlights on a Broadway stage. Just as Rosie had envisioned, Grace was bound to an old furnace, one hand still imprisoned. The other hung limp at her side. Her head had fallen over her chest. Rosie saw no other movement of her body. While she stared, Mike had rushed forward, his hands busily feeling for a pulse.

He had already sheathed his gun. Now he pushed the flashlight in Rosie's direction and barked, "Here, hold this."

Rosie was quick to respond, grabbing the light and aiming it as Mike worked to release the ropes that bound Grace. He set her down gently on the floor and placed his ear against her chest. He nodded in Rosie's direction. "Very faint, but she's still alive."

Rosie was overcome with relief. "Thank God!"

"But if we don't get the EMT guys here soon, I don't know how much longer she can hold out."

They both heard the sirens approaching from some blocks away. "Let's get her out of here now!" Mike said, and scooped her up like he would a small child.

Clutching the flashlight, Rosie led the way as they climbed the stairs and made their way through the kitchen and out the back door.

"Go ahead and flag 'em down," Mike directed. "I'll follow."

As the sirens got louder, Rosie ran back up the walk toward the street in time to see the flashing lights of the first cars approaching. She waved the flashlight and called out loudly: Here! We're here!"

Chris Marino jumped out the door as the vehicle screeched to a stop. An ambulance was behind him and the EMTs were rushing a stretcher and other equipment over to where Mike stood with Grace in his arms. He set her down gently on the stretcher and let the ambulance crew take over while he huddled with his former partner.

Rosie moved closer, noting that they spoke in the short-hand of two people who have known each other well for a long time. Obviously, they were on the same wavelength, sharing information, nodding occasionally and—what's this? They're looking in my direction, and—what?—laughing. No, I don't like this at all. Mike gestured for her to join them, and she debated this for a split second before moving closer. The inside of her right palm itched. Just one smart-ass crack, and I'm gonna smack him for sure.

"Just telling Chris how we're gonna have to get you a gold shield."

"Yeah," his former partner agreed, "great job!"

Hmm . . . She looked from one to the other but kept her hand at the ready just in case. Backup units started arriving, and Marino huddled with members of the SWAT team. The latter then headed toward the house with body language that underscored their objective to take into custody any unau-thorized person. At the same time, detectives donning rubber gloves were prepared to collect evidence when the coast was cleared.

Marino then turned his attention back to Rosie. "Now tell me about the conversation between you and this Carolyn Hughs."

In all the excitement with freeing Grace, she'd almost for-gotten. Now Rosie related the strange exchange. "Maybe she did have an appointment nearby. She acted different—kind of weird—not her usual cheerful self."

Mike interrupted. "If she was threatening you, it has to be followed up."

"I couldn't say she was threatening me. She just acted . . . peculiar."

"Whatever."

But Rosie noticed Mike eyeing her in an odd way. Could

he be concerned? She shrugged and changed the subject. "Shouldn't I call Nikki Marcos? He needs to know Grace has been found."

"Yeah, but . . ." He placed his hands on her shoulders and turned her around to face him, softening his voice. "I'm no doctor, but it's possible she's not gonna make it."

Rosie was silent. Curious neighbors were beginning to gather and a reporter Mike knew had just pulled up across the street. He elbowed Marino and pointed: "That's only the first. They'll all be sucking around before long." He swung back to Rosie. "Tell Marcos the truth: His girlfriend's in bad shape."

After seeing the ambulance head toward the hospital, his former partner returned to where they were standing. Marino had just picked up on what they were saying and added, "There's a lot of questions we're gonna have for Ms. Osborne when and *if* she's ever able to tell us who did this. Meantime, I'll be interested in speaking with Carolyn Hughs."

Rosie perked up. "You don't suppose she's the one who engineered Grace's disappearance?"

"This job was more than that. I call it attempted murder."

"Yes, but—"

Mike cut her off. "Why don't you let the cops do their job, so you can pay attention to some of the other stuff in your life?"

"Like what could be more important than finding out who's responsible for this?"

Chris was watching the exchange, unable to conceal a good-natured grin. "Think I'll get going, but I'll be in touch." He nodded to both and headed back to his car.

Mike was looking at Rosie. "Like, why don't you let me drive you home? We can get someone else to get your car back to your place."

For one wild moment, Rosie was tempted, but something

held her back. The timing's wrong, she thought. "Thanks anyway, but I'd rather just drive myself."

Mike pushed out an exasperated sigh. "Suit yourself." He spun around and headed back to his car.

His body language needed no translation, and Rosie almost relented. Nope—I'm just not ready.

Chapter 22

"Nikki went nuts when I told him the good news," Rosie related, propping up the pillows behind her head and so glad to be home.

"I can believe it," Libby garbled, through a mouthful of cold chicken. She hooked the telephone between her shoulder and ear and reached into the refrigerator for another piece. "I could cry for both of them."

"But we still don't know how serious her condition is," Rosie cautioned. "And we don't even know when, or even if, Grace will be able to tell us who did this."

"I understand. Now, tell me more about Mike."

"Like I said before, he was pretty spectacular."

"Uh-huh."

"What's with the *uh-huh*?"

"Oh, don't pretend with me. We've known each other too long."

Libby couldn't see the wide grin spreading across her friend's face. "He was good, that's all," said Rosie, trying to sound cool. She tried to change the subject, but Libby kept coming back to Mike.

"Aw c'mon, you know you like him. He's special . . . like Aaron is to me."

If anything would be the sobering agent in their conversation, the mere mention of Dr. Fingers did the trick. Rosie had all she could do to keep the sarcasm out of her voice. "I'm sure he is, Libby." Then she begged off any more talk until the next day with a noisy yawn. "Guess I'm even more pooped than I thought. Maybe we can talk more tomorrow?"

"Okay. But just tell me one thing. The police—they still have no idea who—?"

"Not at this point, but the bastard's not going to remain anonymous forever."

After she hung up, Rosie reviewed the events of the past couple of hours. Nikki was overjoyed when she'd called him with the good news. She saw him for a few minutes just outside the hospital.

"Please know that I shall always be in your debt," he said.

His dark eyes were naked, and she could see into his soul. *This is a good man, in spite of what the world may think.* The pain of almost losing Grace was clearly etched in his face. "I'm just glad we have her back," she'd said.

Rosie knew he was the only one besides herself whom the police would allow to visit. Grace would be under twenty-four-hour protection, thank God, until the person responsible was in custody. Could that person be Carolyn Hughs? But why? Rosie tried to find some logic in the mysterious circumstances of this past week, but none of the events made any sense. The one thing she did know was that she was exhausted and just glad to be home and in bed. As Scarlett O'Hara would say, *I'll think about all that in the morning.* But just as she was about to doze off, the phone rang.

"So, my little flanken, good news for a change! I hear that

Grace has been found. Does that mean that we can now get on with our lives?"

"Arnold! How did you find out so fast? And do you know what time it is?"

"The answer to your first question is: You should never underestimate me—or my sources. And it's not quite eleven is the answer to your second question."

Rosie remembered her agreement with the detectives. The plan was to acknowledge Grace's rescue but pretend the attorney was near death and her chances of recovery were poor. At the very least, she'd probably suffered brain damage and might never talk again. The object of the exercise was to make the culprit believe he (or she) had gotten away with this terrible crime. A trap was being laid that required time and patience. Both Rosie and Nikki had agreed to the plan. She quickly recited the rehearsed information but didn't wait for Arnold to pump her for any details.

"So, now we both know it's late, and I'm going to bed." Rosie hung up the phone immediately and turned off the ringer. She was so agitated, however, that she put on the television in the hopes of finding something boring with which to fall asleep. Unfortunately, the set had last been tuned to CNN, which was now broadcasting *the amazing rescue of attorney Grace Osborne, discovered after having been missing for more than one week.* The footage showed an ambulance arriving at Long Island College Hospital in Brooklyn Heights and medical technicians transporting a stretcher as uniformed policemen crowded around.

The reporter's voice described the scene in dramatic tones, not realizing the information he was relaying was a prepared script: ". . . suffered probable brain damage . . . The doctors hold out little hope for a full recovery." Around him, flashbulbs popped, sirens wailed and crowds gawked. Praying that the report would never come to be, Rosie turned off the set and read for half an hour. My friend is safe now, she thought, and finally drifted off to sleep, but even then she could not find peace.

The dream, if it was a dream, consisted of Rosie running away from some unseen threat, a person whose identity she could not determine. That in itself was scary because not only didn't she know why she was running, she also didn't know from whom. As a result, everyone in her dream was a dangerous enemy. Against a background of hideous laughter, faces appeared like pop-up heads in a theme park's tunnel of horrors: Hans Schreiber, Nikki Marcos, Arnold Feltman, Carolyn Hughs, even Mike Bartel! Rosie ran and ran, fearful of stopping lest she be caught. She awoke in the middle of the night, crying out for help. Gabby's soft warm head pushed against her arm as if to reassure her that it was only a bad dream and everything would be all right. But whatever sleep came after that was fitful and unsatisfying.

She awoke as the sun splashed its way through the sides of the venetian blinds. Another new and innocent day. She wanted to believe that everything was going to be wonderful again because Grace was once more among them, but her hopeful feelings were soon dispensed by a psychic bulletin: *No. Everything is NOT going to be all right. You must take even more care now than before.*

Rosie pulled out Chris Marino's card from her wallet and dialed his number. His partner answered, and Rosie identified herself. "I was wondering if you heard anything from the hospital."

Adella Parsons was empathetic. "I'm sure you're worried. We are, too. I called a little while ago, but I'm afraid there's not too much to report yet. They're keeping her sedated.

Look, there's no way to make this any prettier. On top of everything else, she suffered a concussion. That plus severe dehydration make brain damage a real possibility."

"Oh, no!"

"Don't give up yet. They say this is a strong woman who was in pretty good shape before her ordeal began—did you know she was a runner?"

"No, I didn't."

"Well, maybe because of that, she'll have some credit in the bank, health-wise."

"God, I hope so!"

"Stay cool, Rosie. We'll let you know."

"Sure. But I can see her, right?"

"There's nothing to see. She's in ICU, and we've got our people there 'round the clock. But if it'll make you feel better, the uniform has your name. Just show him some ID— make that a photo ID—and he'll let you in."

"Thanks, Adella."

The phone was ringing as she stepped out of the shower, and Rosie snatched it before the answering machine kicked in. Mike's gravelly voice responded.

"You okay?"

Rosie stiffened, remembering last night's dream and this morning's warning. "Yes, why?"

"Detectives went to question Carolyn Hughs last night, but she was not at home. And even as we speak, she's still not there."

"Hmm. You think . . . ?"

"Don't know what to think, but I want you to be extra careful."

Rosie was trying to take this in. "Carolyn? Maybe she's gone missing like Grace did."

"Or maybe she knows something that she's not sharing."

"Or maybe she just had plans that had nothing to do with this terrible business."

"What does your crystal ball say?"

"I got a really bad feeling last night when she appeared out of nowhere, but I was spooked anyway. Can't believe she could be involved in such a terrible thing. I mean . . ." Her voice trailed away.

"Look, I'm not sure it's a good idea for you to stay alone."

(Like, he's gonna use this as an excuse to move in?) "So, what are you saying?"

"Maybe you should stay at your folks for a night or two until we figure it out."

"Oh . . ." She backed away from allowing him to hear her disappointment. "Well, that would be very inconvenient."

"So would putting your life up for grabs."

"*Quelle dramatique!* I'll think about it. Meantime, I'm getting ready to go to the office."

"Why? What's so urgent?"

"Well, let's see . . . there's mail, phone, fax . . . I'm thinking I still have a job after all. Want to make sure that everything's in good shape before I go over to the hospital."

"If you say so, but watch your back. See you later." The phone went dead.

That's so typical, she thought. He hangs up to make sure he gets the last word. (What else is new?) Nevertheless, Rosie was getting used to his peculiar ways. Maybe a little bit too used to them.

The message hit her when she stepped outside and locked her front door: *Don't let the sunshine fool you. There's some bad karma in store.* Seventy-six degrees or not, Rosie shivered.

Chapter 23

In spite of the warning, Rosie had a strong feeling that life was meant to improve. All well and good, she thought, and let herself into the office. I can be patient. She placed her purse on the desk and started the coffee. Except for Arnold, the messages on the answering machine had to do with ongoing business and possible future clients. She pushed buttons and took notes, saving the pest's message for last.

"Hello, my little cheese blintz. Now, about the good news. How about a glass of wine to celebrate? I'll call you later for your answer. Say 'yes,' my dumpling; think how happy your mother will be."

(Say you'll leave me alone, jerk. Think how happy that would make *me!*)

Rosie did not plan on staying in the office long, just enough time to ensure that everything stayed on course for Grace's return. She's got to be okay, and that's all there is to it. So she slit open envelopes, made neat piles and thought of Mike, the nice Mike, as she'd come to think of his split personality. He was the counterpart of the nursery rhyme about the *little girl who had a curl right in the middle of her forehead/ When she was good, she was very, very good/ But when she was bad, she was horrid.* And Mike could be so irritating at times. Last night, however, he was magnificent, and she refocused on seeing him scoop up poor Grace in his arms like she was a wounded bird.

Slim to begin with, her boss was even more so after her enforced week of starvation. The doctors were concerned about dehydration, which could lead to all kinds of complications. And what about the concussion? Rosie needed to get over to the hospital and find out for herself what was going on.

All morning, she had the feeling Nikki would telephone. And so he did, about eleven, just as she was gathering her stuff together and getting ready to lock up.

"Yes, Rosie, I'm calling from the hospital, but I'm afraid there's nothing much to report yet. I'm waiting to speak with the doctors."

"I'm glad you called. Actually, I'm on my way over, so I'll see you in just a few minutes."

"Good. Maybe we will both hear some good news then."

Mike had already alerted Rosie to the security coverage surrounding Grace, and she remembered Adella Parson's warning to bring a photo ID, but as she approached the hospital's Critical Care unit a little while later, she was momentarily taken aback when a burly uniformed cop challenged her.

"See some identification?" he asked, getting in her face at the same time.

"I'm Natalie Rosenstein," she announced, fishing in her bag and pulling out her driver's license, "Grace Osborne's assistant." Still, the policeman scrutinized the card and held it up to the light, matching the photo with Rosie's face, allowing his frown to deepen and linger until he was reasonably sure it was one and the same. She assumed it was all right to move forward when he jerked his thumb in the direction of the double doors, even though he continued to eye her suspiciously and keep one of his hands on his nightstick.

Sheesh! I wouldn't want to be a bad guy caught in his sights.

Nikki Marcos materialized out of nowhere and motioned for her to follow him. "She's still not conscious," he whispered a minute later as they stood at the foot of Grace's bed.

Pale blond hair framed the small childlike face with perfect features. With her eyes closed, Grace reminded Rosie of a sprite or pixie from a Hans Christian Andersen fairy tale— only without the power to fly away. An intravenous stand next to her bed dispensed essential fluids and minerals through one arm while a blood-pressure cuff attached to her other arm monitored her vitals. Various electronic devices blinked and beeped, and one felt compelled to converse in hushed tones.

"The doctors are keeping her sedated," Nikki said softly, "so she's not in any pain."

Then why is he whispering, she wondered? He looked pale and tense, and that was understandable. She turned toward the bed once more and bowed her head. If prayers can be heard and answered, she began silently, I offer mine. When she raised her head after a few moments, Nikki was watching her, his eyes glistening. She motioned toward the door and they both went out of the room.

"Can you tell me what the doctors say?" she asked. "Like, how long before Grace will be able to talk with detectives?"

He looked strained. "The doctors are saying that they can't promise anything." He hesitated before continuing. "One of the issues here is . . . possible brain damage."

"But I thought the police were only putting out that

story in order to flush out the guilty person." She shook her head. "Grace brain damaged? I happen to know that's not going to happen."

He stared back at her, waiting for her to elaborate.

"I do have the impression that, as terrible an ordeal as Grace suffered, she will recover—fully."

"Fully? You know this?" Nikki's eyes were wide.

"Yes, but please don't ask me for details." It was true. Rosie's bulletins were arriving more frequently, and she was beginning to accept her abilities as something due her. Maybe I'll start a psychic hotline when we're through with this. (Yeah, I can just see my mother bragging to the dentist: *Well, you see, I have this talented daughter . . .*)

Voices in the hallway distracted them. Mike had just arrived with the two detectives from the Eighty-fourth.

"Here's the plan," Marino was saying. He saw the other two and waited for them to catch up. "Our department will continue to push the story that Grace Osborne is believed to have suffered severe brain damage as a result of her ordeal."

Nikki Marcos held up a hand. "But of course that's not true."

"Of course not," soothed Adella, "but we want the person who's responsible to think so. It'll make it that much easier . . . to flush out the bad guy, that is."

Nikki's eyes were fixed sharply on the detective as she spoke. "I understand."

"It's very important that we don't mess up here," her partner cautioned. "So we should all understand this is something that cannot be shared with anyone. Not family, not friends, not *anyone.*" He looked at his audience meaningfully.

(Check, Chief.) Rosie wondered if she should salute.

A little while later, Nikki returned to his bedside vigil and

the detectives went to speak with the hospital personnel assigned to Grace.

Mike pulled Rosie aside. "How you doing?"

"You sound like a promo for *The Sopranos.*" But her voice
was soft.

"Want to have lunch—or something?"

(Or something?) "Um, sure."

"Wait until Marino and Parsons finish up. Then we'll split."

(Sounds like, your place or mine?)

But just as Rosie was giving in to the idea, Mike got a call
on his cell. He moved toward the window for better reception, which took him out of earshot, but she watched his expression.

Today's not your day, her sixth sense was telegraphing, *but if
it's any consolation, the change in plans has nothing to do with another woman.*

Mike snapped his phone shut and spun around. The frustration on his face said it all.

Rosie ate an uninspired salad alone and headed back to the
office. Her psychic message center began broadcasting as she
rode the elevator up to her floor: *He's ba-a-ck.* Sure enough,
Arnold was waiting for her in the hall when the doors opened
on her floor.

"Good afternoon, my little crumb cake."

A swift appraisal confirmed that Arnold was taste-testing
every one of his pet names for her. His round frame was ex-
panding by the day, and there was no doubt his suits were
protesting the strain. "Yo! Arnold. Imagine meeting you
here." (Like she wouldn't have known? His aftershave bounced
off the walls!)

"Jest all you like, my lovely," he said, in what must have been his version of a knight gone bad. "I'll have you yet."

He offered an exaggerated bow, but Rosie feared he'd split his pants if he bent too low, so she applauded, stopping him before he reached the point of no return. "How chivalrous!"

"Drink with me this evening, fair lady."

"No, kind sir. Drinking with you is not on my agenda."

"Why not?"

Rosie inhaled deeply, immediately regretting it as Arnold's signature scent invaded her lungs. "Because . . ." And then she dropped all pretense. "Because, Arnold, there's no chemistry between us."

"Chemistry," he repeated, and she noticed his jaw working in disapproval. "Y'know, there was once a time when chemistry had nothing to do with relationships, and women didn't get to choose." His voice turned serious.

By now Rosie had the office door unlocked and had moved inside. Arnold followed, slapping his hand against the door, preventing it from shutting automatically. She turned around, read his expression, and felt the hairs on the back of her neck prickling. *What's this?* "Arnold, I really don't have time to fool around."

"See? That's the problem. You think I'm fooling, that I'm a clown, but I've got feelings." He was thumping his chest with the flat of his hand.

Rosie took note of his flushed cheeks and wild, darting eyes. Falling off the edge? She thought of a nuclear weapon gone amok. Quick, say something to calm him down. "Um, my mother was asking about you last night—sends her regards, actually."

"Your *mother*," he spat out.

"I think she's hoping you'll join us for dinner one Friday night." (Well, that isn't such a stretch.)

"You wouldn't kid a friend, would you?" Arnold was not smiling.

This is not working. I'm better off lying outright. "Look, I'll think about having a glass of wine with you later, but right now I really have to get to my pile."

Arnold looked suspicious. "I don't want to be put off like you've been doing, Rosie. I'm not a child, or even a pet, like some *cat* that you can stroke or soothe with soft, sweet murmurings. No. I'm a human being—a *man,* dammit. I want a firm commitment about what time I can pick you up."

But Rosie was still stalled on *cat*. She could have sworn he'd said something like that before. It was almost as though he knew about Gabby. But the only way he could know that is if he'd been . . . spying? She shivered. Now *I'm* getting paranoid. It's gotta be just a coincidence. The jerk wouldn't have the nerve, would he?

". . . a firm commitment."

Rosie forced herself back to the conversation. "Well, how about I meet you at—"

"No. There will be no meeting me later. Give me a time, and I will pick you up *here.*"

Oh, what the hell. I'll humor him; he's not going to bite. "How about four-thirty?" She noticed his shoulders relax somewhat, and he smiled for the first time, so she added, "But I will not make it a late night. My father has not been well, and I planned on visiting my parents this evening."

That bit of news did not discourage him. It was her agreeing to see him later that put the smile back on Arnold's face. Humpty-Dumpty was back in sync and all was right with the world. He left, but not before first waggling his finger and singing out, "Until four-thirty, my little *schnecken*."

It was one glass of wine and forty-five minutes of complete boredom. That's how Rosie summed it up as she rode the train back to Oceanside. Arnold's interest is not only unwanted, it's beginning to take on exaggerated tones, and his manners go beyond gentlemanly: *The way he held my elbow when we crossed the street, his rush to pull out my chair at the table. I know, I know—this is just the kind of shit my mother would love. Maybe that's why I'm turned off. Am I programmed to fall for the opposite of what Mother approves of?—the jerks who take advantage and hog everything for themselves?—like Jean Marc, for instance? If that's true, I might as well quit now.* Only minutes later, she thought of Mike and flushed hot. He didn't belong in either group. Not quite true. He had one quality that her mother would attach to the second group: "Not Jewish, missy—no good!" *Hmm . . . we'll see about that.*

A large woman settled onto the seat next to Rosie on the train, making it necessary for her to scrunch closer to the window side. She was so tense everything was beginning to hurt. It seemed the more space she offered, the more the woman demanded. After a while, Rosie's shoulder felt bruised and she was getting claustrophobic. (Isn't this just the perfect ending to a wonderful day?) Actually, it wasn't the ending yet. She'd promised her mother she'd stop by for a few minutes.

Being with Arnold had put her in a real grouch. *Why do I do it?—this commuting stuff?—back and forth to Brooklyn from Long Island. It saps my strength and takes so much time. And this seat has seen better days.* Rosie had a headache to begin with, now she was getting a backache. *Why don't I just change things?—move to the city and get on with my life instead of spend-*

ing half my days sitting on this Coney Island fun-ride and getting my guts Osterized. I do not need to live ten minutes away from Mom and Dad. I'd still get to see them. Besides, maybe a little distance between us would be healthier for all. Well, all right, healthier for me! Finally, Rosie was beginning to see what had kept her from really growing up. But, was she also thinking she'd be in closer proximity to Mike? The conductor came along, punched her monthly ticket, and Rosie opened her current book and settled in. She hoped the latest Sue Grafton novel would be entertaining enough to take the edge off her tedious session with Arnold. But in lieu of distraction, her ESP voice mail kicked in.

Storms a-brewing, but the winds will clear the field for a new beginning. Yeah, a new beginning, just what I need. Rosie closed the book and stared out the window, watching familiar communities passing by: Valley Stream, Lynbrook, Center Avenue, East Rockaway. A few more minutes and the train would slow down for Oceanside, and she'd be looking at yet another dull evening—alone. After her shower, she'd visit the parents. Then what? Call a friend to take in a movie? Not really interested; she'd rather read. Don't think about *him*. He's not thinking about *you*.

But at a Chinese restaurant just a few blocks from his West Seventy-first Street apartment, Mike was hefting the takeout package and inhaling its teasing aromas. (Wonder if she likes shrimps and vegetables?) He contemplated his plans for the next day. Maybe he'd bring back enough information to nail Grace's kidnapper. Then we can all get on with our lives.

Chapter 24

"You'll eat?" her mother asked as Rosie was coming in the front door.

"Thanks, Mom, but I already had something."

"*Something . . .* that's the problem. You don't eat regular."

Rosie didn't answer. She slid her eyes toward her father, but he was in his favorite escape mode watching a Yankees and Mets interleague game at Shea Stadium.

"So," her mother continued, "how is your young man?"

Rosie knew she was talking about Arnold and bit back the nasty response that came to mind. "If you mean Arnold Feltman, I told you I'm not interested."

"Yes, I know what you told me, but . . ."

Rosie got this sick feeling. A sickness that only grows out of the ability to intuit that Arnold and her mother were communicating behind her back. *What the hell does he do? Give her a goddamned progress report?* "But what, Mom?"

"Never mind." She patted the couch next to her. "Come. Tell me about Grace. Is she going to be all right?"

Rosie remembered the detectives' admonition to guard the truth about Grace's condition. She didn't like lying to her mother, but since she suspected the latter and Arnold were now fast friends, she had no choice. "We're praying she will be, but there is a possibility of permanent brain damage."

"*Gotteniu!*" Her mother clutched her chest. "Did you hear that, Joseph?"

Her father turned his head slightly in their direction, but never took his eyes off the screen. He held up a finger. "One minute, Ida . . . Yessss!" He slapped the arm of his chair enthusiastically. "A two-hitter. Can you believe it? What pitching! What defense! What a ball club!" Now he swung around and faced them. "So, what did you say?"

He showed genuine sadness after his wife repeated the news. "I'm so sorry. When will the doctors know for sure?"

Rosie felt really guilty, so she switched her tone. "Not for a while, Pop, but the doctors say she was in pretty good condition before this thing. That's in her favor."

"I'll pray for her." But the look he gave his daughter said something more. "Uh, Ida, do you have any more of that honey cake? I feel like something sweet."

"Sure! Maybe we'll all have some. I'll make some tea. Na-ta-lie?"

"I'd love some honey cake, Mom. Holler when you're ready." Rosie had already gotten the sense that her father wanted to speak with her alone.

When her mother was out of earshot, he shrugged his shoulders. "So?"

Rosie had no fear about sharing the truth with her father, so she told him what the detectives had actually said. "That is not to say that Grace is in good shape. She isn't, but she has a pretty good chance of returning to her former self."

"Good. I know how much that means to you. And the other things going on in your life? Your friend Mike, for instance?"

Rosie had forgotten she'd shared that with him. She looked down at her hands. "Uh, he's fine."

"Enough said."

And Rosie knew he wouldn't mention his name again until she brought it up. They joined her mother in the kitchen. Plainly, the latter was in a wonderful mood. She babbled on about her bridge cronies and the terrific bargains she and Rosie's sister had found at Loehman's, plus a lot of other unimportant tidbits, but Rosie could see through all this empty chatter. And then her mother got to the place she'd been heading all along.

"So . . . did your father tell you? We have some news. Your aunt Sophie called." She bobbed her head a couple of times for emphasis. "Your cousin Maxine is engaged. *Nu?*" (Rosie thought the only thing missing was a drumroll.) "And she's such a *mieskeit,*" her mother finished.

Her father shot a warning glance at his wife. Sophie was his only sister, and the two women had competed for his affection for the past forty-plus years.

"Well, she *is* a good daughter," Ida amended. "But the boy . . ." She looked sideways at her husband and shrugged her shoulders. "Well . . . a salesman?"

"Ida . . ." her father cautioned.

"I'm only saying."

"You're making trouble, that's what you're doing."

Rosie observed the two of them and wondered if she could get herself home before World War Three broke out. "Look, Mom, Pop—"

"Okay," her mother said, retreating. "I'm happy for them." Maybe I'm waiting to hear some good news for *us.* She looked directly at Rosie. "We're not getting any younger you know."

There was a flavor of Arnold hanging on every one of her words. Somehow the two of them—her mother and Arnold—had gotten together and were planning the rest of her life for her. And just like a DVD set on automatic, the nightmare played itself over and over. She didn't know which one of them, her mother or Arnold, was the aggressor in the deal, but it didn't matter. Her life was going to be hell until the matter was resolved, one way or another. She sighed at the task ahead of her. They have one thing in common, those two, and that's desperation.

Chapter 25

Mike fought the heavy traffic up the West Side Highway toward the George Washington Bridge. The late afternoon sun was still strong, but the humidity had practically disappeared overnight. About time. Mike was more of a cold-weather guy, and his patience was wearing thin with every passing day of the New York summer. Ahead loomed the Palisades Parkway exit. He maneuvered into the right lane, keeping pace with the suburbanites headed home. The farther away he got from Manhattan, the lighter the traffic, and he found it exhilarating to open up the speed. The skyline had long since faded behind him, trading tall concrete structures for small communities punctuated by trees. Real pretty, he thought, different—a place for me to visit but I couldn't imagine living here permanently. That's funny. I've never been a permanent anything—except maybe when Monica was here. A small pang of guilt. Why? Because I want to make love to Rosie? Or—maybe feeling guilty because I haven't been thinking of Monica at all. Yet, if she were here, he reasoned, she'd be the first to encourage me.

Mike envisioned having sex with Rosie. He drove in a happy state for a few miles until the car behind him honked loudly. Apparently, daydreaming was not synonymous with driving safely. Shit! I'd better concentrate. After another twenty minutes, he exited the Palisades, continuing north on the New York State Thruway. The traffic was sparse now, so he slowed, not wanting to overshoot his exit. Ten minutes later, he started paying attention to the street signs. And, finally, there it was: Glenn Manor.

According to his background check, Glenn Manor was an exclusive Betty Ford–type place for nondangerous types. Yeah? Well I'll be the best judge of that. What surprised him was the person who'd been a patient here. Prim, proper, educated, refined. He realized how stupid was his thinking. When he was a cop, murderers didn't wear signs on them. You never know.

Mike pulled his rental into the parking lot, reached into the glove compartment and pulled out a pair of wire-rim glasses and an uninspired tie. He grabbed the well-worn leather brief-case from the backseat and trod the flagstone walkway toward the main entrance admiring the nicely trimmed hedges and colorful hibiscus. He checked his image reflected in the glass doors at the entrance and decided he looked appropriately studious and uninteresting.

"Good afternoon," offered the heavyset woman at the reception desk. "May I help you?"

Mike donned his most serious expression. "Yes . . . I hope so. I need to speak with someone in the records department."

"Records would be right across the lobby, sir, second door on your left."

He lifted his chin and nodded. "Thank you so very much."

The room smelled stale, like it never got an airing, and that seemed appropriate enough. Stacks of papers and yellowed folders were piled on every available table, and cartons took up most of the floor space. "Good afternoon," he said, when a Joe-college type came out from behind a dusty file cabinet.

The kid seemed surprised to receive a visitor in an area that was used mainly for storage. "Can I help you, sir?"

(Oh, give me these small-town types any day.) "Hope so." Mike cleared a small space on top of a nearby table and slapped his briefcase on top. He hauled out his wallet, gave it his usual open-and-close-it-quick treatment, then proceeded to have a huge coughing attack. *Clughck cloghch!* "Richard *cloghch!* Grant. Sorry—*Gmorshand* Claims."

The other backed up a half step. "Can I get you a glass of water?"

"No thanks. Just an allergy. Guess it can't be easy working in all this dust."

"Nah. Doesn't bother me."

"Well, you're lucky. So, you can help me get out of here more quickly by giving me the file on one of your former patients who, by the way, is about to come into an inheritance."

"Gosh. Who is it?"

Mike made a show of leafing through some papers—actually, racing bets, but the kid didn't know that. "Name is . . . got it. Name is Carolyn Hughs, and I believe her stay here was October 2000."

"Uh, I'm not sure I'm permitted to . . ."

Clughck cloghch! "Sorry, shoulda taken uh-hah-hah-CHOO!" Mike pulled a large handkerchief from his pocket and blew his nose noisily. "Shoulda taken an antihistamine."

The young man had backed away toward the wall and was glancing around as though he were looking for an escape. "Tell you what. This dust is really bad for you. Let me see what I can find so you can get out into the fresh air."

"Surely would uh-hah-hah-CHOO!—appreciate that."

"Coming up." He started pulling out drawers from one of the large standing file cabinets. "October 2000, you said?" A few minutes later, he laid the file down on the table next to Mike's briefcase. "Could you excuse me a minute, sir? I'll be back shortly."

"Sure. And I'll be quick. Don't want to be sneezing all over this stuff."

The young man beat a hasty retreat, and Mike went to work on the file, quickly locating the information he was looking for. From his back pocket, he pulled out a small camera and began photographing the pages that interested him, which was practically the entire file. He worked quickly, so that by the time the young guardian-of-all-things-private returned, Mike had all the information he needed. Anxious to get out before anyone with more brain power showed up, Mike held the handkerchief against his face, coughed once more for effect and bowed out of the room.

Riding home, he replayed the strange telephone call he'd received earlier that had started this whole adventure. His Caller ID had only indicated a blocked call—not anything new in this business. What the hell . . . He'd picked up the phone.

"Mr. Bartel, this is Nikki Marcos."

So, the big one was calling *him*. "What can I do for you Mr. Marcos."

"Please, call me Nikki. I have some information that may be relevant to finding the coward who did this to Grace."

"Why are you calling me? Why not the police?" (Mike wasn't ready to invite the intimacy of his first name.)

"A fair question, Mr. Bartel. And the answer is that although I have the deepest respect for the police, they don't have the time, opportunity or creativity to follow up on my information."

It was this last that piqued Mike's interest. "Creativity? Sounds interesting. Where can I meet you?"

"If you can be downstairs in front of your office in the next few minutes, I think I can explain."

"Downstairs, huh?" (What a wonderful opportunity for an ambush. On the other hand, it's an opportunity to finally meet this character in person. And, who knows? Maybe the mystery man has something to offer after all.) "Tell you what, give me about ten minutes and I'll be there."

"Good."

Mike didn't wait ten seconds. He checked his revolver, grabbed his cell phone from the charger and locked his office. Then he took the elevator down to the basement, exited from a side entrance that led into an alley, scooting into the building next door. Less than five minutes from the time he'd hung up the phone, he was standing inside that lobby, observing the street in front. Nothing in sight yet, so he crossed to the other side and melded into the crowd. Just minutes later, a long black Lincoln Town Car with darkly tinted windows pulled up just shy of his building entrance next door. Mike waited a beat, then crossed over to the limo and casually opened the rear passenger door from the traffic side, taking Marcos and the driver by surprise.

"Mike Bartel. How's it going?"

Marcos regained his composure quickly, extending his hand. "So nice to see you, Mr. Bartel."

"So, what've you got?"

"All business, I see. May I offer you a drink?"

Mike shook his head and looked at his watch. "Sorry to rush you, but I've got another appointment."

"Of course. This is about finding out who kidnaped Grace. I wanted to talk with you about Carolyn Hughs and a possible connection." There was no response from the other, so Marcos continued. "Ms. Hughs is, unfortunately, an unstable person. I know for a fact that she was in a facility upstate for . . . problems."

"How do you know this?"

Nikki Marcos stared off into space. "Because Grace and I discussed it once."

Mike respected the silence that followed and studied the man sitting next to him. He thought of his own pain when he'd lost Monica and softened. Maybe there's something more to him than just a rich playboy. His suffering is real. "Tell me about Ms. Hughs—please," he added.

"Bipolar disorder, it's called, also known as manic depression. I understand that the person diagnosed with this condition experiences two extremes of the emotional spectrum—from the highest happiness to pathological sadness. Among the various highs and lows, the individual can manifest suicidal as well as *homicidal* thoughts. And, that person can notoriously exhibit *poor* judgment." He turned to face his visitor. "Mr. Bartel, at one time Ms. Hughs wanted to believe that I could become romantically interested in her. That was incorrect. I never gave her the slightest reason to believe that. But she, or someone else . . ." Marcos's voice broke, and he took a few seconds to compose himself. "Someone has stolen that which made my life complete. None of us know if Grace will ever recover fully from the ordeal. Whether or not it was Ms. Hughs, I do not know, but I will pay you anything, *any* amount to find the one who did this. His face hardened, and Mike could only imagine what Marcos would do if he could lay his hands on the guilty party.

Mike had no reason to believe Marcos was not sincere and silently berated himself for being such a know-it-all shit. He finally said, "Look, money doesn't add any incentive to my desire to find the person who's responsible. Getting back to your information on Carolyn Hughs, that's important. Give me all you got on that. If she's involved in this, I'll know soon enough."

Marcos told him about the facility upstate and the approximate date Carolyn had spent time there. Mike reached for the door handle.

"Can I drop you someplace, Mr. Bartel?"

"No. Going back to my office. And please—call me Mike." They shook hands and Mike was out the door seconds later.

Now, driving back from Upstate New York, he recalled the pain etched on Nikki Marcos's face. He thought of Rosie, her life turned upside down. And he took stock of the information he'd extruded from the files at Glenn Manor. And more than anything else, he pictured how much better life was going to get after he got all this stuff straightened out.

Chapter 26

"So, maybe you'll come for supper tonight." Rosie's mother wasn't asking as much as she was laying out a plan.

(Again with the food.) "I don't know, Mom. Don't seem to have much appetite these days."

"So? *The appetite comes with the eating,* your grandmother used to say. Come, Na-ta-lie," she cajoled. "Your father's always so happy when you're here."

This last was supposed to sell her, and it did. She glanced up at her office clock. "Okay. I'll see you about six-thirty."

Rosie stared at the phone after hanging up. Her mother's voice, it had an extra lilt about it, like she was trying to disguise her real reasons for getting her over to the house tonight. There was only one thing that could make her sound this way, and Rosie was beginning to get an odd feeling. *Focus,* she told herself—take a minute. . . . Ah, yes, plain as day. Her mother's euphoria had something to do with the husband search. Oh, shit! What has she done now?

As she neared her parents' house, Rosie noticed an unfamiliar car in the driveway. The dentist? (No, the buzz in her head said—*Arnold*. I know it's him.) His familiar scent floated like a storm cloud over the pathway that led to the front door. Dammit! My mother has gone and done it this time! Rosie was so angry she had to take a couple of deep breaths before entering the house, but enter she did.

"Na-ta-lie!" Her mother's voice reached high up the scale, and she was greeting her with the exuberance extended to a lottery winner. "Come, dolling."

While her mom held out her arms for the traditional hug, Rosie flicked her eyes at Arnold and gave him a hard stare. Then she moved over to her father, who looked like he'd swallowed *traif*—not that eating nonkosher food was any worse for him than seeing Arnold at her parents' home was for her.

"Surprised?" Arnold was grinning as though putting one over on Rosie would melt her heart, but if he had any sensitivity he would have known better. *As if.* His presence hung in the air like the smell of sweat in the crowded subways of August and was just as welcomed.

"Arnold." She pronounced his name, not even trying to disguise her disgust. He recoiled, but only for the space of time it would take to squash a bug. Never one to be discouraged long, he was soon chatting merrily, offering his latest take on Grace Osborne's recovery. "All this time, I was thinking maybe she'd just taken a few days away from the office." He helped himself to some chopped liver and crackers, then turned to Mrs. Rosenstein. "You can't imagine how hectic trial work can be."

Rosie's mother made big eyes, then rolled them at Rosie. She seemed to be saying: *See? You could be married to a busy lawyer.*

"I have a headache," Rosie announced. "I may not be staying long."

Her father's face filled with empathy. "That's understand-able," he said. "You've had a lot on your plate."

Rosie nodded gratefully. "Yes, you're right. I'll probably make it an early night."

It was difficult to know who looked more disappointed—Arnold or her mother. But the latter wasn't about to quit so easily. "Come now, Na-ta-lie. I cooked one of your favorites tonight: stuffed cabbage."

"Mom, didn't Dad have a stomach attack the last time you made that?"

"It was stuffed peppers," she corrected her daughter, and turned to her husband. "And tonight, I'm keeping a special eye on you, Joseph."

Arnold, the outsider, observed the family he longed to be part of, waiting for the moment when he could join in the conversation and maybe more: Rosie wore her coldness like a shield; her father was immersed in his baseball game; and the mother's expression showed her frustration. Well, it would take a lot more than Rosie's snippiness to discourage him. He and Rosie were meant to be together. Her mother agreed. At least the two of *them* understood each other.

She'd been encouraging when he spoke to her the previ-ous night, complaining about Rosie's petulance. They'd spent a lot of time on the phone lately. *You come to dinner,* she'd said, *and I'll see to it that Na-ta-lie comes, too.* She knew how he pined for her daughter; how he'd waited patiently for the girl to come to her senses; how no sacrifice was too much for him; how he'd do just about anything to claim her. They were destined for one another. Any fool could see that. What was Rosie being so aloof about? Even her mother kept reminding her she was not getting any younger. Well, neither was he. He wanted her to take the right path. She was looking for magic maybe? Well, he could make enough magic for the two of them. If he wanted to, he could even snap his fingers and make things disappear.

Rosie was glad to leave early. The evening was a farce, a pretense on everyone's part. Arnold filled the void, answering her mother's questions about his parents:

"They're not well, unfortunately. Believe it or not, they've returned to Florida. Dad's cardiologist is there. He's been having problems, and they didn't want to start with someone new."

"What a shame!" her mother cooed. "I was looking forward to meeting them."

Right! Rosie imagined the two sets of parents planning the wedding. Her mother in all her glory, crowing to aunts, uncles and cousins that her daughter had caught a *lawyer!* Her dad trying to be a good host under the most trying circumstances. And Arnold, how long he'd waited to have Rosie as his personal plaything. It'll never happen—not in this lifetime.

How the evening dragged! She and her dad let the other two do most of the talking. They held a silent exchange with their eyes. Finally, Rosie begged off early, announcing that her headache was worse. Her mother called her into the kitchen and bawled her out for not being more pleasant to Arnold.

"He's *your* guest," Rosie reminded her. "But believe me when I tell you, he'll never be your son-in-law." There was a rush of silence, and (oh, happy day!) elation—not guilt—filled Rosie's soul. Why had she waited so long to claim the freedom that was her due?

Her mother was seldom at a loss for words, but this time, Rosie had hit the target. Mrs. Rosenstein's mouth opened

and closed several times, but no sound came forth. Then she
pulled some shtick she hadn't used since Rosie was a child.
She clutched her heart dramatically and stared off into the
distance. Her daughter kissed her on the cheek. "Love you,
Mom, but I'm not seven years old anymore." She walked to
her car, but her feet never touched the ground. *Damn, that
felt good!* Rosie now understood how the persecuted must
have felt when the civil rights movement produced its de-
sired result: *Free at last; free at last/ Thank God Almighty, I'm
free at last!*

She thought about this as she drove through an unexpected rainsquall on her way back to Oceanside. Pushed by
the wind, sheets of water washed over the windshield, making
the wipers impotent against the force. Visibility was nil, so she
slowed to fifteen miles per hour, driving by instinct and familiarity with the local roads. But suddenly, the car emerged
into bright light. *Just like life,* Madame Volante would say,
nothing is ever all black or white.

Recalling her mother's attempt to lay a guilt trip, she
summoned back her declaration: That's right, she reaffirmed,
I'm not seven anymore, or twenty either. It's time to stop letting
people control my life, and that includes anything connected
to Jean Marc. So, she told herself: You had an experience—all
right, a big-time experience. But it doesn't have to dictate to
you for the rest of your life. Put it away, dammit, and stop
punishing yourself for the mistakes of a twenty-year-old. Get
a life already! Alone in the car, she smiled at the good sense of
it all.

Her apartment was nice and cool. Rosie had left the air-
conditioner thermostat set at sixty-eight and her bed turned
down. After returning a call from Libby, a shower sounded
good. The faucets were going full blast when she stepped out

of her clothes, feeling totally liberated. No, Jean Marc, you're not going to impinge on my life anymore. And, no, Mom, you're not going to make me feel guilty anymore.

Rosie began to sing: *You'd be so easy to love/so easy to idolize all others above/so nice to come home to/*so ta-da-da-da-da-de-dum to. The rest of the lyrics escaped her for the moment, but it didn't matter. The Cole Porter song bounced happily off the wet tiles. Rosie's voice was pleasant, and she could hold a tune. She lathered her hair with a new herbal shampoo, drinking in the clean smell. While she waited for the conditioner to do its job, she soaped up a washcloth and squeezed it over her body. Rivulets of thick foam rolled lazily down the curves of her breasts and belly and onto the dark area between her legs. The hot water felt good, liberating and *optimistic.* Yes, she decided, that would be the operative word. She rolled it around on her tongue—optimistic. A few minutes later, she reached for a towel, draped it around her head, turban style, and stepped onto the bath mat. That's when she knew she was not alone.

Rosie's heart took the express elevator down. Scared but alert, she stood frozen on the bath mat, willing herself to stay calm. In one motion, she turned off the bathroom light and reached for her terry robe, wrapping it around herself and tying the sash. Then she peeked around the bathroom door.

Her room was exactly as she had left it with her soiled clothes in a heap on the floor. The stillness both calmed and agitated her. Someone's near, she knew this. Not in her bedroom she could see, but close by. She eased out of the bathroom and along the wall of the bedroom, turning off the light switch and standing silently in the shadows. Right before the room went dark, she'd caught sight of Gabby, wide-eyed, her back in an inverted U, ready to spring. They both knew that someone was near. Her own breath came short and deep, accompanying the beating pulse in her neck. The bedroom door didn't have a lock on it. This had annoyed her when she first rented the place. But she'd reasoned that since she was the only one going to live here, what difference did it make? Rosie closed the door anyway, slipping a chair under the doorknob. Then she inched over to the night table and grabbed up the portable phone, quickly bringing it and Gabby back with her to the bathroom. Before she locked the door, she glanced toward the bedroom window, remembering Mike's warning about the *unfinished symphony,* the staircase that offered easy access to her bedroom. She was too panicked to be annoyed about the fact that he was right.

Mike answered on the second ring. "Yeah?"

He sure had winning ways, but now was not the time to quibble. "Mike," she whispered huskily. "It's me."

A lot of brash retorts came to him, but Mike's instinct told him this was not the time. "What's up?"

Again, she whispered. "I think there's someone here."

"You're home?"

"Yes. I just got out of the shower, and I felt . . ." No, she told herself. Don't get started with the stuff he doesn't understand. Instead she said, "I closed my bedroom door, but there's no lock on it, so I locked myself in the bathroom."

"Did you call the police?"

"No. I called you."

He couldn't resist. "I'm very flattered, but I can't get there as fast as the local police. Call them—now!"

"Okay. I just felt a little foolish."

"Do you want to feel like a dead foolish, too?"

"Okay, okay. I'm dialing."

"Then call me on the cell. I'm coming over."

"No, Mike. That's not necessary, that's—" But it was too late. Typically, he'd already hung up.

After dialing 911 and reporting a trespasser, Rosie slipped quietly back into the bedroom and snatched up some clean underwear, a pair of shorts and a T-shirt. Except for the muted bathroom nightlight, she dressed in the dark, her heart pounding. *Where are the police already?* She searched the top of her dresser and night table for a possible weapon to defend herself, finally opting for a flashlight, and trying to imagine how it stacked up against a gun or knife. It seemed an eternity before she saw the flashing lights of the patrol car. Only when the uniform policemen were coming up the walk did she venture outside. A cool breeze had replaced the earlier showers, and on it rode the faint echo of cinnamon. Could it be? She froze in mid-step.

When they asked her if she'd seen the intruder, she had to admit she hadn't. But the police noticed tire tracks in the mud across the street, an area that was in a direct line with the complainant's home. They began to investigate. No car was there now, but the large beams of their flashlights scoured the area for possible clues. Rosie knew they wouldn't find any, but it didn't matter. *She* knew who the intruder was.

When Mike appeared, one of the policemen came over to his car, but Mike already had his wallet open. "Retired from the Eighty-fourth," he said, "friend of Ms. Rosenstein's." The other nodded and went back to what he was doing. Mike put his hand on Rosie's shoulder. "You okay?"

His touch surged through her like an electric current, opening a door to something warmer than friendship, and she was hard put not to fall into his arms. He repeated his question, but his voice was softer.

"Oh . . . yes, thanks." She didn't want him to take his hand away.

"What happened?"

She repeated what she'd told the police.

"So you didn't actually see anyone."

"No, but . . ." Should she tell him? "But I think I know who it was." Rosie's eyes were searching the dark. Mike turned her around to face him. "I smelled his aftershave," she said.

"Feltman?"

She nodded.

"Sonofabitch! Okay, let me give these guys a hand. See if I can turn up anything." He grabbed a large flashlight from his glove compartment and shone it along the grassy area next to the house. After another twenty minutes, he and the uniforms huddled. Then the latter headed back to their car, and Mike came up to Rosie. "Nothing."

She didn't want him to leave. "Can I tempt you with a cup of coffee and some of my mom's strudel?"

Mike smiled, cupped his hand under Rosie's elbow and steered her toward the door. "Thought you'd never ask."

While Rosie prepared the coffee, Mike walked through the other rooms. When he returned, he said, "I made a few adjustments in the bedroom."

"Like?"

"Like your drapes. You don't need those fancy thinga-mabobs that hold the curtains apart. I took 'em off so the drapes cover the windows. Want to know what the weather's like? Turn on the radio or get dressed and go outside." He spotted Gabby under the table. "Hey, puss-puss, c'mon out."

"She doesn't take to strangers." But even as Rosie spoke, the cat was inching toward Mike.

"C'mon, girl," he said softly, "that's right . . ." Gabby made a liar out of her mistress as she glided toward Mike, accepting his caresses. "Yes," he crooned, "you know what you want, don't you?"

Why did she get the feeling Mike was really talking to

her? Nevertheless, Gabby's willingness to make friends surprised her. Totally out of character, and she said so.

Mike rinsed his hands under the tap. "Smart cat," he tossed at her. She didn't answer him, and noticed he hadn't moved. She opened the cabinet and reached for two mugs. He glided over and stood behind her. "Get those for you?"

He slid his hands along her shoulders and up her arms toward the shelf, evoking chills. Her fingers were already clasping the mugs when he folded his large hands around hers and guided them down to the counter. Rosie's legs were unsteady, and she felt her nipples harden. He pressed up against her, and she dropped her head back on his chest. He turned her around so they were facing each other. His eyes were hungry. He closed his face over hers. She leaned in. Their lips met and they gave themselves to the surging currents.

It was a simple fact of nature—undeniably physical—and something so very much needed on both their parts. Mike swooped her up and carried her into the bedroom. He lowered her gently down on the bed. She peeled off her shirt, and he slid his hands underneath and expertly unsnapped her bra and removed it. She reached toward his belt buckle. Seconds later they were both naked. No words were necessary.

Later, Rosie asked, "Will you stay tonight?"

"Yes."

Arnold had indeed been watching through the window earlier. After Rosie left her parents' house, he couldn't wait to get away from the mother, the clinging bitch. And of course, he knew where Rosie lived; he'd been there before—several times. He knew the street to turn off, knew the quiet, perfect spot to leave his car, knew the way his and his beloved's lives were meant to be. He was already quite experienced in climbing up the outside of the stucco house. He did so this evening, brushing aside the clematis and English ivy to get a better view. He'd observed her through the window, watched as she'd removed her clothes, all but her panties and bra. She kept a clothes hamper in the bathroom. He knew this, too. As his love disrobed, he imagined her removing her things for him on their wedding night. He envisioned himself possessing her, making love to his angel for the first time. She'd be modest, of course, but he would show her how manly, how strong was her new husband. His lovemaking alone would give strength to the credo that now that they were married, she would always defer to his bidding. Then something he hadn't planned on occurred.

She knows. How could she? He never made a sound. Nevertheless, he observed her reaction when she sensed his presence. She was frightened. He wanted to assure her that she need not be. He watched Rosie sneaking across the room, glancing about before taking the phone back to the bathroom. Reluctantly, Arnold retreated to his car and left the area, his mission unfulfilled. On the way back to the city he mused on her unexpected reaction to the events:

Grace's disappearance opened a whole avenue of possibilities. He surely thought Rosie would flounder. She should have required help, certainly direction, and that's where he could have come to her aid. He was meant to be the strong shoulder on which she'd lean. Maybe Grace could have been rescued, and he, Arnold, would have been the hero. But it didn't work out that way. Things got out of hand. Rosie didn't follow the script. Now that meddling private detective Mike Bartel has pushed himself in where he wasn't invited. Certainly, something would have to be done about that.

Chapter 27

Mike drove them into the city Monday morning. "Stay away from the guy."

"Easier said than done." Rosie reminded him that she'd found Arnold at her parents' house. "My mother thought she was making a wonderful surprise for me. It was a surprise, all right."

"How does your father feel about him?"

Rosie sighed. "He doesn't. Tunes everything out but his baseball these days. What can I do? Arnold just keeps coming up to the office. Nothing I say discourages him. Have to admit you were right. He's a stalker, all right."

"Let's hope that's all he is."

Rosie turned to him. "What do you mean?" She thought about it for a minute. "You think Arnold had something to do with Grace's disappearance?"

Mike didn't answer her. He was thinking that when he got into his office, he'd hit the computer and see if couldn't dig a little deeper into Arnold's background. "We'll see."

They talked about Schreiber and the restraining order that Rosie had signed. Mike didn't want to worry her, but it was his experience that a restraining order was no sure thing.

"That Schreiber's a volatile nutcase, but his alibi seems to be legit. According to his neighbors who, by the way, have no love for the guy, his son actually was with him all weekend. The guy had no time or opportunity to snatch Grace and stash her away in that basement. Believe me, if there was a shred . . ."

"He's such a likely candidate."

"Doesn't make him guilty though. Not so sure about Carolyn. She's another weird one." Mike revealed what he'd learned about her from his visit to Glenn Manor. Rosie's reaction surprised him.

"That explains it."

"What?"

"That weird feeling I get whenever she's around. You think . . . ?"

"Door's open. Look, Rosie—"

"Don't say it."

The car slowed down for the traffic entering the Van Wyck Expressway, and Mike began complaining about the futility of living on Long Island when one worked in the city. "How do you do it?"

Rosie didn't answer because she was in the process of working through that very question. She segued back to their former discussion. "No two ways, Carolyn has some airs. Guess Grace had her own reasons to step away from any friendship they might have had."

"Let me tell you, until we get to the bottom of all this, you may be better off staying away from the city. Too many crazies involved."

Rosie was instantly amused. What is it about you guys that make you think you can take over? You know . . ."

Mike held up a hand. "I know what you're gonna say."

"Oh, you're psychic, too?"

"Whatever that means." He reached for her hand and kissed the inside of her palm. The last place he wanted to be at that moment was in the car, but he urged himself to stay with the program. When they got into Brooklyn, he dropped Rosie close to her office and went to return his friend's car. He wondered if he'd be going home with Rosie later. Damn, last night was great!

He thought about how she'd moved underneath him when he'd entered her the first time. She responded like a starved orphan. Well, he hadn't had much of anything in a long time either. Her skin was smooth and soft, her breasts firm, and she had the hips of a real woman, not some emaciated, bony cadaver. She had a lovely body and knew how to move it, arching up to meet his thrusts. His excitement was intense, and it was all he could do to keep from coming too soon. When they finished, he rolled over next to her. Neither spoke. After a while, he traced his finger along the curves of her body. There was no one in their world at that moment but the two of them. Rosie reached up to smooth back his hair and smiled. "You're something else," she'd whispered, and that seemed the right moment to begin again, only this time, he was in no hurry. Thinking about it now got him going again, but Mike held himself in check. *Gotta hold all that till later.*

Mike turned on his computer when he got to his office and logged on to the Internet. *Let's just see if I can dig up a little more information on my favorite stalker.* Not too long after, he began printing out his findings. He grunted with satisfaction. *You never know what you're gonna turn up.*

Chris Marino and Adella Parsons, meanwhile, were sitting with Sam Pixel, the novelist, in his apartment on Eightieth, off Park. Pixel seemed amused by the detectives' questions, but he responded with British good humor.

"Yes, I was with Ms. Hughs Saturday a week ago." He began to smirk. "Um, I hope you don't expect me to describe in detail what went on." Neither detective reacted, so he continued. "I believe we went out for a quick bite, then returned here and . . . oh, well, did the Saturday-night thing." He winked, in case they didn't get the full import.

Adella thought he was a pompous ass, but didn't show any reaction. However, she was thinking that he'd be the last guy she'd want to get it on with. Apparently, he never suspected because he eyed her knowingly, as if he would be glad to illustrate in graphic detail—and having sex with a black woman would not be a problem. (Later, honky.)

Pixel wasn't Marino's type either. He wouldn't even want to go fishing with the guy. He observed the writer's clumsy attempts to seduce his partner and recalled her prowess in the martial arts. Hell, I hope he does overstep himself, I've got a front-row seat to a guy going to hell in a handbasket. Still, Marino thought they might be able to squeeze out some information before they let him go, so he threw out a dart— what the hell.

"Was Ms. Hughs any different than usual?"

The other raised his eyebrows as if to say, where to begin? "Different, how?" But with the detectives leaning forward (wide-eyed and attentive) how could a ham actor like Pixel refuse? "Grace has a history of being different," he continued, leering at his audience. "A little wild at times, if you know what I mean."

Like, this guy really doesn't like to kiss and tell, thought Adella, who nevertheless maintained an interested expression.

"She can run the gamut of emotions," Pixel went on, and

suggested that Carolyn liked to participate in sex games. "Of course, I, for one, have no objections."

Of course not. Adella called upon all her police experience to refrain from overreacting. "We're talking S&M?"

"Yes."

So much for bedroom secrets. Later, the detectives would share this information with their lieutenant, describing another side to the very proper Ms. Hughs:

"Just because the woman's got a law degree and also excels in the bedroom, doesn't mean she couldn't fit a kidnaping into her busy schedule," Adella pointed out. "This Pixel accounts for her time on Saturday night only. The victim went missing sometime between the end of Friday's workday and Monday morning. The way I see it, there's still plenty of other blank space to account for." Her partner agreed.

"I thought you liked the watch repair guy for this one," their lieutenant said.

"We did," Marino answered, "but the neighbors we interviewed can vouch that he had his son with him all weekend. No way he'd could have done the snatch, disabled the vic and left her in that basement without leaving the boy. Now we like the Hughs broad even better."

So, let's dig a little deeper," their boss urged.

Adella was still pondering Carolyn Hughs and her taste in kinky sex. Was it possible she might be capable of something even more avant-garde?—like kidnaping, for instance?

Chris Marino reached Mike on his cell. "Sorry I couldn't take your call before." He explained they were interviewing Carolyn Hugh's latest lover. "Hot stuff, buddy, you shoulda been here." He winked at Adella to make sure she was enjoying the joke, too. Mike asked his former partner to relay the gist of the interview, and Chris was only too glad to comply, ending with "whips, handcuffs and all that good, clean fun."

On his end, Mike was thinking how neatly this erratic behavior fit in with his discoveries from Glenn Manor. "I've got some information in my hands right now that will add to your happiness, if you're gonna be there awhile."

"You bet." Marino's curiosity was piqued, as was his partner's.

Mike came along about twenty minutes later and gave them a rundown of his discoveries. "This bipolar disorder thing leads to some crazy behavior." He scanned his notes: "depression, sleep problems, feelings of failure . . . and big emotional swings from one end of the spectrum to the other. And, get this—*poor judgment*. All in all, it's possible that an intelligent, educated woman like Carolyn Hughs could wind up doing some pretty bizarre stuff. Did she have a motive for kidnaping Grace Osborne? If jealousy counts, I'd have to say yes." Mike told them about the letter from Nikki Marcos he'd found in her apartment. "And it was my conversation with Marcos that sent me to Glenn Manor in the first place."

"So," Marino said, "he turned her down cold. Think that made her mad enough to boil over?"

"*Hell hath no fury . . .*" Adella sang out.

Her partner agreed. "Let's pick her up."

Chapter 28

Rosie picked at her sandwich but hardly tasted anything. She was also keeping a sharp eye on the door. She had the impression that Arnold was thinking of her, and even if he wasn't in the immediate vicinity, she knew the son of Frankenstein had something in the works. At the first opportunity she'd tell her dad that he followed her home last night, and that Mom should stop encouraging the weirdo. She jumped when the phone rang, but knew instinctively it wasn't him. No, *he* likes grandiose surprises.

"Hey, Libby, how're you doing, hon."

"I wanted to talk with you about Aaron." Libby sounded defensive, and her voice grew noticeably softer. "Maybe now, that you're getting closer to Mike, you can understand. Are you still mad about you-know-what?"

"Mad? Oh, I'm not angry with *you*."

"Well, don't be angry with Aaron either."

"Why not? I think he's acted very irresponsibly. I mean, what was he thinking? Actually, what were *you* thinking?"

"We're in love, Rosie."

"In love. Hmm . . . is that what you call it? Look, I realize the last thing you need right now is a lecture, but—"

"Aaron's really happy, you know. He's always wanted a child."

"You mean, he and his wife have no children?"

"That's right."

"So, it's even less complicated than I thought . . ."

"I know where you're going with this, Rosie, but Stella—Aaron's wife, is very fragile."

"Fragile . . ." The space of time that followed equaled the mysterious gap in the Nixon tapes. "Hello, Libby, are you still there?"

"Um, like I was saying, Aaron has told me that Stella has, um, emotional problems, and . . . well, any news like this right now could send her over the top, if you know what I mean."

Rosie kept her mouth shut while she ran this past her brain. (Let me get this straight: This married bastard helps himself to the smorgasbord, and then negotiates his obligation? I know it takes two, and Libby wasn't always the brightest bulb, but why does she have to swallow the crap he's dishing out?)

"But anyway," her friend gushed, "Aaron said he'll pay for all the costs."

Rosie wanted to scream out, *big fucking deal!,* but contained herself long enough to inquire if, after Stella recovered from her fragile state, Libby and Dr. Fingers had any future plans.

The sarcasm floated right past her friend, who was beginning to sound more and more like Marilyn Monroe. "Right now," she breathed, "Aaron thinks we should concentrate on having a healthy baby."

"Of course. No use gumming up the works now." She didn't know if Libby had absorbed the layers of sarcasm but offered a phony giggle anyway.

They spoke another few minutes, with Rosie latching on

to what she now knew was her only role in this affair: that of loyal, keep-my-big-fat-mouth-shut friend. She also reminded herself that when one is pitched up sexually, the brain falls dead. Should she claim she'd never experienced the lapse herself? All she had to do was remind herself about last night:

She remembered how he'd carried her into the bedroom—how the pounding in her chest had obliterated all possible objections; how she'd wanted him to make love to her; how hungry they both were; how there was no pretending on either of their parts. And then, the second time. His gentleness was so unlike the Mike she thought she knew. Her face grew hot now, while her psychic message center sent a redundant flash: *You've found the right one at last.* Yeah, right! And I don't even need to pay a fortune-teller. I also don't have to explain this to my mom.

The phone rang again, and she knew it was Mike even before she picked up.

"So, am I gonna see you later?"

Her stomach did the elevator thing, and she pulled in a deep breath before answering. "Ummm."

"I'll take that as a 'yes.' Watch yourself," he added, before his usual, hasty, no-good-bye exit.

Rosie stared at the phone after replacing the receiver, then looked toward the door, half expecting Arnold to appear. Strange. He hadn't put in an appearance all day. Well, why should she question her good fortune?

Arnold was attending to the messages that had accumulated on his answering machine over the weekend. When he and Natalie were married, he was certain she would be able to organize these things as his practice grew, but he had no intention of having her work in the office full-time. No way. They would start a family, and he was a firm believer in a wife being a stay-at-home mother. Maybe his own life would have been happier if his mother had spent more time at home instead of inventing reasons to be involved elsewhere, like Hadassah, or her friend Miriam's knitting store, or Mrs. Kleinman's down the block. Anything to get away from his father. That was the problem. Not so with Mrs. Rosenstein. What a *balebosteh!* Such a cook! He assumed she'd taught her daughter the basics, so they would at least eat well. And the father? Well, he'd come around after a while, just as his daughter would, when the two of them saw the reasonableness of this perfect match. It had to be soon. He was tired of waiting.

Ida Rosenstein was thinking the same thing. What's the matter with my daughter? Arnold is the perfect catch—Jewish and a lawyer. What more could she ask for? These things cover a lot of territory: money, prestige and, we shouldn't forget—respect. Love, shmuve—that's in the movies. How can I make Natalie understand that affection comes with time? It was certainly true in my case. Joseph was a quiet man when we were first introduced. That's how it was in those days. Parents made *shidechs* for single children—and children did the right thing. Today it's all different. Now I get an argument! Is this any way to show appreciation? This is a perfect match. Trust me.

The same character occupied Rosie's thoughts but in an entirely different way: Arnold needs to have his head examined—literally. Maybe the wiring inside melted during an electrical storm, something like the Frankenstein experiment. And a full moon trips his sensor? Well, it's a sure bet not

everything's attached up there. Stalking? That's an understate-
ment. That was no mystery man last night. That was Arnold.
What normal person does such things? *Arnold is not normal.*

The psychic flash made her head spin, and Madame
Volante's energy moved through her. *Listen to your natural instinct, chérie.* Rosie was sincerely trying to do so, but something was blocking the process. She could only determine
that Arnold was no longer someone to take lightly. She tried
to see or feel beyond this scant information, but could not. At
least, not yet.

Mike scanned the information Chris had provided on Arnold's
background: Apparently he'd spent most of his life in Brooklyn.
Born at King's County Hospital on February 16, 1966 to
Mildred and Isaac Feltman, his family lived in a modest section of Flatbush, not too far from the old Ebbets Field. And,
just to keep things all in sync, Arnold graduated from Brooklyn
Law School. No background in sports or any other extracur-
ricular activity. A nose-to-the-grindstone existence, Mike
thought. Not very stimulating. To his credit, however, Arnold
was also admitted to the bar in Washington, D.C. Maybe his
only trip outside Brooklyn's jurisdiction, Mike thought wryly.
So, why couldn't he locate his parents? Obviously, they'd made
it out of Brooklyn—courtesy of son Arnold? What a stand-up
guy!

Chapter 29

Carolyn Hughs took stock of the work that had been accumulating on her desk. Had she taken her medication this morning? She couldn't remember. Well, she had better remember; it was damned important. Too many things to keep track of. If her assistant hadn't deserted her . . . new job, she said—great opportunity. Right. And what was she supposed to do? The work was piling up. Of course, Rosie would be ideal. Hopefully, Grace will never recover. I can get her business, maybe her guy *and* her paralegal. What a coup! All alone in her office, Carolyn was the only one who could appreciate the joke, but the telephone cut into her euphoria.

"Law office of—yes, this is she. Ah, yes, Detective Marino. What can I do for you? This afternoon? No, that would not work for me. I have to be in court at three, and I've got tons of stuff to process. My assistant has deserted me, and I haven't had a chance to replace her. My casework is piling up, and—what? *Urgent,* huh? Gosh, detective, everything's urgent these days. . . ."

Marino took that as an opening and kept the conversation going with bullshit and flattery, especially the latter. "So, whaddya say?" he finally pleaded and received a throaty giggle for his efforts. After a short pause, Carolyn's voice took on velvet tones. Marino grabbed a pencil and started scribbling on a pad: *The broad's coming on to me.* He shoved the note across to Adella, who rolled her eyes and gave a thumbs-up.

Marino decided to capitalize on his investment and lowered his voice to a more intimate tone. "Oh, c'mon, help us out here." He paused for effect. "How about four-thirty? Think you might slip by about then? Great!" The detective winked at his partner after he hung up. "Learned it all from Mike."

But it was Adella who greeted the lawyer when she came by later that afternoon, though the latter appeared to be searching for someone else. The detective had no doubt that someone was her partner. She offered Carolyn a warm smile. "Detective Marino will be along in just a minute."

Carolyn didn't hesitate. "Oh, that's fine. It's just that," she studied her watch, "I have another appointment."

Adella led the way to one of the interview rooms and offered her guest some coffee, which was politely refused. Marino came along after a minute and smiled warmly at their guest. "Sure appreciate your coming over."

"How can I help you, detective?" Her eyes were totally focused on Marino, who was trying to remember how Mike played the game. He lowered his eyes to half-mast, but the effect was more like a guy who desperately needed some sleep.

Carolyn made a show of looking at her watch. "As I mentioned on the phone, my time is very limited."

Adella thought it best to lend some effort before they lost the fish altogether. "We're looking for any information that will help us find the person or persons who kidnaped Ms. Osborne."

"I understand that, but why do you come to me?"

The detective didn't miss a beat. "We know you and Ms. Osborne have a history . . . that is, you've known each other for many years. Thought you might have some idea of some particular problem she was having—maybe a dissatisfied client?"

Carolyn appeared to be thinking this over. "Unfortunately, nothing comes to mind. Besides which, Ms. Osborne has an *inordinately* high success rate." She stared off into the distance.

"That right?" Adella prompted.

Carolyn lifted her head regally and smiled back as though she were looking down from the queen's balcony.

"Did she have any enemies you know about?" Marino asked.

"None that I can think of. Everyone just *loves* her, don't you know?" If resentment could be measured in yards, Carolyn's offerings would cover a football stadium.

"Would you count yourself as one of her fans?"

"What on *earth* do you mean?"

Still smiling, Adella leaned forward. "Do you find that a difficult question?"

Carolyn jerked herself to attention, once more checking her watch. "If there's nothing more . . ."

Marino straightened higher in his chair and lifted his voice to a new notch. "We're not done here." He ignored the other's glare. "On the day Grace Osborne was rescued, you were observed in the vicinity where she had been held prisoner for the past ten days. What were you doing there?"

Carolyn paled, her eyes narrowed and she gathered her purse in preparation to leave. Her breaths were short, angry, but Adella ignored the drama. "Where do you think you're going?"

"I don't have to sit here and listen to this nonsense."

"Is that what you call it?"

"It is when I'm being accused of God-knows-what!"

Adella displayed an easy smile and softened her tone. "There's another way to look at it," she said.

"Really!" Carolyn showed no sign of lessening her annoyance.

"Yes. We're trying to eliminate the innocent. You can help us by explaining your presence that evening in that particular location so we can concentrate on looking for the one who really is responsible."

"My presence there is my own business; my reasons are personal."

"I understand. But if they have nothing to do with the case, it will make it easier all around if you share them. Of course, we will protect your privacy."

Marino was growing impatient. "Like, we're trying to find out who kidnaped that poor lady and treated her so bad that she may never recover, and you're giving us this personal crap!"

Carolyn's eyebrows lifted as hazel pupils stared from frozen banks of white, giving the appearance of an angry cat staring out of a snowdrift.

Marino ignored her snit and continued. "As you yourself pointed out, Grace Osborne seemed to have it all: a good legal practice, a faithful assistant and lotsa friends." He paused before emphasizing his next words. "She also had a rich guy who was willing to move mountains if she flicked a finger." The subject remained silent, so the detective continued. "Maybe someone resented her for all that bounty." Innuendo hung in the silence that followed.

Carolyn pressed her lips together. "Well, I *certainly* couldn't say." Anger raised the color in her cheeks as she pushed her chair away from the table. "If you decide you want to ask me any more questions, detectives, call my attorney." She didn't wait for a response, but rose from her chair and left the room.

"Yeah," Adella taunted, "you definitely have her eating out of your hand."

Her partner shrugged his shoulders. "Whaddya gonna do? I didn't expect her to kiss my ass, but if she's got nothin' to hide, why'd she get so pissed?"

"You didn't expect her to thank you for more or less suggesting that she was involved in the Osborne thing, did you?" Adella held up a hand. "I just thought of something else. According to what Mike found out, Osborne has that bipolar disorder problem. Is she taking her meds or what? And how does that impact her weird behavior?"

Marino was already reaching for the phone. "Maybe I can save myself some time by checking with Mike." He punched some numbers, then shook his head and left a message. "Gonna have to wait on that."

"Okay. In the meantime, how do you feel about having another go at Schreiber's neighbors?"

"Even though the ones we talked to say he had his son with him all weekend?"

"Yes, because he still had the best reason to harm Grace Osborne."

Rosie closed the office about two o'clock and headed over to the hospital. She found herself going through the same routine with the same guard who insisted on reviewing her identification. Nikki came over to vouch for her and they moved inside to the waiting room. He looked as limp as yesterday's latkes.

"The doctors tell me that Grace's condition is unchanged." He pronounced this last like a doomsday bulletin.

Rosie was moved to anger. "She doesn't deserve this! All she ever did was try to help people." She stopped herself from further diatribe, reminded that Nikki didn't need any revving up. If she knew anything, it was that she wouldn't want to be in the schmuck's shoes who was responsible. The Greek had a big reach. Right now, he had a strange, faraway look about him that suggested he knew exactly what to do with the guilty party.

The temperature around them seemed to drop suddenly. A glance at Nikki indicated that she alone was affected. What's going on? She checked around, but all appeared normal, if you can call the waiting room outside an intensive care unit normal. When Mike stepped out of the elevator minutes later, Rosie put the weather change out of her mind. She watched Nikki's reaction as the other strode toward them and was surprised to see the cordiality between the two even though Mike had briefed her on their recently established detente. When Nikki went to check with the nurses for the umpteenth time, they moved over to a couch on the far side where he grabbed for her hand. A wild impulse coursed through her and she imagined a cake on a bakery shelf sitting alongside a lot of other cakes and wanted to cry out, take me! What in the hell was wrong with her? And why doesn't he say something? Oh, please . . . he's going to tell me he's thought it over and there's nothing in the relationship but wild sex—on his terms—and only when he feels like it.

"Listen," he finally came up with, "gotta take care of some stuff. How do you feel about a drink later?"

How do I feel? About a drink? later? She wanted to say *YES,* but suddenly remembered the date she'd made with her friend. "I promised Libby—you don't know her—we've been friends since kindergarten, and I . . ." She could hear herself babbling like a runaway toilet, but for some unknown reason had lost the ability to shut her mouth. "Mike, I'm sorry, I—" His eyebrows started climbing Mount Everest, and she figured he must be thinking she was shallow, deceitful, a money-grubbing, lying . . ."

"Don't sweat it."

"No, it's not like that, it's—" But he was grinning one of his "gotcha" smirks, and any guilt she'd felt a minute before evaporated and the old itch-in-the-palm-of-her-hand annoyance returned in a flash. This guy knows just how to reach me. Before she could say anything, he grabbed a hank of her hair gently and crooned, "You're excused."

Before Nikki returned, Mike gave her a rundown on the day's events. Rosie was not surprised to learn about Carolyn's illness. Her sixth sense had been telegraphing for some time now, and weird, wild and wacko were only a sampling of the signals.

"So, is there a connection to Grace's kidnaping?"

"Just watch your step."

Duh. Like, she was planning to invite Carolyn for a sleepover? But before she could offer this wise summation, that strange chill that hit her earlier returned. Mike noticed she was shivering. "You okay?"

"I'm not sure."

He started doing the eyebrow thing again, but Rosie reached out and put a hand on his arm. "Mike, be careful. I feel . . ."

A question formed on his face, but Nikki returned at that moment, and they both looked up eagerly for an update. The other shook his head. "Nothing new yet, but the doctors still feel there's a chance."

Riding the train back to Long Island later, Rosie tried to imagine how her parents would react to her giving up her Oceanside apartment and moving into the city. The prospect of looking for another job appealed to her about as much as having a cavity drilled without novocaine, but what choice did she have? The doctors were not exactly exchanging high fives over Grace's chances. Even if a miracle should happen

and life returned to its previous state, she'd had it up to here
with the commuting. She'd been putting off this decision too
long. Okay, what was she leaving out? Mike. Well, maybe
Mike had something to do with advancing her schedule a bit.
And her folks? She saw no earthly reason to tell them about
Mike right off the bat. Think positively. Maybe with time her
mother could get used to the idea. Yeah, that's like suggesting
Mom should try attending church on alternate weekends.
Her father? Well, he was a lot more liberal. Yes, the best ap-
proach was definitely through her father.

Rosie had to admit that Libby was looking radiant when they
met for dinner. This time, they met at Mr. Chong's because
mommy-to-be was craving wonton soup and chicken cashew.
While they waited for their first course, Libby coveted the large,
crisp noodles, dipping them in duck sauce and daintily pack-
ing away enough for two *sumo* wrestlers. Rosie pulled her eyes
away from the orgy and broached the subject that currently
plagued her:

"I'm considering giving up my place and moving into
the city."

Her friend paused long enough to frown and offer, "It's
Mike, huh?"

"Noooo—I've been thinking about this for a long time.
You know that."

"Uh-huh. But it's really Mike, isn't it?"

"Like I said, I've been debating this for a while." Rosie attempted to imitate Mike's eyebrow thing, but the other
seemed unimpressed.

"Have you mentioned anything to your folks?"

"Not yet. Listen, Libby, we're not sixteen anymore." Rosie

gave her the hard stare as if to emphasize the obvious. "Talking about parents, have you given them the glad tidings yet?"

The waiter arrived with their soup, and Libby shoved the empty noodle dish at him and made big eyes. "Could we have a refill on these, please?" To Rosie, she said, "Actually, I did."

"And?"

"And . . . while they may not have approved of the timing—I told them Aaron and I would be married as soon as his divorce became final (to which Rosie's eyebrow thing now resembled Groucho Marx's famous tic)—they were *thrilled* to know they would be grandparents." She didn't finish up with *so there!,* but it was implied.

"I see. Well, I give you credit for clearing the air. Um, has Dr. Fingers indicated just when he plans to start the ball rolling vis-à-vis divorce proceedings?"

Libby scooped out a generous helping of crunchy noodles from the second bowl and sprinkled them on top of her soup. She spread them out evenly before answering. "Remember I told you Aaron's wife was fragile? And I hate it when you call him by that name."

"Fingers?"

Libby stared back hard but didn't answer.

"Sorry." But Rosie didn't sound apologetic. "Okay, okay, I won't tease you anymore." In her heart of hearts she was thinking, my poor, deluded preggy friend has about as much of a chance of having her Doctor Fingers marry her as I do of winning the lottery. What are the chances of that happening? Latest figures are one in a hundred and fifty million.

Mike dialed his former partner after listening to his voice mail. "What's up?"

Marino told him about the interview with Carolyn Hughs. "She won't give up what she was doing on the block where Grace Osborne was discovered, but I sorta recall you telling us something about a doctor she sees for her wacko problem. Isn't he located in Brooklyn somewhere?"

"Yeah, come to think of it. Hang on." Mike fished out his notebook and started flipping pages. "Sonofabitch. On Pierrepont—that's only a block away from where Rosie met her. Doctor's name is Waldenheim, Dr. Max J."

"So," Marino said, "maybe she did have a legitimate reason to be there after all. Guess I can understand her reasons for not wanting to share. None of anyone's business."

Chapter 30

Your stars are all lined up today with pleasure and promise in your forecast. Yeah, right. Just let it be cooler with less humidity, and I'll be satisfied, Rosie thought. It was as though someone up there heard her because when she opened the window a crack she found the muggy stuff had moved on. For how long? Never mind, I don't question miracles. Along with a general feeling of well-being, a strong premonition urged her to be selective about what she chose to wear this day. Okay, I won't quarrel with that. She went to her closet—maybe something that says *let's talk?*—and picked out a short sleeve, two-piece navy linen with white piping on the lapels and metallic buttons with a U.S. Navy motif. This one had a skirt for a change. Why not? she argued with no one in particular. My legs happen to be damned nice. I keep hiding them in pants. *Do you realize what you're doing here?* her censor prodded. Yes! And stop trying to make me feel guilty. She marched to her dresser, opened her lingerie drawer and lifted out the new lilac bikinis with matching bra, daring her conscience to argue. After her shower and morning coffee, Rosie carefully applied some makeup, slid into her new clothes and winked at herself in the mirror. Not too shabby.

At the office she returned phone calls while opening the mail. The latter had gotten pitifully thin lately, she noticed. Curiously, there were no messages from Arnold on the answering machine, and he wasn't lurking nearby. She wanted to believe he'd given up but knew better. Mike called around eleven.

"Sooo . . . tied up with some dear old friends tonight?"

That thumping in her chest was so loud, she almost couldn't hear her reply. "Actually, I've got nothing planned for tonight."

"How about dinner and . . . whatever?"

The whatever part drew her attention. She heard herself give a breathless, "I'd like that," and tried to imagine what his reaction was.

Actually, Mike produced an instant hard-on. "Pick you up there around four."

She barely had time to acknowledge the plan before she heard the click and he was gone. He sure likes to leave graciously. She spent the rest of the day trying unsuccessfully to distract herself. About ten to four Mike knocked on the office door. Rosie was glad she'd started freshening up fifteen minutes before.

His appraisal was such that she began to wonder if he could see clear through her dress to her lilac underwear. "Will it take you long to close up?" he asked. She remembered answering, but wasn't sure what because she was too fascinated watching his eyes move up and down the length of her. He made no secret of what was on his mind and was in fact moving toward Rosie when the phone rang. He held nothing back: "Fuck it! Don't answer."

Of course, she didn't pay any attention. "Law office of— Oh, hi, Mom." She waggled her finger at Mike, who shrugged his shoulders as if to say *How should I know it's your mother?*

"No, nothing new." (Wouldn't you know she'd call now. It's like she's got long-distance x-ray vision.) "How's Dad? Uh-huh. No, tonight's not good." She smiled at Mike. "I have plans." He gave a thumbs-up and nodded for emphasis. "Okay, Friday. Right, see you then."

Mike took the receiver from her and placed it firmly in the holder. He picked up her purse from the desk and handed it to her. He then put his hand under her elbow and guided her toward the door. "Questions?" he challenged. She shook her head.

Downstairs, Mike hailed a cab and gave the driver an address. "It's a little early for dinner, but I know a nice place for drinks. Game?" She didn't see the necessity of bothering to answer.

The *nice place* turned out to be Mike's apartment. Rosie took notice of the location when the taxi stopped (Columbus and Seventy-first, no less), certain Mike must be putting her on. But when the doorman came out to open the door and nodded familiarly at Mike, she figured it was all part of a Fellini film. She had a difficult time putting together the tough, sometimes rude, former NYPD detective with the classy building they were about to enter. Italian marble floors, Persian area rugs, an embossed wall covering and antique mirrors greeted them in the lobby.

Mike pressed the elevator button and eyed Rosie, well aware of her reaction. When she didn't speak right away, he raised his eyebrows and smirked. "Nice, huh?"

She offered a quiet "Yes," trying to keep her voice from sounding as though a shuttle was just launched. My mother would just *plotz.* Uh, not so fast. Maybe we're here to visit a friend or close relative? But no, the key fit the lock, and they entered what turned out to be Mike's very own apartment, a

neat (he must have been working since four in the morning
to get it looking so nice) one-bedroom layout with parquet
floors and area rugs in bold abstract designs.

An upgraded music station dominated the living room
where an extensive collection of vintage seventy-eight and
thirty-three records were stored. Rosie caught the names of
several performers: Billie Holiday, Miles Davis, Josephine
Baker, Lionel Hampton, Duke Ellington, Peggy Lee and on
and on. She was impressed. This is serious shit, she was thinking. So, if we ever get too old for sex, we can talk about the
golden age of jazz.

Mike appeared to enjoy her reaction. "Not too bad,
huh?" Instead of waiting for an answer, he headed into the
kitchen where she heard the clinking of glasses and rattling of
cellophane. He returned carrying a tray that held a bottle of
wine, two glasses and a bowl of pretzels. But wait! This obviously experienced seducer was not finished setting the scene.
Before filling their glasses, he slipped a CD into the machine
and the smoky voice of Peggy Lee crawled into the room like
a seductive fog. He handed her a glass of wine and watched
her as she took her first sip. She read the message in his
eyes—those two blue orbs that had the ability to project
everything from arctic ice to Caribbean heat. At the moment
they were promoting the latter. Just as he began to move toward her, the phone rang. Mike never took his eyes off her.
"Fuck it," he muttered, and reached out for her. Rosie went
right into his arms, happy she'd chosen to wear her new lilac
bikinis.

"So tell me about this apartment," Rosie asked later. They
were lying side by side in Mike's bed, still somewhat breathless from their lovemaking.

"The apartment . . . yeah. Four months after Monica

died, my mother passed away, too. Big mountain to climb, losing my two favorite people in this world."

Rosie wanted to reach out to comfort him but didn't want to insert herself into what was a private moment from Mike's past. Maybe he appreciated that because he went on to tell her that memories of the life he and Monica had shared in their small apartment were there to haunt him every evening when he returned from work. "I decided the inheritance from my mother couldn't go into a better investment than this condo, which was just coming on the market. I took the timing to be an omen."

"Is that when you left the department?"

"Yeah."

They lay next to each other, neither talking, for several minutes, then Mike said, "Okay, now it's your turn."

"How do you mean?"

Mike propped himself on one elbow, grinned down at her and arched his eyebrows. His expression said, *I've got all the time in the world.* After a brief pause, Rosie told him about Jean Marc.

"That explains it."

"Explains what?"

"How come you're so distrusting."

Rosie didn't answer him right away, but she knew he was right. "My mother thought she was raising a princess. Guess I swallowed that line, too. Took me a long time—too long—to realize there are no shortcuts."

"So you returned to the States and went back to school."

"Yeah, and—"

"And you stopped trusting everybody."

"I suppose . . ."

"Until you met me."

She shoved him playfully in the chest—his marvelously muscled, masculine chest that she found herself wanting to put her head down on and never leave, but she knew that once they got started, they'd never stop. "Hungry?" she asked.

"Yeah," he answered, "but . . ."

"Seriously, I have to think about getting back to Long Island yet."

"No, stay." He pulled her closer. "I mean it. I'll order something in. Stay with me tonight."

Actually, Rosie's initial hesitation had to do with logistics: *Well, I can rinse out my undies, and I do have enough emergency makeup in my purse.* Then the other, unacknowledged fear manifested itself: *No, Mike is no Jean Marc. And if I can't tell the difference by now, I should get hung. My mother? She wouldn't approve of any of this. Right! All the more reason to stay.*

Now it was Mike who was having second thoughts: *What in the hell did I ever think I was doing? Couldn't leave well enough alone? A glass of wine, a roll in the hay and dinner was all she wanted.* But deep down he didn't believe this. Her face was still on his chest and, wonder of wonders, he felt her lips move and heard her whisper, "Yes."

Chapter 31

Although Rosie floated into the office the next morning, she was hardly aware that her feet touched the ground. Then her sixth sense sent a message reminding her that life is a combination of ups and downs: *Be prepared for some unpleasantness today.*

The first thing that greeted her was the blinking light on her answering machine. There were three messages. The first was Arnold's unwelcome voice in a tone that put her back to her seventeenth birthday when she'd stayed out too late and incurred her mother's wrath: "Where were you last night, Natalie?" Arnold demanded. Damned nerve, she thought and pressed the delete button. Nikki's call came next. He sounded weary, so understandable. The doctors were going to try something new, but he didn't sound optimistic. Rosie realized that if Grace did not recover, there would be some drastic changes in her own life. How we take things for granted until something comes along to pull the rug out. She pushed the button for the remaining message, and Carolyn's British tones sang out:

"*Really,* Rosie, I've decided we ought to make some permanent arrangement. It doesn't look as though Grace will be resuming her practice. *Actually,*" her voice dropped down to a conspiratorial mode, "I don't want to deal with Stephanie or her excuses anymore either (pronounced *eye'ther*)." Then she returned to her original chirp: "So, at your earliest opportunity, let's do talk!"

"Let's not!" Rosie said aloud to the answering machine, and stared down at it as though it were the enemy. Altogether the three messages might have detracted from her astounding time with Mike, but she wouldn't let that happen. I'm not going to allow anything to spoil that. Except—the bad feelings she'd had earlier were still there. Rosie didn't know what they meant, but she was primed for anything.

"Mike," she'd said earlier, "I've got some strange vibes."

He'd started getting cute: "Oh? We're getting back into the woo-woo business?" (Like, what else should she have expected?)

"Please," she'd cautioned, "watch your back. I mean it!"

"You sound like a remake of *The Ghost and Mrs. Miniver.*

"Don't get cute. I'm serious."

"Yeah . . . yeah . . . yeah. . . ."

In the afternoon, Rosie headed back to Oceanside still thinking about their conversation. She was sure she'd be talking with him later but didn't expect to see him until tomorrow, which gave her ample opportunity to worry about the pigheaded fool until he came out to spend the weekend. Dinner at her folks' tonight was not something she was looking forward to. Should she have invited Mike? Not without having a conference with her father first so he could help keep her mother from threatening suicide. Still, the bad feelings that started her day persisted.

★   ★   ★

Mike looked up when Arnold walked into the bar that night. Hadn't seen the sleaze in a couple of days and would have been just as glad to skip tonight as well. But, no, the jerk was headed his way. Confrontation? Like, pistols at dawn or something? Mike doubted it. Arnold didn't have the balls.

"Well, Mike . . ."

"Arnold."

A full minute passed without a follow-up by either. So much for scintillating conversation.

"Seen Natalie Rosenstein recently?" This from Arnold.

"Na—? You mean Rosie."

"The name on her birth certificate is *Natalie*."

"That what you do in your spare time? Read birth certificates?"

Arnold's tightly pressed lips spread into a wicked smile as the color in his face deepened. "And what do you do in your spare time? Take advantage of innocent women?"

"Innocent women . . . oh, you mean Rosie? No, actually, in my spare time I read death certificates."

Arnold's pumpkin face looked perplexed. "Death certificates?"

"Yes, came across some interesting ones today, actually. Hey, my condolences. I didn't know your parents were deceased."

The other's face went from angry flush to shiny wax in seconds. "What right do you have—"

"Hey, it's public record. But you know, the thing I don't understand is why you told Rosie's family that your folks were down in Florida. What's up with that?"

"That's none of your business."

"As I said, the information is public record."

Arnold was silent for a minute, but his jaw was working

in anger. Then something must have clicked in his head because he suddenly smiled and seemed to do a complete turn-
around. "Hey, you know . . . there's no reason for us to be
battling here. Maybe we should just have a drink and talk
about some of these things like two rational human beings."

Was that the lawyer part talking? Mike was surprised and
began to wonder what the schmuck had in mind, but it
shouldn't be a total loss, a drink might bring him some more
information, so he shrugged his shoulders. "Hell, why not?"

"What are you drinking?" Arnold asked.

"Dewars, rocks. What'll you have?"

"No, this one's on me. I insist."

The whole scene was beginning to resemble a poker game.
See ya and raise ya— "Oh, what the hell! Sure. Go ahead."

Arnold ordered two Dewars, and they toasted to the
World Series, peace on earth, the end to terrorism, Grace
Osborne's recovery and a couple of other things before actually drinking. Mike was surprised at Arnold's one-hundred-
and-eighty-degree turn. While making small talk, and trying
to see where this was going, he studied the man he and Rosie
had come to know as "the stalker." Somewhat out of shape—
pudgy even, Arnold Feltman's ever-expanding paunch prevented his jacket from meeting in the front, button to
buttonhole. Dark circles under his eyes indicated the man was
probably not sleeping well. His face was drawn, troubled—
due, no doubt to his sick obsession over Rosie. Well, ain't that
just too fuckin' bad. He was gonna have to get over it because
nothing would ever come of his sickness. Crazy to think he
ever had a chance. Stupid? No, Mike didn't judge him that
way. He suspected the guy was crafty—sneaky, maybe, but not
stupid. He had to have some brains to have completed
Brooklyn Law School. *Whap!* Mike heard the thud of some-

thing hitting the floor. The two of them looked down and saw Arnold's wallet.

"Oh, damn," said Arnold, who made a big thing of trying to wiggle his ass off the edge of the bar stool.

"No, I'll get it," Mike said, who thought it was the least he could do since the other was buying.

"Thanks . . . Hey, you're not drinking," Arnold complained after Mike put his wallet back on the bar. He lifted his glass for another clunk.

Mike took a healthy swig, thinking Rosie would not believe this scene, which he intended to describe to her in detail when he saw her on Saturday. Right now, his job was to pull what he could out of this asshole and try to see if there was any hope of curing him of his addiction to Rosie. Another few minutes of mental dueling and Mike came back to his appraisal. Yeah, that's what it was—an addiction. *I just said that—an addiction. Damn! I must've swigged too fast.* He was beginning to feel the effects of that last gulp.

"Hey, you okay?" Arnold inquired.

"Me? Sure."

"Want to maybe get some fresh air?"

"Whaddya think? I'm drunk?"

Arnold was smiling openly. "Certainly not. Just thought maybe you'd feel better with some fresh air." He put some money down on the bar and got off the stool, a lot easier than when he was struggling earlier, Mike thought. *What's going on?* Rosie's earlier warning returned. *Please, watch your back.* That woo-woo business. But maybe I should be paying more attention.

When they got outside, Mike just couldn't find his balance, so Arnold gripped his elbow. "Here, let me give you a hand. . . ."

★ ★ ★

Rosie couldn't shake the bad feelings she'd had all day. *Something's just not right.* All the time she was showering and getting ready to go to her folks, her ESP was screaming a message: *LISTEN UP! Something's not right.* Okay, but what? She spent some time with Gabby who was thoroughly annoyed that her mistress chose to stay in the city last night instead of coming home and taking care of her like she was supposed to and verbalized her displeasure with a loud *Neeyeh!* "Yes, I know you were upset, sweetie, but I had something really special I needed to take care of." And Rosie began humming some of the music they'd listened to before winding up in Mike's bed for the first of several sessions. Gabby seemed unimpressed, but dipped the tip of her tongue in the bowl of milk anyway. Rosie checked the mirror before locking the door, wondering if she could wipe off the goofy expression before her mother latched on to what her daughter had been up to. She practiced a few openers to throw her off the course. *So, Mom, what's new with the family?—or—Did you see that ostentatious wedding on TV last weekend? Honestly!* Why was she feeling defeated even before she began?

Her father greeted her with a hug and a choice of a glass of wine or a *shnapps.* Now he's reading *my* mind. She chose the whiskey. "Need to talk with you, Dad," she managed, just before her mother came out of the kitchen to greet her.

"So, Na-ta-lie"—she patted the cushion on the couch next to her—"what's new?"

Rosie went into a cheerful, three-minute filibuster of absolute nonsense while her father just sat and listened. His frown and wrinkled eyebrows asked questions. All at once, the light dawned, and he broke out in a grin. He *knew!* And what's more, Rosie couldn't wait to tell him more. And all of this was going on behind her mother's well-meaning back.

When the latter went into the kitchen to check the soup, her father leaned forward.

"You have something you want to tell me?"

Rosie took a deep breath, searching for the right words to begin. In the background, they could hear happy humming, making them both aware that Rosie's mother was in an especially good mood. Her father waited patiently for his daughter to begin, his all-knowing smile barely hidden.

"Dad, it's like this," she began, and poured out her feelings for Mike. "Please understand, we're not talking marriage or anything. I just feel he's the right one. I know I want to be together with him, and he feels the same way." The humming inside segued into the opening bars of "The Sound of Music."

Her father held up his hand. "I know things are different with you young people today. I don't understand it, but I'm not so old or close-minded that I can't accept. Your mother? Well, that's a different story. In our day, if we met the right one, we got married—period. Today? It's different. And on top of that, your mother never imagined that you might fall for a *shaigetz*."

Dad, he's special."

From the other room, Ida Rosenstein's unmusical voice pierced the moment: *Ta DUM dee dee dum* . . .

"I'm quite sure he must be," her father said, "for my very special Natalie to have fallen in love."

The volume from the kitchen increased without warning . . . *LA LA LA MUSIC!*

Both father and daughter cringed.

"Uh, that's another thing," said Rosie, hesitating. Mike calls me Rosie."

And under the moon . . . (Joseph Rosenstein covered a smile).

"Like your friends have been doing for years—I know."

"Yes, you do, Dad, but Mom . . . I can see her having a *knipsch*."

. . . and over the sun . . .

Her dad half turned toward the kitchen. "It will take a while for your mother to get used to the fact that none of her plans worked out. Mike is neither Jewish nor a professional." He shook his head but never stopped smiling.

Ta dum dee dee dum . . .

"Mike's had a lot of sadness in his life. He lost his wife—cancer."

Her father shook his head. "I'm so sorry." He hardly had time to express his shock when a loud call from the kitchen pierced the tender moment:

"Sit! I'm bringing the soup."

Rosie jumped up and headed toward the kitchen. "I'm coming to help, Mom." She heard her father whisper, "We'll talk more after."

. . . LA LA LA LA . . . and the happy music—brings a song to my heart and will all end well.

Chapter 32

Something's terribly wrong. Rosie felt sick in the pit of her stomach when she returned home from her folks', but it wasn't the food. Say what you will, her mother was still a terrific cook. No, what bothered her was the feeling that something awful was happening again, and she was certain it had to do with Mike. When he hadn't called by eleven, she tried his home. Then she dialed his cell. No answer on either one. This is how it was with Grace. Could the same sick person be doing this again? Peace was something that eluded her for most of the night. The following morning, after continually trying Mike's phones and pager without success, she pulled out Chris Marino's card from her wallet and left a message on his voice mail. He called her back within ten minutes, and she told him of her concerns:

"I know something's really wrong, Chris. Do you think you might get someone to go over to his place and check?"

Marino thought about this briefly. "Sure. I can do that." He was pretty sure his friend was taken with this Rosie chick, but knowing Mike, he might also have tied one on the night before and stayed over whatever broad's house he'd been buying drinks for. "Give me a couple of hours. I'll get back to you."

"Okay—call me." But the day would pass without any further word.

Chris Marino made a couple of calls after he spoke with Rosie and was finally rewarded when he got hold of the bartender who was on the evening shift at Casey's. "Yes, Mike was in last night. No, he didn't get smashed. As a matter of fact he only had two drinks. Left with a friend. Female? No, one of the lawyers from the courthouse. Not a regular, but somebody that he'd seen a couple of times before. They seemed to be having a good time, him and Mike, before they left—kinda arm-in-arm, so to speak. Mike appeared to be a little wobbly. Hey, maybe Casey's wasn't the first bar he'd stopped in. Yeah, sure, glad to help."

Marino was scratching his head. Something didn't sound right. Mike wobbly? And what friend? He checked the time. Today was supposed to be his day off, but what the hell. He told his wife he had to take care of something and took off for Mike's place. A little while later, he was dialing his partner. "Hey, Adella, got a curiosity here. Wanna give me a hand?"

"Does this have anything to do with one of our cases, or are you freelancing? 'Cause today's the day I promised myself a manicure. My nails look like shit."

"Indirectly . . . sort of—freelancing, that is."

"How *indirectly*?" she asked, studying one of the many badly broken nails on her right hand.

Marino screwed up his face. "Has to do with Mike. Seems he didn't come home last night. And before you offer some snappy shit about how the brothers hardly ever get home on Friday nights and why should you care if my former honky partner is screwing around, let me remind you I'd never desert you even if you are the damndest, smartest black woman I ever knew."

"You finished?"

"Yeah."

"Where do you want me to meet you?"

"Casey's—half an hour. And thanks!"

Marino had contacted the bartender he'd spoken to earlier and asked him to meet them at the bar. Cliff Peterson had been tending bar at Casey's for three years. A thin, pale-faced man on the other side of fifty, he had long ago learned to keep his face free of judgment (even if the customer was pissy-eyed drunk). He knew all the regulars and many of the once-in-a-whilers. Then he began to demure. Peterson claimed he was plenty busy the previous evening and protested that he might not have noticed if Mike had been drinking before he came into Casey's.

Marino pushed his face closer. "Don't give me any of that I-keep-my-nose-clean shit, or I'll have to recheck your history going back a few years. Computers make that real easy."

Peterson hardly missed a beat. "He came in sober. Then I poured him a generous Dewars before his friend arrived."

"Tell us about this *friend*, Cliff," Marino said.

"Well, like I said, the place was hopping—Friday night and all, and maybe I didn't get such a good look."

"Why don't you tell us about the so-so look you *did* get," Adella urged. She smiled, luscious lips framing white teeth into a dazzling smile. Her eyes sparkled with the promise of better things to come, and the bartender looked like he would fall over.

"Uh, he was familiar, but I just don't place his name. Seen him in here, but not regular, if you know what I mean."

Marino nodded. "How about a description?"

"Kinda pudgy y'know? When he first come in, didn't look like the two of them were such great friends. But the next thing I know, the other guy's sitting down next to Mike and ordering a round—on him."

"Pay cash or a credit card?"

"Cash. Actually, now I remember: He dropped his wallet. Mike picked it up for him. I got busy, and the next I know, maybe ten minutes pass and the two are headed out the door. Like I said, Mike was kinda shaky. The other guy had to help him out. I was surprised 'cause you know Mike can hold his liquor."

"Yeah," Marino said, "Mike can do that all right." He nudged his partner that they were finished, but she turned back for one last question:

"Would you recognize the other guy if you saw him again?"

"Sure. Probably. I guess so."

When they got out in the street, Marino said, "Are you thinking what I'm thinking?"

"If you're guessing that someone slipped Mike a Mickey, yeah, but I would have thought Mike's too smart for that."

"Except, if you're fishing a wallet off the floor, you ain't got your eyes on top of the bar."

"True. And is the 'pudgy' guy the same one I'm latching on to?"

"If you mean Arnold Feltman, it is."

The detectives called the squad room to get Feltman's address and telephone number and headed over to the Ocean Avenue address. There was no answer when they rang the doorbell, so they called him on the phone, but the answering machine kicked in. They left no message.

In between, Marino and Adella kept trying Mike's home

telephone, his cell and his pager without any response. Marino started tapping nervously on the steering wheel while they sat in their unmarked car across the street from Arnold's apartment building. Adella recognized his agitation, but decided to wait a bit before offering soothing platitudes. She knew his friendship with Mike Bartel went back a long way, and she respected that.

Time seemed to crawl, Marino's tapping increased, and small talk between him and Adella had long ceased to suffice. It was now three o'clock in the afternoon and Arnold had still not returned. Suddenly, Marino shot forward. "I ain't waiting any longer."

Adella looked at him. "You got a plan?"

"Yeah, I'm going upstairs and letting myself in."

"Without a warrant?" The look he threw her made her rethink the question. "Okay, you want me here watching your back or upstairs?"

"Stay with the car and keep your eye on the entrance."

"You got it."

Marino returned twenty minutes later. "Clean. No weapons. No Feltman, either. Wonder where the slob can be?"

"I'm thinking we get hold of his photo and take it over to Casey's for an ID just to be sure we're not chasing the wrong guy."

That suited Marino, so they headed back to the Eighty-fourth. On the way, Adella suggested they give Rosie a call, too, just to be certain that Mike hadn't checked in with her. "Okay, but don't give any details yet till we have some definite info."

While her partner went scrounging for Feltman's photo, Adella put in a call to Rosie. "Just checking in," she said, when Rosie picked up on the first ring.

"Have you heard from Mike?" asked a concerned Rosie.

That answered Adella's question, leaving an even bigger blank. "No." She knew Rosie was no dummy, and didn't treat her like one. "But we're following some stuff right now." Not wanting to leave too much room for her questions though, Adella quickly added, "We'll get back to you later," and hung up.

With a grainy photo of Arnold Feltman in Marino's pocket, the detectives retraced their steps to Casey's Bar. Cliff Peterson identified Arnold as the guy who left the bar with Mike the previous evening. When they were outside, Adella asked, "Where do we go from here?"

Rosie was mulling the same question, but because the detectives chose not to alarm her, she remained ignorant of the developments—a mistake that might have resulted in tragedy.

Chapter 33

Arnold had been standing in front of her office door for at least ten minutes. He could hear the phone ringing inside, but no one answered. For the twentieth time, he checked his watch. Where is she? This was most annoying. It took another five minutes before he heard the elevator doors open, but his beloved's face sported a frown as soon as she spotted him.

"Arnold, what are you doing here?"

"I think that's pretty obvious, my little knish."

"Stop already with the food business! I'm not a tray of hors d'oeuvres."

"You are to me, my angel."

Rosie inserted the key into the lock. "What is it you want?"

"Not a good attitude, Natalie." Rosie didn't rise to the bait, so he continued. "Let me be frank. You are the one I've waited for all my life. I'm ready to discuss a serious, permanent relationship." He rocked back and forth on his heels like an Orthodox Jew *davening* at temple on the High Holy Days.

Apparently, this was Arnold's version of a marriage proposal. She fought her desire to laugh out loud. No two ways— this guy is a real flake, but I don't want to piss him off. So, how to handle this, other than throwing up?

"Actually, I'm not really prepared for a permanent relationship," Rosie offered, striving to maintain a straight face.

"Not prepared," he repeated, but an uneven blotch of
anger spread across his cheeks. "What sort of preparation do
you require?"

Uh-oh. "Look, Arnold, this is neither the time nor place
to discuss this kind of thing."

"Just where and when would you like to meet?"

Shit! Walked myself into that one. "Let me call you."

"That's bullshit and you know it!" Arnold didn't try to
disguise his wrath. "Listen, Natalie, maybe you think you're
dealing with a moron. And if that's so, then you've made a big
mistake. When Grace—when she disappeared you could have
leaned on me. What do you know about running a law office? I was there for you. Did you ask my help? No!"

Rosie was squirming inside. *What is he saying?*

". . . I've given you every opportunity to cooperate, but
you just keep stringing me along."

Opportunity?

"Now, let's understand something: Time marches on. Your
parents are happy with me. And I'm tired of waiting for you
to *come around*. You've already had many opportunities. Too
many. Come to your senses because time's running out." His
chest rose and fell like someone trying to pump air into a flat
tire, and anger had turned the tips of his ears red. He looked
like a bomb waiting to explode. Rosie knew she had to come
up with something very creative. Every psychic particle of her
told her that this was not just a clown, but a really bad man.
Quick, think of something!

On the rare occasions when her parents had a disagree-
ment that appeared to have no reasonable solution (from her
mother's perspective), the latter would resort to star quality
on the Yiddish stage. She would make a show of shaking her

head slowly, rolling her eyes up and looking at the ceiling, searching . . . searching for the voice or image of the Higher Power to rescue the situation. Rosie called upon these memories now, clutching her throat for extra emphasis. She must be doing a fairly reasonable imitation because Arnold had halted his tirade and was staring at her.

"You remind me of my mother," he said, but his voice was devoid of sentiment.

Was that a good thing, she wondered? She cleared her throat. "I just can't talk about this right now, Arnold. I feel . . . too emotional." (Sigh.) She guessed her act went over well because the jerk was smiling—maybe too broadly. Rosie could see evidence of his morning bagel still plugged in between his upper teeth.

"We will settle this later, Rosie—one way or the other." This last sounded somewhat menacing and to complement the tone, Arnold's smile segued once again into a glare. Should she assume that her next chance would be her last?

Rosie closed the office after an hour, finally admitting that Grace's practice was on permanent hold. The phones weren't exactly ringing off the hook, and even if they were, there was no attorney in residence to respond. She checked to make sure that the computer and all other equipment were turned off, took a last look around and locked the door behind her. Rosie didn't count on seeing Arnold in the lobby downstairs, but it was too late to retreat. He'd already spotted her.

"Oh, good," he said, rather cheerfully. "I was just going to get something to eat. Please join me."

This didn't sound so much like an invitation as it did a direct order. Rosie imagined a refusal on her part might lead to permanent disability, but she'd take that chance. "Oh, Arnold, that's so sweet, but—"

"There are no buts, Natalie. I thought you understood that when we had our little conversation earlier." He started guiding her toward the exit.

Rosie chided herself. This is ridiculous. It's broad daylight. What the hell am I afraid of? But she *knew.* "I am not hungry, Arnold. You go ahead." (And maybe I can escape.)

"I'm not going alone." That strange smile crept across his face like a trail of picnic ants. He pushed her along, his weight underscoring his advantage.

Rosie searched the area for a familiar face. Finding none, she considered screaming. And if he's not doing anything more than inviting me for a sandwich at Nathan's, won't I look like a jerk? Now they were out on the sidewalk, Arnold was hailing a taxi, and the light dawned: Oh, shit! He's got more on his mind than hot pastrami on rye and a dill pickle. *Do not get into the cab with this love-sick lunatic!*

Things happened so fast after that, Rosie would wish later she'd had a video camera with her: In the midst of struggling against the mountain man, help arrived in the shape of a familiar long, dark limo with tinted windows. Theo, who was fast becoming her permanent bodyguard, bounded from the car and hustled Arnold away while Nikki guided her back toward the limo. Once again, Rosie found herself in debt to the mysterious man.

"I told you I would protect you. It's true, as you so clearly pointed out the last time, I was not able to prevent the tragedy that occurred to Grace. But I always learn from my mistakes." And, once again, he was offering ouzo to calm the nerves.

Rosie shook her head. "Thank you anyway. I . . . just don't know what got into him." She had a rough idea but was afraid to say it aloud, certain that Nikki would personally escort Arnold to the Greek version of the gas chamber without troubling the state with all the nonsense of a trial.

Theo had returned to the car, and Arnold was nowhere in sight, but Rosie couldn't contain herself any longer. She told Nikki about Mike. "He's disappeared. I can't believe it's happening all over again."

Nikki asked a lot of questions, but Rosie could only repeat what she'd told Chris Marino. "I know they're looking for him. I need to help."

"Can you do whatever you did the last time to help locate Grace?"

"I'm going to damned well try! But I need to contact the detectives who are looking for him now."

The other nodded and handed her the phone. "Theo will drive you anywhere you say." They were just approaching the main entrance of the hospital where Grace was still fighting to regain her identity. "I'll leave you now, Rosie, but you will be in good hands. You know how to reach me." And he was out the door before she could thank him.

Neither Chris Marino nor Adella Parsons was available, Rosie was informed. She left an urgent message for one of them to call her. Then she took advantage of Nikki's offer and asked Theo to drive her home.

After Theo deposited her safely at her apartment, Rosie began pacing up and down her small living room, her arms hugging her shoulders. Where is Mike? This feels like a *déjà vu*—the sadness with Grace. Oh, God! I can't believe this is happening again. *And if it is, you know what you have to do,* her inner voice insisted. Yes, meditate—go into a trance like she did before the vision of Grace's location appeared. Rosie's options were clear: If the police were floundering, she had to use her own powers to find him.

But relaxation is the key to meditating, which is not an easy thing to do when one is agitated. How the hell could she become less tense when she was as tight as an old spring? Rosie tried several settings: the kitchen, the living room, the bedroom. Gabby was curled up on her bed, pretending not to notice when Rosie walked in. The pet was too comfortable to be shifted and stretched her legs straight out, proclaiming that section of the bed was her spot. Rosie reached out to stroke her warm, soft fur and murmured, "I know you fell for Mike the minute he cooed sweet nothings to you. Hussy. That's what you are." She realized she could have been talking about herself. "Yes," she said aloud, "guess I'm guilty of the same."

Rosie lay down next to Gabby, who was now purring with happiness since her mistress was not chasing her away after all. Somehow, the combination of lying down and cooing to her loving pet calmed Rosie, too. Her own pulse slowed down to something more normal, and she was able to close her eyes and lower her shoulders from up around her ears. *Mike, where the heck are you?*

A graveyard for over-the-hill cars and trucks . . . She'd been here before. . . . *Old, battered, paint-peeled cars, wrecked pickups, treadless tires, mounds of metal and jackknifed junk decorate this deformed mountain of castaways. Maneuvering up the uneven hill of rust, searching for signs of life. A small creature darts out from underneath an abandoned Jeep. This is no time for distractions, no room for mistakes. The area's deserted and growing darker by the moment. Only one streetlight is working, not enough to penetrate the dusk. Wading around mysterious bundles of garbage and noisy tin cans.*

Mike, I'm here! Give me a sign. Nothing. But this is the place. It has an unholy familiarity. A squeak and a clunk of metal. A mouse scoots across the path. Mike! Still no answer. Light's almost gone. Have to do something, but the street sign's facing in the opposite direction. Get a landmark! Old brick apartment building across the street. Difficult to see now . . . got to keep the focus—five stories, looks deserted, two broken windows fourth floor. What else? Growing misty . . . gone.

Rosie was still holding on to Gabby when she came out of her trance. She sat up on the edge of the bed and reached for the phone. This time, her call was answered. "Chris, I think I may know where Mike is."

Chapter 34

Rosie parked her car on Gold Street, half a block from the Eighty-fourth Precinct, as Chris had suggested. He was waiting for her and handed her a placard. "Here, put this on your dashboard with the seal facing outward." At any other time, she would have enjoyed the thrill of parking illegally and with an official NYPD identification on her car, but she was so anxious to find Mike, she followed directions quickly and locked her car. Adella had moved to the backseat of the detectives' unmarked Chevy Impala and indicated that Rosie should sit up front.

"Look," Rosie began, "I don't know how this is going to evolve. . . ."

Marino put his hand on her arm. "It's okay, you don't have to explain. Whatever you did to locate Grace Osborne, do it again for Mike, and I'll be eternally grateful." He turned the key and started the car. "Now, where to?"

"It's a deserted junk lot—old cars, trucks, garbage—stuff like that. I don't know the location, but I got the impression it's not too far from the court area."

Their car was moving, but not fast. Adella asked, "Any landmarks?"

"No, sorry, just a mountain of junk. Oh, God—Mike—He's got to be all right."

Adella leaned forward from the rear and put her hand on Rosie's shoulder. "Stay strong; we'll find him. Just keep concentrating on what you might have noticed." Her voice was calm, even toned, and Marino decided to stay out of it for now.

"Rodents—don't know whether they were rats or mice. Bundles of garbage."

"What kind of bundles? Plastic bags, paper sacks, or what?"

"Both. Some of it smelled really foul."

Marino was maneuvering around the area, beginning with a five-mile radius. If nothing seemed familiar to Rosie, he'd increase the perimeter. He drove slowly, evenly, hoping something would spark her memory. After fifteen minutes, he remembered a deserted lot on West Ninth, and headed there, but when they arrived, Rosie said it didn't look particularly familiar.

"But I just remembered something else. There was only one streetlight that was working. The light was very dim, and it was difficult to see. Then, too, the only street sign was facing in the wrong direction, so I couldn't read it."

So now they had added some dimension to this crazy ride. Since it wasn't dark at the moment, this last piece of information wasn't helpful—yet. Soon they were approaching another dumping area, but Rosie pointed out that all street signs seemed to be facing correctly. "Besides, this place is too small. The one I'm thinking of was much bigger . . . and piled higher with old cars and trucks and junk—huge hunks of bent, rusted metal—and tires! Did I say? There were lots of old tires, too."

Adella had an idea that maybe Rosie could remember more if she were less uptight and gently proposed she consider closing her eyes and concentrating on the visions she'd seen right before she'd called Marino. "We need your help, Rosie. No one but you can lead us to Mike, and every minute counts."

Rosie was only too glad to try, so Marino parked the car alongside Prospect Park, turned off the motor and opened the windows. The only sounds that could be heard at the end of this late Saturday afternoon were some children skateboarding just inside the park and mothers gossiping on nearby benches while rocking their carriages. With the two detectives remaining quiet, Rosie closed her eyes and silently commanded herself to return to her trance state of earlier. Marino caught Adella's eyes in the rearview mirror, but neither spoke.

"I remember something else!" Rosie sat up straight. "There's an old brick building—deserted, I believe—opposite this dumping place. Five floors, it has, but some of the windows on the fourth floor are badly broken." Marino started the motor and headed out. "I believe the building's facing west," Rosie continued, "because right before everything went dark, there was a reflection in the windows of the skies and setting sun. And . . . and . . . (Rosie was becoming more animated) the sidewalk next to the lot was all cracked, like nobody used it anymore. It's a real old area, and the street nearest the old building—the part nearest the sidewalk—is partially made of cobblestones." Rosie was panting when she finished. "Does this help?"

"Damned straight," Marino assured her. "I think I've got a better idea where this lot is located." In the back, Adella sat straight up in anticipation.

Ten minutes later, Rosie was jumping up and down in her seat like an excited child. "There!" she pointed. "That's it!" Their car was approaching an old area that had, remarkably, many of the nuances of her description.

"Good stuff, Rosie!" Marino yelled. He was trying to stay calm, but his adrenaline was pumping.

In the backseat, Adella was punching her fist in the air. "You're terrific, Rosie, wanna come to work for the Eighty-fourth?"

"Just let Mike be okay, is all I ask."

Marino called the precinct, gave them the location, but told them he and his partner were not going to wait for backup. "You know where we are, so start sending us the good guys." He told Rosie that he and Adella were going to check things out. "You stay put."

"No way. I'm coming."

"Yeah, Mike said you were a stubborn broad. Okay, but stay behind."

Both detectives checked their belts for guns, mace, flashlights, pagers and the like. Rosie estimated the equipment they carried must add at least twenty pounds to their fighting weight and watched in fascination as, with drawn guns, they moved effortlessly up the hill of rotting, rusted, useless trash.

"Wait!" Rosie called from the rear, "there's something else I just remembered." But Adella put her finger to her lips, shook her head and frowned. "But it's important," Rosie insisted. Now Marino turned around, a question on his face. "Look for a long mark—a deep line," she called to him. "It'll be like an arrow directing us to Mike."

"Huh?"

"I'm thinking it would be like a line, but it's not like it's painted; it's like a . . . groove, like something heavy being dragged along, and it caused a . . . yeah! A deep groove in the surface." Even Rosie shook her head.

Marino was struggling to digest this information. He looked at his partner, who raised her shoulders in bewilderment. Rosie had dropped back and was walking along the perimeter of the lot. Adella signaled Marino to hold up. They watched as Rosie retraced her steps. Now she stood on the broken sidewalk and studied the surrounding buildings. This section of Bedford Stuyvesant could be summed up in one word—depressing. Rosie pointed beyond Marino, and both detectives followed her finger.

"The other side," she said. "We're on the wrong side."

Marino and Adella came back down to where Rosie was standing and pointing. Sure enough, on the far side of the lot, an old brick building climbed into the early evening sky. "See?" Rosie said excitedly, "the fourth story? There's the broken windows!"

Marino grabbed her shoulders. "Good job! He gave his partner a nod. "Think we've got ourselves a genius here." The three of them headed around the lot.

"Careful," Rosie cautioned, "lots of broken glass." As they got closer, she gasped. "And look! there's the line. It's showing us where Mike is." She was indicating an indentation in a small section of earth at the edge of the lot.

With Marino in the lead, the three of them carefully picked their way up the mountain of discarded fenders, broken glass and garbage. Sure enough, a recent track consisting of a single groove wound around and up through the maze, ending at the rear of a dented old wreck. Marino drew his gun, but Rosie waved her arms frantically and shouted him off. In the next few seconds, all three could hear faint thuds coming from inside the trunk

"No, wait!" yelled Rosie. "It's Mike!"

Marino replaced his nine millimeter in its holster but motioned to Adella, who drew hers. After trying unsuccessfully to open the trunk, Marino quickly searched the grounds nearby and selected a rusted hunk of flattened metal from a nearby pile. He pushed Rosie back with one hand and locked eyes with Adella who, after sweeping the scene around the car, tightened her hands over the gun. Marino inserted the substitute crowbar into the seam of the trunk as the other two held their collective breaths. With one huge effort, the trunk lid popped open, exposing the bound, gagged, but very alive Mike Bartel. Marino helped his former partner to a sitting position and the others rushed forward to untie the ropes. Rosie carefully removed the duct tape from his mouth, and Mike drew in a gulp of air and began cursing.

"Sonofabitch drugged me . . . didn't know what the hell was happening. That fat fucker, when I get my hands on him . . ." He paused for a breath. "Oh, jeeze, guys, thanks!"

"Here's where you owe your thanks, pal." Marino pushed Rosie forward.

Mike didn't hesitate. He reached out and pulled her toward him. "Was it some of your woo-woo stuff?" She shrugged her shoulders, then nodded. "C'mere," he said, not in the least embarrassed, and wrapped his arms around her. "Thanks." Rosie felt her face grow warm, then everybody started talking at once, throwing questions at Mike, until he cut through the din with, "Hold it! Let's get out of here first, then we'll take it one at a time."

"Maybe you forgot how this works," his former partner said, pulling out his cell phone. "Can't just leave. I gotta get the crime team out here. Then you can give us the details, so we can pick up your drinking buddy."

"Cute," said Mike, waggling his forefinger at Marino, "but you're right. Let's do it by the book. And you might want to get hold of your FBI guys and the D.A. This has the same blueprint as Grace Osborne's disappearance."

Rosie was thoughtful. "Yes, this makes sense, sick though it is." She related Arnold's earlier rantings about how, after

Grace disappeared, she—Rosie—was supposed to have leaned on him for help.

". . . In other words, fallen into his arms like he had scripted," Adella said.

"By the way," Marino asked, "how did you know about the groove that led us to the car?"

"I . . . just *saw* it. Can't explain how, and it became a direction indicator. But I'm thinking it was caused by something that Mike had been dumped into to make it easier to drag or push him along." She rolled her eyes toward Mike, expecting some smart-ass crack.

"Like a wheelbarrow," Adella offered. The group considered the uncomfortable spectacle, so she added, "Definitely not first class."

While they waited for the forensics specialists, Mike related how he'd got suckered at Casey's. "Give Feltman his due: he's sneaky. That means we gotta watch out for this guy until he's locked up." He pointed at Rosie. "So, it's not a good idea for you to be alone anywhere until then." He had yet to find out about Rosie's earlier experience with Arnold, but he noticed Marino nodding knowingly. "What?"

"We've already put out an APB." His former partner provided a quick rundown of what he knew. "Feltman's not stupid, just possessed." And he rolled his eyes toward Rosie for emphasis.

Mike suggested they remove all temptation. "There's no reason," he said to Rosie, "why you can't take a hiatus from the office until and *if* Grace is able to continue her practice." The others agreed. "And another thing: Don't even consider staying in your place either." For emphasis, he dipped his chin and his eyebrows took flight. He looked directly at her as though he had some other site in mind. Rosie knew where that would be. Her blood pressure responded to the surge in her solar plexus, but she managed to keep a straight face. The other two were waiting for a clarification.

"If I have to," she said, "I can stay with a girlfriend (though she knew that was not what Mike had in mind). But what about Gabby?"

"Talking about her cat," Mike said to the others, perfectly aware that their lives were becoming an open book. The arrival of the crime team saved them from any further discussion.

After ensuring the area was secure, Marino offered to drive Mike back to his place. Rosie reminded them that her car was parked on Gold Street. "Tell you what," Mike said to Marino, jumping on the opportunity. "I know you need to get back to the precinct, why don't you drop us off at Rosie's car. We'll take it from there."

Mike's former partner flicked him an *I'll-bet-you-will!* expression, but nobody argued.

Rosie was surprised that Mike was content to sit on the passenger side while she drove. She'd always considered herself a good driver, but figured he'd bring the ME-MAN! thing into the picture. He was silent, and she supposed he was reliving the buried-alive experience. Then he started shooting questions at her:

"How did you figure out where I was? What exactly told you I was in this deserted lot?"

"Is this how you used to interrogate prisoners?"

"Just call me curious. Y'know, I could have suffocated, and that would have been the end. Guess that's what your friend *Arnold* had in mind."

"Yeah, my *friend*, all right."

"Never mind. This guy is capable of some mean stuff. I'm tying this together with Grace's abduction, but I'll be damned if I can figure out what his motive was. We've got to keep you out of sight until we get him."

"So, what did you have in mind? Like, I should stop breathing until you catch him?" She could feel his eyes on her, and was immediately sorry she had mouthed off.

"Here's what we're gonna do," he said, ignoring her snit, "and this is not negotiable. We're gonna hang together. Wherever you go, *I* go. Got it?"

Rosie had to laugh out loud. "That means you're coming with me to my folks' on Friday for *shabbes* dinner?"

"Yes, smart-ass, that's what it means."

Rosie took a deep breath. (*Oy.* This means guns will be drawn at the old corral.) She said, "For now, though, I'm planning to drop you off at your place. I'll call Libby from there, then go home and pick up a few things and go over to her place."

"Or, you could just park in front of my building while *I pick up a few things* and we go back to your place. You don't get it, do you? I'm not letting you out of my sight until that dickhead is in custody."

Rosie's heart was pounding. *This is the real thing, you dummy. He's saying he doesn't consider you a one-night stand.* So they finally agreed to do it Mike's way.

"Now, tell me, how did you know where to find me?"

"Look, I live a normal life—or I try to. The past couple of weeks haven't exactly been what I'd call normal. Then, I got this feeling. Can't explain how these thoughts come to me, but I knew something was wrong when you didn't call. And it was bad, so I called Chris, and the rest—well, you know the rest."

Mike reached over and stroked the back of her neck, but

Rosie pulled his hand away, laughing. "I've been driving a long time and never had an accident. But if you continue to distract me like that, I make no promises. . . ." *Now here comes the proposition.*

Indeed, they were only minutes from Mike's apartment when he cleared his throat. "Ah, I always wanted to say this: My place or yours?"

(What did I tell you? Now, what am I going to do? I yell at Libby for letting Dr. Fingers take advantage of her. So, what am I doing? I can just hear my mother saying, *Time is passing, Na-ta-lie.* Ah, such words of wisdom!) Rosie slowed as the light turned red and swung around to Mike. "How about you throwing some stuff together and we head out to Long Island before the rush hour discourages both of us?"

His eyes lit up. "Okay by me. You can park in front. I'll tell Stan to keep an eye on your car."

Rosie gathered that Stan was the doorman. "Sounds convenient, but in the interest of time, think I'll wait in the car." Mike couldn't hide his disappointment. (Like, maybe he thought I was up for a quickie? As if.) He came down twenty minutes later, showered, shaved and carrying a fair-sized satchel. Rosie couldn't resist. "And how long were you planning to stay? A month?"

"If that's how long it takes." His eyes lit up, complementing a wicked smile. "Now, are you gonna start this thing or not?"

Chapter 35

The moon and Jupiter are in perfect alignment for you today. Take a chance; there will seldom be a better opportunity.

Mike lifted the cup of coffee to his lips but never took his eyes off her. Rosie could feel the heat rise in her cheeks. He didn't even try to disguise his thoughts. No cover-up, just naked lust and an aggressive desire for more. More? Ohmygod! The man was tireless. But even she realized this activity couldn't go on forever. One or the other of them would have to be resuscitated. Besides, she hadn't returned her mother's phone calls. The last thing either of them wanted was a visit from the Oceanside police inquiring if there was anything wrong. She could imagine them knocking on the door, saying they had been contacted by a Mrs. Rosenstein who was worried about her little girl who wouldn't return her phone calls.

"I'm going to be calling my folks this morning. Would you consider driving over with me later? My mom's called a couple of times, and—"

"Sure."

"Did I hear you right? You said 'sure?' "

"Why not?" He looked amused.

Where to begin? "Well, for one thing, you could never make the first team."

"Was it something I said?—or, better yet, something I did?" He was leering at her wickedly.

"Don't be cute. It's my mother. She has this, uh, thing about religion."

"And me not being Jewish puts me out of contention even as a *friend?*"

"Somehow I don't think *friendship* is of prime importance to my mother. Her focus is more in the husband market."

"Oh."

"Here's your hat; what's your hurry?"

Mike slid to the edge of his seat, giving the impression that he was about to bolt and run. Now Rosie was laughing. "Relax, I'm not interested in getting married," she said. "Anyhow, my mother has poor judgment in that area." She described the impression Arnold had made on her. "She thought he was a prince. I can't wait to tell her the truth about her first pick."

"Was your dad also hot for Mr. Chubbs?"

"No way. Arnold has no interest in sports. That let him out of the running to begin with. At best, Dad found Arnold boring, which made conversation practically nonexistent."

Now Mike perked up. "Your dad sounds like a very astute man."

"That he is." Rosie began carrying the breakfast things over to the sink.

"Why don't you let me do that, and you go get dressed . . . or whatever." Mike's eyebrows were going uphill again, and he broke out in a meaningful grin.

"Okay, but no more 'whatevers' right now. I have to pick up a few things at the market, and Gabby's almost out of food. Um, if you behave, I'll let you come along."

He laughed and gently shoved her out of the kitchen. "Get going—or else!"

Later that afternoon, they headed out to Long Beach. Rosie had phoned her dad earlier and told him she was bringing Mike, knowing he'd need a lot of time to prepare her mother. The question was, which mood would the dear woman be in when they arrived. There were several choices: There was the-last-day-on-earth scenario, the I-will-not-surrender theme or the silent treatment, any of which would give her mother the opportunity to display her acting talents. They only had a little while before they'd find out the verdict.

Her parents' reactions were no surprise. Rosie's dad perked up as soon as Mike broached his favorite subject: "How about those Yankees? Some season, huh?"

Happiness sparkled in the older man's eyes like Rosie had not seen in years. "You are a fan?" To Mike's "sure," her dad proceeded to the testing area: "And who would you pick for MVP?"

"Jeter, of course. He had over thirty home runs, two hundred hits, a hundred-plus RBI's and a warehouse of double plays. He's the man!"

Her father's reaction was predictable. He slid his eyes toward his daughter as if to say, "so you finally brought home the right one." He and Mike continued until Ida Rosenstein put in an appearance. She moved toward Mike with her hand extended stiffly and without any prompting, but her mouth was set in a less than happy mode. The two shook hands like well-trained warriors who would never fight together on the same team but nevertheless believed in the same cause. In that sense, Rosie was the issue. She and her dad exchanged eye signals that could be interpreted as *not every day is Sunday*, a family saying, which loosely translated meant something like, "you can't win 'em all."

Mike and her dad downed scotch before dinner, but Rosie held herself to one glass of wine after they sat down at the table. After all, someone responsible had to drive. Her mother faked it altogether, having nothing to drink before or during dinner. She's really in a snit, Rosie thought. She imagined her dad's instructions to her vis-à-vis the evening— "One: keep your mouth under control, and two: pretend to be pleasant to Mike-the-*goy*."

Long before their visit ended, Rosie knew it was a hopeless situation. My mother will never give in any more than she will ever accept the truth about her choice of a husband for me. Her Arnold turned out to be one big zit, and she can never accept that. But the evening was not a total loss. Rosie hadn't seen her dad so happy in years. This last of course annoyed her mother even more.

Rosie helped with the cleaning up, hoping to bring her around, but it was a lost cause. Ida Rosenstein had put her money on the wrong horse, and she couldn't forgive herself. While she would eventually come to grips with reality, her hopes for her daughter's prospects were presently in disarray.

Not so, Rosie and Mike. They were about to embark on a future together that, while not exactly what Rosie's mother might have had in mind, was nevertheless more than either of them could have envisioned.

Epilogue

Exactly eleven months and two weeks had passed since Rosie led Detectives Chris Marino and Adella Parsons to the trunk of the old car where Mike had been unceremoniously dumped. Despite all the technology available to the FBI and NYPD in the months that followed, Arnold Feltman was never found. Mike theorized that he'd skipped the country, but all their efforts to locate him through Interpol had failed thus far. He must have changed his looks, possibly with the help of a plastic surgeon, and whichever country he had immigrated to, he must be working and . . . on and on went the theories. In the end, they all concluded that Arnold was much smarter than any of them had ever given him credit for. In short, Arnold Feltman was the Ira Einhorn of the twenty-first century. And, while Einhorn was eventually brought back to justice for the 1977 murder of his girlfriend, Holly Maddux, he had managed to enjoy thirty-plus more years of freedom than he was entitled to. Was Feltman on a similar tract?

Arnold was wanted for questioning in the kidnapings and attempted murders of Grace Osborne and Mike Bartel. (The police were also interested in talking to him about the suspicious deaths of his parents some years before. The cause was determined to be a faulty gas valve in their home—the very same house in which Grace Osborne had been held prisoner.) Some might conclude that Mr. Feltman had discovered a simple means to eliminate controversy in his life.

While Ms. Osborne made a complete recovery, she never resumed her law practice. She did, however, marry the eccentric and very rich Mr. Nikki Marcos, well-known international hotel-chain owner and diamond king—after his divorce from his third wife, of course.

Ms. Osborne turned her practice over to a former colleague, Carolyn Hughs, who, after extensive treatment at a facility in Upstate New York, managed to stabilize her illness enough to become one of New York's leading adversaries for abused women and children. One of her best known cases involved a custody battle between Ms. Jane Fisher and Mr. Hans Schreiber. Ms. Hughs not only won the case handily in a courtroom duel with the famous attorney, Harvey White, she ensured that Ms. Fisher retained sole custody of her son and also saw to it that Mr. Schreiber was convicted of bigamy and deported to Germany, where he would never again bother the gentle Jane Fisher.

Rosie accomplished more than even she had ever imagined. Mike proposed all right, but marriage was not on the menu (which suited them both). Their union was business, but not strictly—which also suited them both. Mike's private-detective practice became known as Bartel & Rosenstein and featured not only the former NYPD detective but also the very talented Natalie Rosenstein, professional clairvoyant, whose proven services were becoming more in demand from police and government agencies throughout the metropolitan area. During their first vacation together, which was as close to a honeymoon as the two ever got, Rosie and Mike visited Madame Volante in Paris. Nearing eighty, the amazing lady was as sharp as ever and as all-knowing as Rosie remembered. Upon meeting Mike, whom she liked immediately, she said grandly, "Zis ees ze one for you, *ma chèrie*. Not like that *con!*" She spit to emphasize her dislike for Jean Marc. "If you say so," Rosie demurred. She really wanted to join her former mentor in a let's-rip-the-bastard-apart session, but figured she was so far ahead of where she ever thought she'd be, she could afford to be generous and just let it ride.

Alas, Rosie's friend Libby's life was still in limbo. She and Dr. Aaron Finkel, aka Dr. Fingers, had welcomed a healthy nine pound-plus baby boy into the world six months before. Libby grandiosely assured Rosie that the good doctor was working hard to secure a divorce from fragile wife Stella, and that it was only a matter of time. Meanwhile, the happy new father had found a pleasant apartment for her and the baby only a few blocks from his ob/gyn practice. That way he could come home for lunch and their little family could visit together. (These visits often included a matinee for Mommy and Daddy.) Unfortunately, they hadn't yet figured out a way for him to spend the night. "But," ventured Libby, "we're working on it!" Of course . . . and Arabs and Israelis have been fast friends for years.

Rosie's father had found a friend in Mike. He was delighted to discover that sports was not all they had in common. The two freely indulged in animated discussions on everything from politics to history. This last surprised Rosie, who never suspected Mike's depth. When he teased her about her so-called "woo-woo" talent, she could ride him on his nodding acquaintance with Adolph Hitler and Stalin.

Rosie's mother had her own demons to conquer, however. Still a work in progress, Ida Rosenstein had to live with the knowledge that she had been wrong. How could she have misjudged that nice Jewish lawyer? And now the worst: she suspected her daughter was "living in sin." Never mind. She loved her Na-ta-lie, though she struggled with the conflict that Mike would never convert. Getting them to marry would just take a little extra work on her part.

Just the same, the proposal Mike offered on the way back to their apartment on Columbus Avenue had nothing to do with a preacher or a rabbi, but Rosie was more than up for it. They sang old Ella Fitzgerald and Louie Armstrong tunes all the way back to Manhattan.

At the same time, on a distant kibbutz in Israel, a rotund man dressed in black (with kosher curly sideburns peeking out from under his yarmulke) was just concluding a welcoming speech to a group of recent arrivals: "So, don't mistake my good nature with stupidity," he said, in an unmistakable Brooklyn accent. "There is only one way of doing things here . . . and that's mine!"